A delicious read with a great story plot of twists and turns. Complete with a taste of mischief, passion and faith!

I felt like I was one of Starli's friends.

Kay Cooper
K's Kookies

Carole Brown's Knight in Shining Apron is a romantic mystery and an excellent read. Her characters are so real I keep thinking I know them personally. You will know them too.

Molly Noble Bull, Writing contest winner author of **The Rogue's Daughter.**

Cozy romance meets cozy mystery! Romance is in the air... Or is it? Mystery interwoven with a light-hearted romance makes this a book to snuggle with. Enjoy it with your fresh brewed cuppa coffee or not. Although romance is not my usual cuppa tea, I can certainly recommend this clean read with suspense that'll keep you guessing with every turn.

Emma Right, author of children and **teen fantasy and mystery books**.

Praise for award winning author
Carole Brown

I enjoyed **Knight in Shining Apron**, the second book in the Appleton, WV, series, even more than **Sabotaged Christmas**. Carole Brown writes with a touch of humor, just enough mystery-suspense to keep the reader turning the pages to see what happens next, and a nice mixture of sigh-worthy romance. Looking forward to the next book in the series.

Carol Ann Erhardt,
Christian Romantic Suspense author of
Joshua's Hope and the **Havens Creek Series**

Just the title made me smile. A really good mystery, a nasty villain and a heroic man who cooks is a bonus.

Lisa Lickel,
author of the **Buried Treasure Mysteries**

Carole Brown has outdone herself with this sequel to **Sabotaged Christmas** in the Appleton series. While the romance is threaded throughout, the mystery is intriguing enough to keep the pages turning. Highly recommended.

Knight in Shining Apron is a must read for any who love romantic mystery.

Barbara A. Derksen,
author of the Finders Keepers Mystery Series
and the Wilton/Strait Murder Mystery Series

Carole Brown does not shy away from the tough issues of life, as I recall from reading her masterful novel, **The Redemption of Caralynne Hayman.**

Domestic abuse is not something that is discussed over the kitchen table, but needs exposure in books by authors like Carole Brown. **Knight in Shining Apron**, in the Appleton, WV Romance Mystery series, presents the debilitating effects from abuse on the victim's psyche in a sensitive and understanding manner.

The reader empathizes with Starli as she tries to cope with ongoing intimidation from the brother of her recently deceased abusive husband.

Living with secrets presents challenges that interfere with Starli's ability to forgive and trust. Carole Brown writes in music and ice skating as therapeutic tools for Starli as she strives to maintain emotional balance.

The plot of this novel is realistic enough to add depth to a formula romance.

The suspense from the social issues resulting from the antagonistic brother-in-law, mysterious damage to Starli's restaurant, the secretive background of her newly hired chef, and other happenings adds up to several late nights of page turning for this reader.

The setting in Apple Blossoms' chef kitchen stirred up the culinary juices while reading the novel.

The satisfactory resolution of the domestic abuse issue and other subplots merged with the happiness of the romantic elements finally coming together.

Well structured. Well written. Well worth curling up with hot chocolate and cookies.

Cleo Lampos, Storyteller, Speaker, Author of:
Rescuing Children: Teachers, Social Workers, Nuns and Missionaries Who Stepped into Shadows to Rescue Waifs

Knight in Shining Apron

An Appleton, WV Romantic Mystery

Carole Brown

Story and Logic Media Group
Printed in the USA
... For the discriminating reader
...because we believe story *needs* logic.

Knight in Shining Apron: © 2016 by Carole Brown
Series Title: An Appleton WV Romantic Mystery

 **Published by STORY AND LOGIC Media
Group, New Carlisle, OH 45344
... For the discriminating reader...
Because we believe story *needs* logic.**

Cover Design by SAL media
Printed in the USA

ISBN 13: 978-1941622278
ISBN 10: 1941622275

Library of Congress Cataloging-in-Publication Data
Brown, Carole
Title: /Carole Brown
ISBN   (pbk)

    1. Series fiction   2. Cozy Mystery   3. Romance   4.
Inspirational fiction

I.   Title.   Library   of   Congress   Control   Number:
2016941169

Note From The Author

"It's impossible," said Pride.
"It's risky," said Experience.
"It's pointless," said Reason.
"Give it a try," whispered the Heart.
                              -- Unknown

If anyone could experience these sentiments, it's Starli Cameron, my protagonist in this book. I needed her to come to life. Thus I had to do quite a bit of research.

- **Abuse.** From my first book to this one, where I touch on it, I've studied quite a bit about abuse. It's a hard topic, but necessary if we don't want to go through life with our eyes closed. *Because of this research, I could pen correct reactions from Starli--her fears, her doubts and troubled spirit.*

- **Music:** specifically classical piano. Listening to the professionals playing the difficult and beautiful renditions--many created by past composers--was inspiring to say the least. *I was able to capture Starli's emotions when troubled, how the music affected her and the response from captive listeners, some of whom may not have understood but still felt the passion of the music.*

- **Ice Skating:** researching this beautiful sport--one that I've always enjoyed as an amateur--gave me details of the various moves that ice skaters must practice and perform as a second nature. Being in top form physically and mentally is absolutely necessary. Starli is strong and fit, and though not a professional, she was talented enough to perform for the town's benefit.

- **A business and becoming a chef:** I sought out different employee positions and what it takes to run a business, particularly a restaurant. I learned about the art of becoming a chef, their habits and talents in developing recipes and food, the idiosyncrasies with their personal items of business. *As a result, I could, if and when needed, pen an occasional employee position. I knew that excellent chefs--like Sir Joel Peterman-Blair--cared for and were particularly careful of their knife sets.*

I couldn't have done it without all the avenues open to writers: personal experience within my own life, interviews with those involved in the situations, the internet, YouTube, and most of all, books.

Dedication:

To Sharon, who goes above and beyond her labors of love and work for others.

Carole Brown

An Appleton, WV Romantic Mystery

She can't run away
from her past. Will the
new chef help or hurt?

Apple Blossoms
Restaurant

Knight in
Shining Apron

Chapter One

Starli Cameron slashed off the last name on her list, the last possible candidate.

It'd been a long day, in spite of loving her work, so saying that was saying the impossible—for her—because she'd never said it before.

She had to admit, she was picky when it came to her beloved restaurant, Apple Blossoms. Anything and anyone to do with it came with high scrutiny from her. She wanted the best and only that for her business.

That last chef applicant, with his incessant sniffing, had driven her crazy. And what about the pompous one who'd strutted into her office with his fake Italian accent itemizing his demands. She'd not had a chance to say a word about *her* requirements. Good thing too. His dismissal had been fast—although she hoped, politely done.

She ripped the paper from the tablet, crumpled it and tossed her pencil to the tabletop just as the loud pounding began.

Hurrying to the front door, hoping it would be one of her best friends—Toni or Caroline—so she could let off some steam, she flipped on the porch light and peeked through the peephole.

An eye glared at her, and she jumped back, heart beating like a woodpecker determined to get at the insects behind the tree bark.

Roland Stratton.

He can't see me.

"Starlie-e-e. Open up before I beat down this door." He accompanied his words with a couple more loud bangs from his big hands.

God, please, not again. Starli gripped the door casing. "What do you want?"

"Think you've got it made, don't you? While Ryan is decaying in the ground, his wife is playing the high-rolling, successful business-woman to the tilt. You couldn't even give him a son, could you?"

Dear Lord, please help me. A knife twisted in her heart. "No. That's not—"

"Don't bother to deny it." The voice roared, anger resounding through it. He kicked at an empty flower pot, sending it down her steps to crash at the bottom in a hundred pieces.

"I have to make a living." Desperation surged through her. She hated the whine in her voice.

"What about the five hundred grand he left you? Remember that measly amount? Did you squander it? Hoard it?"

Starli's insides froze a little more. Was Roland Stratton, Ryan's brother, after the money? Too late. It'd all gone toward opening the restaurant.

She recognized the feelings raging through her. Anger, hurt, dismay, defeat. But she didn't want to address them. Didn't even want to acknowledge them. She peeked through the hole again.

Her husband's brother staggered over to one of the porch stands and stared down at it. Then drawing back his leg, he gave it a vicious kick and sent it sailing across the porch.

"I went back to school and started the

14

restaurant. That took money—"

"You're as stupid as Ryan always said." A coarse laugh grated through the door. "Too stupid to live. But you did, didn't you, Starlie-e-e? Ryan died, but you lived."

Starli pressed her head against the door. When he moved away soon after Ryan's accident, she'd thought she was done with the Strattons, that she'd at last find some peace. But he hadn't stayed away. His police reassignment back in Appleton scared her. She knew what the Strattons were capable of.

What could she say to pacify him? Anything? Nothing?

"Look down at that ugly finger of yours, Starlie-e-e."

Starli's gaze dropped to her left pinkie. The crooked one. The reminder. Fear thudded in her chest.

"I think you need another reminder." His coarse, drunken laugh drowned out the bang, bang, bang his fists repeatedly applied to the wooden door.

"No." The single, whispered word exploded from her throat.

The sudden silence played in her ears like a dreaded dirge.

He was gone. For now.

Chapter Two

Joel Peterman-Blair stepped further into the kitchen and leaned against a counter, his gaze fastened on the red-haired guy who wielded the large knife like he'd had plenty of practice.

The man's gaze lifted as if just aware someone different had entered his domain.

"Hi. Uncle Lawrence—Manny sent for me." Joel moved forward. "Wouldn't know where he is, would you?"

Suspicion, then disdain flickered in the brown eyes. With a frown, the man pointed the blade. "The new helper, are you? Last one we had just walked out. You're kind of old for the position."

Abashed at the man's bluntness, Joel stiffened. Old? Who did the bloke think he was?

Joel started to speak, but the man plowed on. "But if Manny wants you, Starli must have agreed. Who am I to complain?"

The knife flashed in the sunlight streaming through the huge windowpane over the sink. None too pleased at him, he seemed.

"Over there. Start on those pans. And you're too dressed up. Tomorrow, come without the tie."

Joel winked at the girl cutting vegetables at a large table. The man had mistaken him for a hired helper. *What a joke on Uncle Lawrence when he finds me doing dishes.*

A monstrous apron hung on a peg beside

the door. Joel tied it around his waist and rolled his sleeves above his elbows. When he turned on the taps, the hot water gushed into the sink. He poured a lavish supply of soap into the spray and dug in.

When was the last time he'd washed a pan? He couldn't remember. He wouldn't want his lady friends to see him, but.... His whistle matched his washing pace.

Behind him the swinging door whooshed open, but he paid it no mind.

Joel eyed his progress. He'd made a serious dent in the pile of pans. One more, and he'd have the bunch done.

"Who *is* this?" A surprised female voice slashed through the quiet kitchen.

"It's the new guy Manny sent to help out." Red-haired, knife-wielding guy growled out the words. "I thought you approved it, or I would have checked with you first."

Joel stacked the last pan and turned, water and suds dripping from his hands.

The most exquisite creature he'd ever seen waltzed across the room. Her white-blond hair, captured in a ponytail, bobbed with every step.

Giving him the once-over, was she? He allowed himself another quick glance, nodded, then lowered his gaze. Might as well play along with the charade. His lips twitched. "Ma'am."

Tall and slender, she glided closer, her deep green eyes blazing with distrust. "Who are you? You've got soap suds all over the floor."

Mirth swelled inside him, but he swallowed the temptation to laugh. He wouldn't have been surprised to see her stretch one long finger in haughty accusation at him, declaring,

"Off with his head."

The substantial puddle on the floor seemed to be shimmering in amusement, but he ignored the implications and nodded toward the back door. "Through there. I thought all employ-hired help did that." He risked staring into her eyes.

She frowned, her perfect brows forming a V over the bridge of her straight nose.

"You must quit that frowning." Joel hid another smile and couldn't resist teasing her. "You'll be old before your time."

"What do you know about frowns and women?" Her crisp voice reproved him. "You're a mess."

Joel looked down at himself, soaked from the dishwater. She was right. He was a mess. Beneath the apron, his red silk tie had bled onto his white shirt. Bully. What an impression he was making.

"Ma'am, you, on the other hand, look like one of those delicate Japanese water lilies."

Her eyes sharpened.

"Only fairer. Much more so."

"Are you Irish? Your baloney is as thick as our autumn fog." Her tone snapped at him. She definitely wasn't believing his flattery.

He felt his lips stretch wider. "Nay, My Lady, but my great-granny was."

Her red lips curled, and a snort emanated from her slender throat.

Very unladylike, but somehow impressive.

"Manny didn't hire you. I don't know what your game is, but it's up. Now. Get out."

He looked at her and the three employees standing behind her. The two women's sudden angry faces glared at him. Red-hair clutched his deadly knife. Joel raised both hands, but before he could speak, the kitchen door swung open again.

"Joel? You're here? Why didn't you call me?" Uncle Lawrence's proper voice filled the room. He gripped the doorframe and gaped. "*What* are you doing?"

"The dishes." He gave a nod toward the sink, then crossed the room in long strides to gather his uncle in a wet hug. When at last he broke away, Joel laughed and pounded his uncle on the back.

A wide smile lit up the maître de's features. He turned to the woman. "Miss Starli, my nephew, Sir Joel Peterman-Blair."

If a trumpet fanfare had blared out the announcement, it couldn't have been any more impressive.

"*Sir?* This man is your nephew?"

Joel bowed slightly, amused at her shocked tone. "At your service, ma'am."

"Stop calling me ma'am." She snapped.

"Yes, m ..." Tongue in cheek, he spoke to his uncle, but his gaze remained fixed on the woman. "Mind telling me who this queen is?"

Manny glanced at Joel, but elaborated on his explanation to Starli. "My *English* nephew, the chef I told you about."

"But 'sir'?"

"The Petermans have the ancestry, the Blairs the, er, money, and Joel has the title. Hence, my relationship with the scoundrel." Manny's eyes twinkled.

"I see." Skepticism edged her voice. "Can he cook?"

"Can I? Ma'am—excuse me—Miss Starli, you haven't eaten until you've tasted my scones." Joel swaggered a little. He turned to his uncle. "And who is the lovely lady, Uncle Lawrence?"

"Ms. Starli Cameron. She owns Apple Blossoms and will be your employer."

Had he bitten into an unripe persimmon? His lips wanted to purse into a sour moue. "I see."

As if just aware that her employees were standing defensively about her, Miss Starli sighed. "It's okay, Louis. This...guy is Manny's nephew. Regardless of how he entered the restaurant."

She turned to Joel. "This is Louis Dupree, the assistant chef, and the kitchen help, Camille and Juanita."

Joel turned to the women and bowed slightly. The younger girl erupted into giggles. The older one looked pleased and bobbed her head. Only then did he switch his gaze to Louis, the red-haired man. There was no friendliness on his face, only mistrust and a bit of anger.

Joel hesitated, knowing full well a little humbleness would go a long way to making friends with this man. "I'm depending on your help, friend."

Louis made no answer, only inclined his head, his hand gripping the knife handle as if he thought to use it for protection...Or something else?

So much for humble pie.

Joel debated on whether to say more, but returned the nod, then followed his uncle and Ms. Starli out of the kitchen. Once in her office, she motioned for him to sit. His uncle edged toward the door.

"Manny, you're welcome to stay if you wish."

That sounded like a plea. Afraid of him, was she?

Again, Manny's gaze went to Joel even though he spoke to Starli. "I'll let you and Joel get acquainted."

What was his hurry? Something was up his uncle's sleeve if he had to bet on it.

He turned back to the woman sitting on the opposite side of the desk. Her gaze, fastened on the doorway, darted to him, flicked away, then edged back to him. She drew in a deep breath.

"Why are you here?"

Had Uncle Laurence not told her? "I thought you knew. Uncle Laurence said you needed a chef."

"Do you jump whenever Manny—your uncle—tells you of someone's need?"

"I'll let Uncle Laurence explain it to you." Joel crossed his legs and settled back into his chair.

"Manny told me you're an excellent chef."

"I am that."

She frowned at him. "Conceited, aren't you?"

"Convinced."

His snappy reply must not have done anything for Miss Starli. Her frown deepened.

Joel wanted to laugh.

"So Manny wants you to help us out for a time. Are you willing? What's your usual remuneration?"

Should he overcharge her to bring her down a bit? No. There were better ways to do that. He named his price.

"Are you worth it?"

"Every penny."

"That's rather steep." Starli's cheeks reddened. "If I hire you, I'll expect at least a five year agreement from you to stay on."

Joel's only reaction was a lifting of one eyebrow.

~*~

Manny's nephew sat back in his chair, one long leg crossed over the other. In spite of his ruined clothing, he exuded confidence, mirth, and warmth. Did he think this meeting a joke?

Starli's mental hackles stood straight up. She scowled at his smiling face.

"Haven't you ever heard the good book say laughter is good for the soul?" He peered at her as if he thought she never read the Bible.

"I read the Bible, Mr. Peterman-Blair. Excuse me, *Sir* Peterman-Blair."

"Joel will serve nicely. May I call you Starli?"

"No, you may not."

Now why had she refused? She never insisted any of her employees be so formal, but this man really got her. Time to take control of the situation.

"The five year agreement?"

"I'll think on it."

"Are you saying you won't stay five years?" Starli eyed him.

"Let's review our options in the morning. Shall we?"

"I insist you start in the morning." Might as well up the pressure a little.

"I'll just have a bit of a look around, if you don't mind. What are your hours?"

"Mine?"

"Sorry. The restaurant hours?"

"We open at four and close between ten and midnight. Depending. You'll be responsible for the evening meal and overseeing the kitchen staff."

Starli's gaze rested on the lock of golden blond hair that fell across his forehead. She jerked her gaze away. "Then we'll see you in the morning."

He strode to the door, then paused. His voice brought her gaze back to his face.

"You really should smile more often. You're a beautiful woman, and beautiful women should never frown. Have a nice evening, Ms. Starli." He snapped a jaunty salute at her.

The door eased shut behind his tall form. For a long moment there was silence, then the sound of soft whistling drifted through the closed door.

What on earth had Manny gotten her into? If she'd ever seen trouble, this man and his casual air was it. He thought he could charm his way into what he wanted, did he?

Think again, Sir Joel Peterman-Blair.

She just hoped she hadn't put her beloved restaurant at risk.

Chapter Three

Starli stared at the opposite wall in her office the next morning. Images projected, then faded, on her mind's eye.

Ryan's obsessive buying.

Ryan's drinking.

His mental and physical abuse of her.

His threats that he'd hunt her down if she tried to leave him.

The women in his life plodded one by one across her mind-screen, their taunting smirks forever branded on her soul.

His flirting eyes and cocky confidence. So sure he'd win her.

And he had. She shuddered and rubbed her little finger.

Her mind whirled from the terror of her past life. She shook her head and struggled to bring her breathing back to normal. No. It was over. Ryan could never hurt her again. Pastor Haag had encouraged her to trust God for protection and healing.

But what about Roland Stratton? Why had Roland shown up at her door? Revenge? Savage delight in tormenting her? A plan to hurt her? Greed?

Prayer like a solace formed in her heart, and she let it rise heavenward, hoping to extinguish the niggling doubts eating at her nerves.

She reached for the small-sized note she'd found after Helen, her last—and excellent—chef had left behind hidden in her private desk in the kitchen. Her sudden resignation after her employment with Apple Blossoms from its beginning, had been both upsetting and disappointing. Of course, she'd understood that Helen's ill sister had need of her. Of course, she understood the short notice she'd given. But what she didn't understand was why the woman had hidden this.

This note that read like a threat. A death threat.

Starli didn't have to re-read it. She knew it by heart.

Don't delay. Your sister is ill and needs you as you well know. I demand your resignation from Apple Blossoms immediately. If I don't hear of it within a week—and I will hear—then don't expect to see your sister alive again.

A hand touched her shoulder, and she jumped. Raising her head, she steeled her face to blankness.

Manny. Her taut nerves relaxed. In spite of his invitation to Joel, he was still her friend.

"Starli. What is wrong?

When she made no comment, he continued. "Remember, we are in this together. Tell me."

She loved his 'we.' Made her feel so not alone. Yes, she was independent, and she wanted it that way. She allowed few people into her life, and even fewer to know of the fear that dogged her life.

"Thanks. It's your nephew. I'm not sure he's...well, he doesn't seem to be...he might not..."

The crisp blue eyes staring into her own didn't question her right to ask questions, but was there a bit of—what was it?

Disappointment? Sorrow?—in them? "Are you worried that Joel won't be good enough, Starli?"

"Of course not." Could she make him understand her reservations about the handsome chef?

"You're wondering if Joel can cater to our West Virginia clients suitably?"

She motioned. "Sit down, Manny."

Back ramrod straight, he obeyed although his obedience went only so far as to allow him to sit on the edge of the cushioned office chair.

Starli studied her maître de, her headwaiter. That was his official title, but he was much more than that. He'd been one of the first she'd hired.

She'd met him years ago when she was still in college at one of the best restaurants in the city. His English bearing, his precise speech and impeccable manners had impressed her as a man who was conscientious about his work. When his eyes had met hers after a rebuke from her fiancé, Ryan, they'd conveyed sympathy for her and disgust for her soon-to-be husband. Their relationship had deepened into real friendship.

Now he cared almost as much as she did for the restaurant.

She rubbed her forehead and wished the headache would go away. "So what shall I do? You know Louis is not capable of serving as Apple Blossoms head chef."

"No, he is not the man for the job." Manny tapped his lips with one finger. "I believe Joel is prepared to begin immediately. He took home several of the recipe books, and if I know him, which I do, he spent the better part of the night familiarizing himself with the most popular ones."

"Do you think he can be ready? Shouldn't he have some time to acclimate himself to Apple Blossoms?"

"I believe you requested he begin today?"

Was that condemnation? Her cheeks heated at the thought of Manny hearing about her unreasonable demand from his nephew.

"But Joel will need little time for that. He's experienced, adaptable, and very, very good. He studied at Julliard's." He stopped and peered at her. "You do know what that means?"

"By all means, tell me." She did know, but she wouldn't deprive him of his tale. Starli allowed a smile to widen her lips, aware she was mimicking Manny's English speech.

"I have a brother-in-law still in England."

Starli perked up. Ah, Manny was going to relate the reason Joel had rushed to West Virginia at his uncle's bidding. "Go on."

"Edward is Joel's father. He married my sister who died some time back. When Joel showed such ability and interest in concocting some really good recipes, even while still in his O-Levels, er, upper high school grades, I knew his talent should not be wasted. I determined he should have his chance." He paused. "Excuse me for bringing this up. Edward would have rather his money be spent on Joel studying law, or some other such fancy."

A chuckle escaped her lips at the thought of someone describing law as a "fancy." Starli leaned forward, fascinated with the story.

"What happened?"

"It was my money, and I offered it because I knew his father would never encourage or fund his choice." A wry smile curved Manny's lips. "Joel, being Joel, went with his—excuse me—gut feeling. He proved to be far wiser than his rather—hmmm—unsteady father. He went to Julliard, won several awards while there, and even before he graduated, became one of the most sought after chefs in England. The career fits him."

That tale made her even more uneasy. Nervous tremors spread through her stomach. "And what makes you think this famous nephew of yours will want to stay in West Virginia? And at Apple Blossoms in particular? I hardly think so."

"He became quite ill while at his last job and cancelled all his work." Manny folded his hands together. "He's much better, so coming here might be the sort of thing he needs."

"Ill? Will it hinder him here? I want a permanent chef, not another one I have to replace in a year's time when he decides to go back to wherever he lives. Or because he's ill." Starli knew the tart tone showed in her voice and hated it. Manny didn't deserve it.

He sat up straighter, spread his hands. "Do you not need a chef now? If we are to keep the high standards you—we—have created for Apple Blossoms, then we have no other choice. He is available for a period of time and is an excellent chef. He can do nothing but good for our restaurant."

That made sense. And what else could she do? She would not settle for mediocre. If she could not have an excellent chef, she would shut down Apple Blossoms. Starli winced. It would kill her, but she'd do it rather than run a second-best business.

"I know you've talked of him at different times and mentioned a couple weeks ago his availability, but why did you send for him? We hadn't made a final decision." Starli struggled to keep her voice normal. Manny didn't need to know her feelings were hurt he'd taken matters into his own hands.

For the first time since she'd known him, Manny's face tinged red. "I took the liberty of sending for him because I thought perhaps you would say no."

Manny, who was always so careful to not offend, so proper, had been afraid of her answer? Was that why she felt the need to justify herself? "I've always trusted your judgment. Don't you know me better than that?"

"I beg your pardon. But you've never made any pretense of hiding your distrust of most males. I've sat back for the last three months and watched you reject each candidate. Just last week you passed over two good chefs who would have served us well."

Starli couldn't have felt more shocked than if a hand had suddenly begun writing on her office wall. "Manny? Am I that bad?"

"Bad?" Manny shifted his position. "No, never. But you are overly cautious, to the point of..."

"Phobia." Starli finished his sentence for him.

Her maître de spoke but Starli didn't hear.

Manny, her beloved friend and head waiter, had criticized her. She roused to answer him. "We'll give Joel a trial run. Say, six weeks. What do you think?"

"You'll not regret it."

The door swung open, and Joel peered in. His face glowed with humor.

"Talking about me, were you?"

~*~

The expression on her face was worth his acting. Time to pull her out of the dumps. "Are you frowning again? I thought I told you..."

"Don't tell me what to do."

"I wouldn't dream of it." Joel strode on into her office without waiting for an invitation and crossed his arms. "But would Her Majesty allow a humble servant to make a suggestion?"

"No, I won't."

"Then I bow to your superior knowledge." Joel gave her a slight bow. "Although it was information I thought you might like to know."

She studied him with those big emerald-colored eyes. There was hesitation and curiosity in them, and he waited...

"What are you talking about? If it's something I need to know, then tell me."

It was his turn to study her. He wasn't use to telling tales, but why on earth would the man be standing in the hallway...

"Hmmm. Not sure it's any of my business." He eyed her to gauge her reaction. "Why would Louis be standing outside your office doorway?"

"Perhaps he wanted to speak to me and knew I was talking with Manny?"

More like eavesdropping. Was that

breathlessness he heard in her voice? Her gaze flashed to his uncle, and something passed between them. Would they fill him in on the secret?

Obviously not. "Is My Lady ready to show me the ropes?"

"Manny, would you?"

But Manny hustled to the door and shook his head. "I think Sir Joel wants his new employer to explain things to him."

Was that a sly grin on the old fox's face? What did he have going on in that brain of his? Joel turned just in time to catch Starli's heavy sigh and disgusted look.

"I say, I'm not bad company at all, if given half a chance." He paused for effect. "At least that's what all the little ladies at home tell me."

"Mr. Blair—or whatever your name is—you are not home."

His prospective boss crossed her arms on her desk and glared up at him. Was it a defensive mechanism? For what? Prickly, she was, but fearful?

"Let's get something straight. If you're to work here—and I appreciate you offering to do so, considering your uncle's high praises of you—we will work best together strictly on a professional level. Is that plain enough?"

"Very. Should I knock before I enter? You don't prescribe to the open door policy?" Joel disciplined his twitching lips.

If her frown could deepen, it did.

"I don't know if this is going to work." Starli sat back and shook her head. "If it wasn't for Manny..."

"Loosen up." Joel straightened. "Come walk

me through your restaurant."

She drew in a deep breath.

Resigning herself?

"One more thing I want you to know. We schedule in a few special events through the year. Only a select few, but they must be topnotch. We have one coming up in a week." She gave him a searching look. "That is the real reason I'm hiring you."

Otherwise I'd send you packing.

The unspoken words hung between them as plain as unflavored yogurt. Joel understood perfectly.

If he hadn't owed his uncle, would he be here? No. He took another glance at the woman across from him. Well, maybe.

She stared at him for a moment, then rose and moved to the door.

Joel followed her out. Her back was as stiff as if old-fashion starch had been poured into it as she led him through the restaurant.

He was impressed. The whole building reeked of cleanliness--and not the antiseptic, medicine-y odor that so often plagued other establishments. A delightful smell of something spicy and delectably appetizing pervaded every room. Floors clean, no smudged walls, crisp, attractive tables. Bathrooms spotless. Kitchen organized and as neat as a busy area could be.

In front of the back door he'd entered yesterday, he gave Miss Starli a questioning look.

An impatient expression flicked across her features.

If you must.

He shoved open the heavy door and waited

for her to precede him.

"Must you orient yourself to the outside, too?" Her sarcasm bit into his joviality, but he ignored it.

"You might want to say something to your cleaning boy about leaving the door unlocked." He nodded at the younger man spraying the back car park.

Her only answer was an annoyed glare.

They circled the building in silence. Joel studied the restaurant, surprised and pleased at the quiet, elegant look of it. He hadn't thought it would be so up-class. He took his time walking around, glad to see the windows sparkling, the landscaping simple and attractive. Eaves painted, foundation in good repair.

Back at the rear door, Starli snapped. "Satisfied? Does it meet with your approval? Sir?"

"Quite." He pursed his lips in a silent whistle. "I think I'll give it a go. Providing that you greet me with a big smile every day."

"If that's what it takes to get you to stay, feel free to take off now." Starli reached for the door handle, but Joel beat her to it. Sighing, she stalked ahead of him, saying nothing but walking straightway out of the kitchen.

The gaze of the three kitchen workers lit on him with varying degrees of curiosity.

He gave Camille a wink, grinned at Juanita, and nodded at Louis.

The women cast furtive grins toward their departing boss, but Louis ignored him and with a sour expression, concentrated on the meat he was slicing.

When Starli walked on, Joel paused long enough to say, "Have you a good start on dinner?"

At Louis' gruff assent, he went on, "I'll be back in a jiffy. Want to check on something. When you get a minute, cut me as many steaks as you can from those goose necks in the freezer."

He headed down the hallway to the offices. Starli and Manny stood together talking, but both paused.

"Wanted to ask. Isn't there a flat that goes with the job? I could batch with Uncle Laurence for a few nights, but really need my own place."

"The apartment cleaners will finish in the morning. You're free to move in any time after that."

Joel's gaze moved to his uncle. "Will you have time to check on a vehicle for me? You know what I like and know where to ask better than I do."

"I'll take care of it."

A scream rent the air. Joel turned as the kitchen door slammed open. Louis stood in the doorway.

Together, chef and owner moved, but Joel beat her through the door. "What happened?" he snapped.

"Oh, sir, Juanita's sliced her finger off." Camille pointed, hysterics in her young voice.

He shouted orders as he leaped into action. Juanita sat sprawled on the floor, a bloody mess in her lap. Joel knelt and inspected the injured digit. Thankfully, Camille's hysterical declaration was untrue. Juanita's finger was severely cut, but definitely still attached.

He accepted the clean white cloths Starli handed him and asked, "Someone call the squad?"

"Manny did."

He slipped an arm around the shaken woman.

Ten minutes later, the squad arrived and within a short time they sped away. Joel turned back to the kitchen. Camille stood still. When she didn't move, he peered at her. "Are you all right? I'll especially need your help now that Juanita won't be able to work tonight."

She didn't answer, only raised a hand and toppled over. Joel caught her and eased her to the floor.

His gaze went to Starli's face.

~*~

Fortunately the restaurant was quiet right now. Joel had left Starli tending to Camille who'd refused to be sent home although Starli was being just as determined to make her employee rest in her own personal office. Poor girl. Scared her badly, it had. But he was positive the faint had been a faked one.

He'd taken the opportunity to head back to the kitchen. He wanted a head start on those steaks, and marinating them was the key to the tenderness they needed.

Louis stood muttering, the knife slicing through the air as well as decimating the tomato. His face was a dark mask of bull-like rage. He didn't bother to look at Joel.

"What happened?" Joel prompted

"Stupidity," the assistant chef muttered and gave an extra loud chop to the poor tomato.

Joel eyed the abused vegetable and wondered if he should jump to its defense. "Juanita was careless?"

"She was stupid." The man flashed Joel a look. "How many times I have told her how to slice the tomatoes, and can she follow the directions?" He gave Joel no time to answer. "No. She cannot do this one little piece of advice."

Joel felt his lips pulling, begging to smile, but he held it back. He'd sensed enough this morning to know Louis' trust would not be an easy thing to gain, and he needed that to do his job properly.

Why had Louis been listening in on Manny and Starli's conversation earlier? That's what he'd been doing. His posture of hugging the wall, his tilt of the head all screamed 'eavesdropping.' He'd been startled when Joel had walked up behind him. He'd not jumped or said anything, but the glare and the sudden departure gave him away.

"Well, my man, it looks as if it's just you and me to get ready for tonight. We'll need to work like mad men to have all things as they should be."

Louis' face didn't rearrange into agreeableness, but he gave a quick nod at Joel's implied request, swept the squashed tomato aside, and reached for a new one.

Satisfied the man would do his best, whether for him or Miss Starli didn't matter. Right now, Joel was thankful for what he could get.

Chapter Four

"**A**m I interrupting?"

Even before she raised her head, Starli recognized the voice. Stewart—or better known to his friends in Appleton as Stu—Stroth. He'd certainly been a friend to her through the past few years of her life besides an excellent banker and her go-to person for business advice.

He might be a bit too serious—too much like herself, as Caro insisted albeit with a teasing grin plastered on her face—but he was an excellent banker. She just wished he wasn't so adamant about pushing their relationship to something else.

"Come in, Stu." Starli gave him a friendly wave. "What are you doing here during banking hours?"

"Dad asked me to check that all was ready for the banquet." He walked into her office, unfastening his coat. He patted his collar and shoulders. "What a nuisance. I believe I've lost another scarf."

"Nothing new there. You're always doing that." She laughed at his disgruntled expression. "When have I ever not been ready? Menus are planned and the food prepped. Toni's offered to do the flower arrangements early Friday morning, and all waiters are healthy and anxious for the extra work. I hear almost everyone's accepted the invitation."

"Good. I told Dad you'd have everything

under control, but you know him." Stu nodded, his jelled, short-cut hair shining in the ceiling light. A darker blond than her new chef, but still very, very attractive. "I wish you weren't entertaining us though. You could have gone as my date."

"But I am. Your dad specifically requested me."

"I know. Still...I heard you've hired another chef. Was my information correct that he came from overseas?" Stu frowned. "I wish you would have asked me to run a background check on him. You can't be too careful, and I'm always willing to help out. You know that."

"I do, but he comes highly recommended by Manny."

"I see."

But did he? He was more disturbed than she'd ever seen him, and Stu never got upset— at least, not with her.

He jumped to his feet and strode to her window staring out it for seconds before returning to his seat. His features had cleared. "I don't like you taking chances like this. It could affect the loans you need. But never mind now. We'll work around it."

Starli nodded agreement unsure of what to say at his untypical behavior.

"Are you busy tonight? I need to run to Charleston for a quick 10-minute business meet. We could enjoy dinner at the LaCrost..." He pulled two tickets from his jacket pocket and waved them. "...and take in the Mountain Men concert. Always enjoy their singing."

You do. How many times did she have to explain to the man she couldn't get into the bluegrass music with any real enthusiasm? "I can't, Stu. You know, next to Apple Blossoms, LaCrost is a favorite of mine, but I'm swamped today. I won't be free anytime early enough to enjoy an evening with you. It'll be late before I can even think of going home, and it's already pushing afternoon."

His frown indicated an argument was coming. She'd endured them before, so stopping it before it started was the wise angle.

"I'm really sorry, Stu. I could do with an evening off, but I just can't tonight."

"That's the third time this month, you've weaseled out of a date with me. If I didn't know better, I'd think you were avoiding me."

Great. She'd have to spend fifteen minutes pacifying the man. It wasn't that she didn't enjoy his company occasionally or hadn't appreciated his help through the years. He attended church, but not regularly, and often she'd wondered if his attendance wasn't for the chance to sit beside her. But he'd been active in social affairs around town and was well-liked and looked up to by the town people.

Oh, well.

"Stu. How can you think that? You've been such a friend through the years. I'll never be able to thank you enough for all you've done for me."

"And that's why—"

"Exactly. You know very well how busy we both are. It's just been crazy getting our schedules to mesh lately." She leaned forward, hoping to convey her sincerity. As much as she appreciated him, he didn't quite measure up to her status of an intimate friendship. "I thought the aftermath of the Christmas and New Year's season would be slower, but it hasn't even hinted at that."

He stood abruptly. "Starli, I think we could go far together. Think about it. I'm ready."

She stared at him. Was she wrong? Making a mistake in not agreeing to what he wanted? He was a fine man, polite and generous with his time when she'd needed him. He was stocky-built like his father—Appleton's mayor—but worked out regularly and kept himself trim and in shape. And truth be told, fun to be with, when she deigned to give into his invitations. If only...

"Soon, Stu. Soon."

He sketched a wave at her, and to give him credit, a smile of forgiveness, as he strode out the door. "I'll hold you to it."

And he would.

~*~

"Starli?"

"Yes, Camille?"

How many more interruptions would she have today? Inwardly, Starli sighed. But she'd always tried to be available for her employees, open-door policy, as Joel had jokingly put it. Today was no different, busy or not.

The young girl peeking at her from the doorway had a saucy grin on her face. To look at her, you'd never guess she'd fainted dead away earlier.

She'd hired her at Caro's request, and Caro was the modern day, Appleton, West Virginia's real life Joan of Arc, as she and Toni liked to tease their friend. Camille was a sweet kid in a lot of ways, but underneath the exterior of vibrant youth, Starli suspected resided a layer of toughness. How deep that went was anyone's guess. She truly hoped the girl was a step up from her shiftless family.

"I wanted to talk with you."

"Come on in, Camille."

The girl—was she nineteen or twenty? She couldn't remember—waltzed into Starli's office and sat in the chair opposite her own. She stared down at her lap for a long moment, a satisfied smile on her face. Then she looked up, and her features settled into an earnest, make-you-understand expression.

"I've decided what I want to do with my life."

"You have?"

"Yes." Her head nodded. "I want to be just like you."

Oh, dear, what did she have in her head now? Starli had no time to ask questions.

"I can't think of a person I admire more than you. So-o-o, I've signed up for piano lessons. When I have more time, I'm going to practice my ice-skating. And I want to own my own restaurant business someday. Like you. So I was thinking..."

Where on earth had Camille come up with this? Didn't she have enough to deal with, without having a young person dog her heels every hour of the day?

"...if you could give me more responsibility. I think I'd be great as a manager, and you could teach me what I don't know. Sort of be your— what's it called?—apprentice. You know I'm a good worker, and smart. I can learn quick. Will you do it?"

~*~

"Starli, you need to see this."

Manny's grim tone sent her heart speed-bumping through her chest.

"What's wrong?" Starli jumped to her feet and followed him to the front of the restaurant.

He didn't need to answer. She saw it right away.

The dark mahogany reception desk stood in its usual regal position welcoming their patrons and guests with dignity. But slashed across the top lay a foot-long jagged scratch.

Tears filled her eyes at the defacement. She and one of her best friends, Toni DeLuca—now Douglas—had searched, found, and fallen in love with this desk. Toni, being a carpenter, had done the restoration. The piece had added the perfect touch she'd felt the restaurant needed.

She touched the top, smoothing her hand over the defacement. A hand covered hers, and she looked up at Manny. "Who did this? *Why* would someone do this?"

"I don't know, Miss Starli. I just saw it and have no idea when it happened because the log-in register for guests covered it."

Starli nodded. "It's damaged and will never be the same."

"It's damaged, you're correct. But it will be a reminder of how you conquered this, of how it made you that much stronger."

Was that a hint of moisture in those wise eyes?

"I dare say, Toni will be able to repair this even to your satisfaction."

She felt her lips tipping upward at his encouraging words and gave the desk a loving pat. "I dare say you're right, Manny, as you always are."

"I know I'm right.

"I suppose we'll never know who did this destruction. I don't want to accuse or think it was an employee, and can't even fathom one of my friends hurting me like this. A guest is a preposterous suggestion, so who does that leave?"

Their gazes met.

One name flashed in her mind but she wasn't about to say it aloud.

~*~

Starli raced through the black night toward her home and almost reached it, when a giant conveyor belt that appeared beneath her feet, pulled her back. Ryan, on her heels, stretched long arms for her. Thick fingers clutched at her blouse and gripped it. His deep, demanding voice morphed into Roland's loud gruff one and blasted in her ears.

"Starle-e-e, you killed my brother."

"Stupid woman. Stupid, stupid, stupid."

Shrill ringing mingled with his harsh voice. She knew what was coming and raised her arms.

The ringing continued, but Roland's voice faded. Struggling, pulling herself from the depths of the nightmare, Starli at last lifted heavy lids, her blood pounding. She stretched out an arm, touched the nightstand and the ringing phone, but didn't pick up the receiver. Consciousness returned.

Starli's chest heaved, her body, drenched in terror-induced sweat, shook. Ryan was gone, would never hit her again. She struggled to release herself from the tangle of bed covers.

The phone on her bedside table rang without stopping. Twenty times. A pause, then began again.

She groaned and wished she hadn't been so adamant about no answering machines. But she couldn't bear to listen to Roland's constant messages.

Her blurry eyes took in the bare-bones bedroom. The stark simplicity satisfied her, somehow kept the terror at bay. She knew that someday she'd have to forget Ryan's impulsive buying for every piece of modern technology that had once cluttered their home. She'd have to adjust.

But not yet.

Not today.

The phone began its ringing again. How many times had it already rung? She stared at it, then at her clock. 7:30. Who on earth was calling this early?

Manny? Something wrong at the restaurant? Worry nudged her still sleepy brain, and she reached for the receiver.

"Yes? This is..." She heard the huskiness in her voice and cleared her throat.

"Miss Starli? Are you awake?"

Joel Peterman-Blair? What did he want? Her grumpiness edged up a notch. "What? Do you know what time it is?"

"My watch says...hmm...seven-thirty. Were you still asleep?"

Still? He was going to make her admit she was still asleep at seven-thirty in the morning? Maybe she would have been awake at her usual 5:30 if she hadn't stayed awake half the night stressing over Juanita and her finger, which fortunately hadn't been severed in spite of Camille's hysterics.

On top of that, Camille's crazy proposition made her uneasy, and worse, pondering who'd been able to sneak into Apple Blossoms and damage the reception desk. She'd been so keyed up by the time she'd arrived home last night, she couldn't sleep. Normally, after hours of practice on the piano, she'd be calm enough to sleep like a babe. Not last night. No wonder she felt like death warmed over.

"Yes, I was. I happen to sleep in occasionally."

"Of course, I understand. I wondered if you'd like to show me the town."

"Show you the town?" She sounded like a parrot. Was he crazy? Calling her before she was out of bed and asking a virtual stranger to show the sights to an Englishman? Who did he think he was? The king of England?

No, *just* a knight.

She frowned, then saw her reflection in the mirror opposite her bed and lifted a hand to smooth out the wrinkle between her brows. If she had to be around this man very long, she'd be old, wrinkled, and gray before she reached forty. She heard his chuckle, and wondered if he'd read her latest thought across the airwaves.

"I don't think so. Ask Manny to be your tour guide."

On second thought, she didn't want him to corral Manny and spoil his routine. Another sigh escaped her lips.

"You eat breakfast? Let me buy you a

doughnut and some coffee."

"Sorry. I don't eat doughnuts."

"Coffee then? Tea?"

"I can make a perfectly good cup of coffee when I want one, but I prefer tea."

His subdued laugh came through the line, confident and low.

"Come on. Let's go for a leisurely stroll. It'll do you good. Put some pink in those lovely cheeks."

Starli's gaze flew to the mirror again and searched her face. She did look pale. She started to frown, then stopped herself. He was just another man who thought nothing of tossing around compliments that meant little.

"Agreed? Go comb the tangles out of those silky strands of yours. I'll pick you up in fifteen minutes."

"I don't want..." It was too late. Sir Joel Peterman-Blair had hung up.

Starli considered her mirrored self for a good twenty seconds, before throwing back the covers and heading to the bathroom. When the man arrived, she'd put him in his place. He might be quite important in England, or wherever he worked, but he was just a chef to her. The sooner he got that straight, the better off they'd both be. She had no desire to be friends with him. Ever. Period.

Fifteen minutes later the doorbell rang. Starli stood at the top of her stairs. She'd refused to dress up for him, but she hadn't been able to resist the soft white sweater she'd bought last weekend.

The thought crossed her mind to stomp down the stairs preparatory to chewing out Mr.

Sir Peterman-Blair, but she couldn't bring herself to do it. She cared too much for these old, but still gorgeous stairs.

Instead she glided down the stairs and opened the door determined to be firm and steady in her refusal of his friendship.

He leaned against the porch rail, a broad smile on his face that lit up the cloudy day. How could anyone be that handsome and be earthly? Warning bells clanged in her mind. But the first words out of his mouth halted her own.

~*~

Joel caught his breath but didn't pause when he spoke. "I say, you're the loveliest creature in West Virginia."

He saw the surprised twinkle before she doused it. On her guard, was she? Well, his paternal grandmother had passed enough of the Irish to him he could deal with a smidgen of cool reserve from the fair lady.

"Are you ready? Let's get going before your beautiful town comes alive."

Her lips firmed, her body became a statue, almost as if she was in a trance. Then, as if she'd been kissed and awakened by a prince— the thought stirred the laughter inside him— she moved and picked up a jacket before joining him on the porch.

"I've located a coffee shop. We'll have a sip or two of some good coffee in a bit."

He felt rather than saw her glance, but plowed ahead, determined to break through that icy exterior. Somewhere beneath it had to be some warmth. If he chipped at it enough..."I took the liberty of bringing home that great big recipe book at your restaurant and a menu to peruse last night. Some interesting items on the menu. I think I know what is missing to bring your restaurant up to par."

"Up to par?" She bristled at his words.

He held up a hand. "No offense. I meant, if I've judged you correctly, you want only the best for Apple Blossoms. Your meat selections are excellent. And I like that you offer a variety of fresh vegetables. But the desserts—that's where it's lacking in extraordinary choices."

"What do you mean?" Concern edged her voice.

Her anxious face bothered him. Little wrinkle lines deepened between her brows. He wanted to smooth them away, but refrained and hastened to assure her. He did touch her hand in an attempt to soothe her worry, but she pulled away, so he walked on, giving her some space. "You have some good selections on the menu, but I think we can improve those. Let me show you how we can make your desserts topnotch. Trust me."

"Trust you? I don't know you. I trust Manny and Caroline and Toni only."

Ah, ha. Someone had betrayed her trust.

A tiny ripple of anger bit at his insides. Who would hurt this woman? He spoke again and modulated his voice to gentleness. "I see. But I am the expert chef. If I work for Apple Blossoms I'll not have my name blotted by anything second rate."

He met her eyes and held them, daring her in a silent challenge to refuse his suggestion. "I'm sure your current choices are delicious. But what are you running? A roadside joint?

The pub down the road?"

"Of course not." Her face reddened, her words snapped.

"Then..."

She studied him for a moment before conceding. "I'll take a look at your suggestions. Then we'll go from there. I'll want some samples. They must be desserts the locals will enjoy."

"Trust me, Love." The words slipped out before he could stop them.

"Sure." Her lips pressed together.

Her sarcasm was charming, but he decided to ignore it. One thing at a time. "Now that that's settled, tell me about the town.

She drew in a long breath, and he loved the sound.

"Appleton is an old town, with a historical Indian battle between the Shawnees led by Chief Cornstalk, and the white soldiers. Interesting spot that encourages one to use their imagination." Enthusiasm sparkled from her features, and Joel didn't want to take his gaze from the sight.

"The state of West Virginia is famous for its coal mines. Many a family man has made a living deep under the ground. It's a dangerous job, but the main source of income for scores of men. Years ago, children even worked in the mines."

Something definitely bothered her. Himself? Problems with the business? When he spoke again, his tone was gentler than it had been, the teasing gone.

"Doesn't West Virginia have a nickname?"

"Wild and wonderful."

Joel pursed his lips. "That's it. Wild and wonderful. And yet this wild country has produced a regal creature like you."

Her gaze grilled him as she studied him. Measuring. Probing his sincerity with her needle-like judgment.

He pushed on. "Do you ever find the mountains overwhelming?"

"Overwhelming? No. Threatening if you don't respect the obstacles they present in different seasons. Challenging for those who feel compelled to conquer them through sports or sheer daring."

"You like sports?"

She shrugged. "I adore ice skating and have tried skiing. I wanted to take lessons, but have never found the time. I don't care much for the rougher sports either as a participant or a viewer. What about you?"

"I've always liked challenging sports. In college I did pretty well in polo. Since then I've tried hang gliding, a little mountain climbing, some skiing, and most water sports. I even went up a few times ballooning."

"Really? I think I'd like to do that.

"Ballooning? We'll try it sometime, if I can find the equipment and someone to help."

Her emerald eyes shone. Then a cloud settled across her face. She shook her head.

"No, I don't think so."

~*~

Disappointment lodged in her. Starli raised her gaze to a sky that promised a fair day. What fun to sail above the world looking down on everything earthly. She sighed. Not for her and not with Joel Peterman-Blair.

Definitely not with him.

"We'd better head for that coffee. I'm running out of time." Starli urged.

"Right. Let's go."

He set off at a steady pace. Starli liked his stride and matched it. That three miles she ran on her treadmill everyday was paying off now.

Five minutes later, they turned onto the block of the coffee shop.

Laughter exploded from him. "You buy if I beat you there."

"You want to race? You think you can outrun me?" Before she could question her decision, she burst into a sprint. She heard his pounding steps behind her, heard him call out something, but paid no attention. She felt him grasp her shoulder just as she collapsed against the door. Laughing, she twisted around.

Joel brushed at the hair on his forehead, his face inches from hers.

Blinking, Starli pressed her back against the shop. She fumbled for the handle. Was his face moving closer? His lips parted, and she could feel his warm breath on her cheeks. Was he planning to *kiss* her?

"I let you win." He teased in a husky low voice.

"Oh, yeah, right." She jeered back at him. Exhilaration shot through her. "I beat you fair and square. You owe me one supersized coffee."

He patted his pockets. "Oops. I think I left my wallet in my room. You bring any money?"

"Cheater."

He chuckled, and she responded with a

reluctant laugh of her own. Withdrawing a brown leather embossed wallet, he held it up. "Guess I do have it."

With a shove at the door, Joel indicated for her to enter, and Starli swept in. She eyed the menu on the wall, looking for the most expensive drink she could find. If he wanted to issue challenges, he'd have to pay.

Her gaze lit on the coffee shop owner.

Rita Mae Simpson touched her dark hair, fingernails glistening a dark red.

Starli froze. How could she be so casual when she knew Starli despised her past actions? Toni hadn't punished Rita Mae for her twisted acts of hate, had generously shared her inheritance with the woman. But as hard as Starli tried, she couldn't quite forgive the woman for the heartache she'd caused her dear friend.

The owner of The Coffee House eyed Joel, her lips the same color as her nails, and curved up, her whole manner, flirtatious.

"I heard you're the new cook at Apple Blossoms." Her lashes dipped in a slow flirting way.

Joel grinned back at the woman. "I'm the chef."

"Anything I can do to help you get adjusted, just let me know. I know everything and everybody in these parts." Rita Mae's simpering tone purred.

"Sounds like a person I need to know."

Heart as cold as an ice cube, Starli interrupted. "So very tiresome. If we could have some service?"

Rita Mae turned slowly to fill their orders,

her gaze lingering on Joel. Rita crooned in a husky voice. "Big guy, we need to talk."

Starli fought to keep her lips from twisting in disgust. Another flirty man.

Chapter Five

Joel scooted his chair closer to the table, sipped at his steaming cup. Hmmm. Good. He eyed the frozen queen across from him. Was it his imagination or had she iced over after entering the shop? So much for his hope of progress.

He'd been surprised she'd accepted his challenge of a race so quickly. His heart had flopped watching her pump down the sidewalk, abandoned to all thoughts but winning.

Let her win? He'd challenge and let her win every day to see her shadows vanquished.

"Tell me about this special event coming up. What do I need to do to prepare for it? Do you have a menu planned?"

Starli's gaze refocused on his face. She set her cup down carefully as if waking from a dream. "Event? It's our first one of the winter season. The town council is having its dinner for all the business owners in the area. I want no hitches. I'll need to use the mayor and town council for a reference when I expand."

"You have plans to open other Apple Blossoms?" She was ambitious. Joel liked that.

"The plans are in the very beginning stages, but I have begun putting out feelers for the best locations."

"Good thinking. I like women who use their brains for something besides flirting."

"I've had to learn to stand on my own feet."

"So these events—they are to build good

community relations?"

"Mostly, but they're also fun."

"Some special events to keep things interesting." Joel nodded his agreement.

"Sort of. It's a lot of work. I try to keep Apple Blossoms warm and inviting but upbeat enough people feel special when they are there. Classy enough for more important functions." She shrugged.

"What's the menu for these council-people?"

"They requested beef. I thought about our Spinach-Stuffed Beef Tenderloin."

"Perfect. Let's put mashed potato tamales with it and maybe a green bean and tomato salad." Joel cocked an eyebrow at her.

Like porcupine quills, the doubts in those beautiful cool green eyes stood out. Her voice bordered on stiffness when she spoke. "Our previous chef refused to serve potatoes with the beef."

"You want her to serve as the chef that evening?" Joel would not back down. This gorgeous woman needed to know he was in charge. Strangely, he sensed it was vital he stand firm on the menu selections. She needed to know he wasn't her puppet chef.

"Of course not. Don't be silly. If you think the potatoes will work, we'll go with it. *This* time. What's for dessert?"

Joel tapped his fingers on the table. "Let's see. What about a Cranberry Cake with warm Orange Sauce? They'll bite our arms off for it."

"Sounds like a good selection. We don't serve alcoholic beverages, but we have a nice selection of other drinks that'll complement the food."

"I have a drink concoction I mix that would be super."

"Do you create many menus?"

"Sure. I also add my own touch to most items. Didn't Uncle Lawrence tell you about the one I created while still in school?"

Music hummed from his employer's pocket. She pulled out her cell phone and checked the number. White-blond hair fell over her face as she bent her head. Her warm, spontaneous laughter when they'd raced and joked earlier had tempted him.

Almost, he'd been tempted to kiss those red lips of hers.

~*~

Starli didn't recognize the number.

Her gaze drifted to Joel again. Confident. Perfect. Too good to be true. Why did he have to be so perfect?

She frowned and answered.

"Starlie-e-e. Enjoying breakfast with your new man? And leaving your business unprotected?"

The room whirled in a dizzying circle. No. No. She saw Joel turn half away, giving her some privacy.

"How did you get my cell number?" She managed to squeeze out the question between dry lips. She'd just had it changed and no one—no one—but her closest friends had it.

But then, how had Joel gotten it? Her gaze flashed to him and back to the floor.

The coarse laugh grated on her overly sensitive nerves.

"Forgot all about Ryan, haven't you? Glad to be rid of him, aren't you? Going to kill this one

56

like you did my brother?"

Each question slapped her in the face. "I didn't kill..."

Joel swung his chair around.

Roland Stratton gave her no chance to finish. "Oh, yes, you did. You drove him to drink. Drove him away that night in anger. You did it, Starlie-e-e, and I won't let you ever forget it. I'm coming after you and when I get through—"

"But you're the police. You can't do that." She shuddered at the wail in her voice.

"I can. I will."

The connection went dead, and she winced. Hand shaking, she stuffed the phone in her pocket. She didn't look at Joel. Couldn't. She watched a tanned hand slide across the table.

"Is something wrong?"

Starli shook her head. Refuse to acknowledge the threats. Don't talk about them, and they could be ignored. Maybe they'd go away. If only.

She lifted her cup for a sip of coffee, but her hand shook so much it sloshed onto the table. She set it down.

"Someone's bothering you?"

She could hear the steel in his voice.

"It's just a prank call. Don't worry about it. I can handle it." She gasped out the words and stared out the window. Was Roland out there watching her? She jumped as her cell rang again, then groaned.

She knew Joel's gaze never left her. Relief like a warm blanket covered her when she read the number. Caroline Gibson. Fumbling, Starli slid a fingertip across the screen.

"Starli? Is that you? You sound funny."

"It's me." It was so good to hear Caro's teasing voice she wanted to give out an uncharacteristic whoop. A friend. Her gaze flew to Joel. No. He wasn't to be trusted. Yet. If ever.

Caro jabbered in her ear. "I found this awesome concert with what's his name—you know that guy you like so well?"

"Pierre Markus."

"That's him. It's on Saturday, February third. Want to go? My early birthday present to you."

"I'd love it. But I can't leave the restaurant on a Saturday. That's my night to play."

"Nonsense. Of course, you can. You substitute for your other groups all the time. Call in a favor. They love you. They'll be glad for the handsome fee you pay them. And Manny and that new chef can handle things for one night. No. Wait. Let Louis take care of it that night. We'll all go. You ask the chef as your date—he is as good looking as Manny said, isn't he?"

"Hold it right there. There's no way." Starli cast a surreptitious glance at the man sitting across from her, his gaze *still* brazenly focused on her face. His lips curled up in a knowing grin. Could he hear Caroline and her outrageous suggestion? Starli pressed the phone tighter against her ear.

"Then I'll do it."

"No." She almost shouted the objection.

"Take your pick. Either you do it, or I will."

The no-nonsense radiating from her friend left Starli sighing in exasperation. "I can't believe I love you."

"Don't try to change the subject. Which will it be?"

"Okay, okay, slave driver. I'll do it."

"Fine. Then Toni and Perrin, me, and Toby. I suppose he'll want to invite that simpering new friend of his. You and Joel. It'll make a wonderful evening for you."

Joel's white teeth gleamed as his mouth widened. He *had* heard.

She lowered her gaze to the tabletop until Caro hung up. Safe move. Then she shifted and blurted, "Why do you call Manny, 'Laurence'?"

"That's his name. Laurence Manley Peterman. I've always called him Uncle Laurence."

The double chocolate-flavored beverage slid down her throat as she sipped, and she peered at him over the rim. "You must be close and spend a lot of time together."

A flash of shame crossed Joel's face. "Not so much the last few years now that I travel so much. He's always been my champion though, and I know I burden him with many of my problems."

"I haven't heard him complain." Starli's senses sharpened. "How many times have you seen him this past year?"

"Are you insisting I confess all? Worried I'm neglecting my uncle? I have taken Uncle Lawrence a bit for granted this past year. Especially after what he's done for me." A thoughtful frown marred his perfect features.

"Why were you knighted?"

"I've spent several years in third world

countries cooking for various organizations."

"Really? Several?"

"Two and a half years in a couple of African countries. Right before I took the last job I had. A few of the organizations paid a small stipend, but mostly, it was volunteer."

"I think that's wonderful." Starli placed a hand flat on the tabletop. "I wish—"

~*~

The white hand lying in front of Joel was smooth, in spite of the scar that ran across the side of it. He noticed Starli's little finger, the slight crook in it and reached over to stroke it with his thumb. "Looks like a bad break. Childhood injury?"

Starli's face paled. She pulled her hand back and tucked it into her lap. "I need to get going. I'm already late at the restaurant, and I'm never late." She stood, looked down at him. "You'd better get going, too. I think your boss frowns on latecomers."

With that, she turned and walked out, her left hand hidden in a jacket pocket.

A beautiful enigma. Had she purposely ignored his question? Who was threatening her? And most of all, could he help her?

~*~

Starli jogged the whole way home. Why had she allowed herself to be talked into spending time with that romancer? The scorn she'd felt earlier surged again as she thought about his smile at Rita Mae Simpson with her atrocious flirting. Had he done it in fun? Teasing? Or was it his friendly personality?

And had he almost kissed *her*?

She stumbled across a crack in the sidewalk

and bit down harder on her lip than she'd meant to. Who cared why he'd done it? He was being a typical male.

She unlocked and shoved open her door, started to head to her bedroom to change clothes, then strode to her piano and sat down. Her fingers caressed the keys.

If only she'd made different decisions in her life.

If only she'd stayed in school, gone to Europe for her musical studies.

If only she'd never met Ryan Stratton.

If only...

She stared down at her crooked finger, the forever reminder of Ryan's cruelty.

~*~

Starli pulled into the reserved parking area of Apple Blossoms just as the sun peeped from behind a snowy white cloud, bathing Apple Blossoms in a warm golden glow.

Pausing before getting out, she studied her business building, the structure strong, yet pleasant, the windows sparkling and clear, the cozy, inviting but unobtrusive sign that welcomed her diners.

But why, instead of the dim night light that usually lit the reception area inside, was there bright lights coming from the distant hallway?

Had Louis left the lights on last night? Or Joel? Perhaps he'd come straight from their run and The Coffee House to Blossoms? One thing for sure, sitting here in her vehicle didn't answer the questions.

She started to insert the key in the exterior door and realized it was unlocked. A thief? She fumbled for her cell phone, then chided herself.

You're paranoid. Manny's probably here getting an early start on the day.

Edging inside, her guard up, she avoided flipping any lights on. If someone was here who had no business being so, she didn't want to alert them beforehand. She peeked into the dining section and saw nothing amiss, so she moved on into the kitchen and stopped abruptly at the site of the walk-in freezer door standing wide open.

If her heart could have sunk lower than her feet, it would have. Who could have left the freezer door open all night? She'd never known Louis to do such a thing, and Manny was diligent about checking everything, from doors to kitchen produce. There was no one else except...

Starli bit her bottom lip. She couldn't bear to think it could have been Joel. Not because she cared a whit for him, but Manny? She wouldn't have him hurt for any amount of money. He'd been her rock from the moment she'd hired him. And if it hurt Manny because of Joel's involvement, then that made a difference.

Her gaze swept over the meats and frozen foods stocked. Stretching out a hand, she checked one of the meats and winced at the softness. Thawing.

"What's going on?"

Starli was sure later she'd jumped a good three feet off the floor. She whirled. "Why are you here this early?"

Joel Peterman-Blair.

He ignored her question and strode into the freezer. He touched a package of chicken, then another. "Why are these thawing? Is the freezer broken?"

Before she could even open her mouth to respond, he'd moved to the thermometer and stood gazing at it, shaking his head. "This can't be. I checked it myself yesterday before I left. Who's done this?"

He turned slowly, but didn't look at her, only stared as if thinking, his mind a thousand miles away. "I wonder..."

"What?"

Joel turned to look at her. "Never mind. It was nothing." But then he suddenly sprang back into the freezer and began gathering the packages of meat.

He gave her no time to ask questions. The grim set of his lips would have alerted her to the seriousness of the situation even if she hadn't known. A cook she might not be, but a business woman she was. The loss of this amount of meat would set her back several thousand dollars. Dollars she wasn't willing to surrender to whoever had done this.

"Grab what you can carry and deposit it at my work table."

"What are you doing?" she asked even as she loaded her arms.

"Changing tonight's dinner special and getting a head start on the inspired menu I've just had for Friday's banquet." For the first time Joel cocked a grin at her. "I'm saving your skin—er–meat."

"But the city council specifically requested beef—"

"I know, but by the time they've sampled the first bite of my dish, they'll have forgotten they wanted beef." He grinned even wider. "The beef is farther back in the freezer so still well frozen."

And for the first time since she'd met the over confident, overly pushy chef, she was thrilled he knew what he was talking about.

More power to him.

~*~

"I didn't know Camille Findley and that assistant chef of yours were such good friends."

Feeling more relaxed knowing Joel had everything under control for Friday night, Starli smiled at the blond banker as he pulled out her chair. "I don't keep track."

"It's no big deal." Stu settled into his own chair across from hers. "Only I'm sure everyone else was already gone last night. I thought Manny always closed up for you."

Was Stu right, but how could he be mistaken? He'd always been so reliable and wasn't one to jump to conclusions. Perhaps Joel had asked them to stay late to perform some task for tomorrow. Had Louis accidentally forgotten to make sure the freezer door was shut and latched?

She was glad she'd given in and come when Stu had waylaid her as she exited the restaurant this evening. Her plan had been a quiet evening at home, maybe a long soak and an hour's practice on the piano, then dinner and settle down in her favorite chair for an hour's read with Carole Brown's newest Denton and Alex Davies' mystery.

The plan hadn't materialized, but seeing Stu's simple happiness was worth giving up her plan. What would it hurt? He was a good man and a friend.

"Are you sure it was last night? Perhaps they were finishing up some tasks Joel had assigned them."

"I'm sure. But I will say, when I stopped for a latte at The Coffee House before heading home, they were there too." He motioned to a waiter. "She was shedding some of those fake tears she produces quite often. Not sure if they were arguing or what, but Louis looked like a thundercloud."

The waiter approached, and Stu gave their orders.

The brightness of the evening dimmed. Was Camille now working her usual tactics on Louis?

Chapter Six

Friday morning. The councilman's banquet-day had finally arrived. She'd avoided the kitchen for the past few days, but could avoid Joel no longer. Her need to control and maintain order overrode her growing uneasiness when in Joel's presence.

Starli shoved open the swinging door and peeked into the kitchen. Joel stood wrapped in a white apron. A tuft of his blond hair stood straight up. Something must be tickling his funny bone for every now and then a chuckle emanated from his throat.

Caro's insistence that she invite Joel to the concert echoed in her ears. She pressed her lips together. She didn't want to think about that.

"Ah, ha. Our good employer coming to check up on us? To make sure I have everything as planned?" Flour from Joel's hands drifted back to the countertop.

Starli lifted an eyebrow and walked on into the room.

"As usual, I have everything under control." He went on before she could speak—if she'd had a mind to—and nodded at the steaming pots on the huge commercial stove. "We're on target time-wise, so you need have no worries there."

"Good. What's the name of this concoction you'll be serving?"

"A surprise, Love."

"I'm not your love, and I don't like surprises."

His brows lifted as if she'd delivered the most unbelievable news. "I seriously doubt that, but we'll deal with that statement later."

"By the way, Stu told me last night that he saw Louis and Camille here in the restaurant after hours. You didn't assign them extra work?"

"Stu? You were out with Stu?"

He'd honed in on that fact rather than what she'd said. "About Louis and Camille?"

"No, I didn't. And Manny and I were the last ones to leave. I know he locked the doors securely."

"That's odd. How could they have gotten inside?"

"Ask them. Or I will if you prefer."

"I can do it."

He nodded and asked, "Want some Scotch pancakes?"

"Pancakes?" Starli felt her stomach growl. How long had it been since she'd eaten a pancake?

He grinned. "Come on. Just one. I have fresh fruit and my very own blended syrup for your pleasure."

Temptation, temptation. He was so hard to resist. "Just one."

Joel nodded at the stool. "Sit and talk to me."

She'd never felt so indecisive in her life. Joel Peterman-Blair's good looks attracted her. But the alarm bells ringing inside her constantly reminded her to be careful. She felt like a butterfly flirting with fire. "I've got work to do."

"Isn't someone coming in to help with decorations?" Joel measured flour, then whipped eggs in another bowl.

Starli watched his strong hands work in confident moves. "Toni. She has a special touch with flowers. Manny will be here shortly, too. He always makes it a practice to be here before most of the staff."

Starli's breath caught. She'd never seen a man with such dark lashes.

"What's your favorite fruit? We've got strawberries, peaches, apples and bananas."

Her heart warmed. She whispered. "Don't let it get out, but I adore all types of fruit. You choose."

Joel lifted a spoon, batter dripping. "Do you realize that even though I heard you play only the one night, you are my favorite entertainer?"

"Really?"

"The customers love your live music. Go play a couple of songs while I finish these pancakes. Two. I want to hear at least two rollicking good tunes."

~*~

Two songs later—not quite as rollicking as the man had demanded—Joel appeared in the doorway. He strolled over to the grand piano, a tray held aloft with one hand. "Where did you learn to play like that? You didn't study overseas?"

Melancholy twisted her insides. A lost chance because of one bad choice. "No, I didn't."

She could feel Joel's eyes on her, but he said nothing more about her music. Instead he swept a hand toward a table. "Your breakfast awaits, Your Highness."

With a flourish, Joel set down her plate, placed a small glass of juice at the top, then poured her a hot cup of coffee. Smiling, he pulled out a chair for her.

The pancakes looked delectable. Orange slices and crushed pecans floating in clear, mahogany-colored syrup topped the stack of perfectly browned cakes. Starli's stomach growled. She cut a small bite, slid it into her mouth. Her eyelids closed, and she almost moaned in delight.

"A bit of okay, isn't it? Here. Try a couple of these rashers."

Starli opened her mouth to ask what on earth a rasher was, when she caught a glimpse of the small serving plate piled high with bacon strips. Joel laid two of them on the edge of her plate.

"What do you eat for breakfast?" Joel sat opposite her and crunched a strip of bacon.

"Fruit. A slice of whole wheat toast or bagel. Occasionally in the winter, a cup of oatmeal. Sometimes I'll have Louis make a smoothie for me after I get here."

Joel shook his head. "Not much for an active person. You should taste one of my fry ups."

"What is a fry up? Sounds terribly cholesterol-laden." Starli set the bacon back on her plate.

"Probably is, but smashingly good. The works. Sausage and bacon, eggs, fried potatoes and tomatoes, baked beans, and kippers. What else? Oh, yes, fried blood sausage. "

"Double yuck." Starli stood. "I've got to get to work. Thanks for breakfast."

The invitation to the concert she needed to issue to Joel hung like a mirage in front of her. But images like that were best ignored.

~*~

Starli greeted each business owner that evening while Manny and a young college man—one that filled in on special event nights—showed them to their seats. White-coated waiters slipped between tables filling drinks.

When Toni DeLuca-Douglas entered on the arm of her professor husband, flushed and radiant, she leaned close to hug Starli. "We received the phone call for our final approval to adopt the little girl we want."

A lump lodged in Starli's throat. She'd always wanted a child, but Ryan had drilled it into her after years of not conceiving that she couldn't get pregnant. Yet she would not, could not defuse her best friend's happiness with her sorrow. "Toni. That's wonderful. I want to hear all about it."

"We go next week to pick her up. I'm so excited I know I'll never sleep tonight."

Starli hugged her friend close. "I'm so happy for you. Can I do anything to help you get ready?"

"Everything's ready." Toni folded her hand inside her husband's and looked up at his face. "We've been working on the room ever since we suspected our dream would go through."

"Then we'll talk later. I can't wait to see what you've done with it." Starli's friends walked away. She'd had her questions about Perrin Douglas when he'd first appeared in Toni's life, had sensed his troubled soul. It was a good thing now to see how Toni and he balanced the other with their all-consuming love.

With the last of the guests seated, Starli nodded at Manny and turned to her piano to begin playing. An hour of performance during dinner. Following the speaker's notoriously long speech-making, the presentation of the year's best business award, and the evening—hopefully—would go down as another proud notch for Apple Blossom's.

A door banged, and a pompous voice roared indignation. Starli sighed and turned, knowing who she'd see when she did.

Caro's voice, a notch above its usual pitch, joined in the commotion near the entrance. She and her brother Toby confronted the newly elected mayor. Caro's freckled face, flushed and drawn into a frown, radiated frustration. Toby clutched his sister's arm, trying to draw her away from the fat man who presided over Appleton.

She started toward them when the kitchen door swung open. Joel, dressed to the T in a spotless white uniform and tall hat, strode to the center of the room, a platter held high. He lightly tapped on the empty glass on his tray.

The room quieted as if by magic. All eyes turned to the charismatic, confident man.

"I've been given to understand that our Honorable Mayor Stroth..." he inclined his head toward the man "...favors shrimp. Therefore to kick off tonight's event, I've created a new appetizer—shrimp with Creole sauce, just for him. It has my own special blend of spices and a touch of citrus. I'd be honored if Mayor Stroth would sample "Shrimp

Cajun" now."

Starli closed her mouth as she watched the mayor waddle in obvious pleasure toward her chef. Joel hadn't told her he'd created a special hors d'oeuvre for tonight. Why hadn't he stuck to the agreed-upon menu?

Mayor Stroth tasted and pronounced the shrimp and sauce perfect. Joel bowed slightly then raised a hand. "You will want to save plenty of room for our main dish of the evening. Your taste buds will insist its heavenly manna."

He waited till the laughter died down, prolonging his obvious declaration, allowing the interest to build.

"My own specially prepared Spinach Chateaub Thadd. And for dessert, to celebrate this glorious late winter we are enjoying, Chocolate Au Mint crème Brule."

The guests exploded into clapping, their ebullient faces radiant.

Her gaze darted to Joel, and he met it, a glint in his own. What was she reading? Satisfaction? Triumph?

Manny had already seated Caro and Toby, and Starli caught the approving nod he sent his nephew. Joel winked at his uncle and slipped back into the kitchen. Had Manny and Joel been in cahoots, their minds working in smooth harmony to keep the evening quiet and productive? To make it a success for her?

Joel had certainly created a diversion from a possible serious flare up tonight. She couldn't fault him for that. She supposed artists, creative chefs couldn't help themselves. Creating menus and tempting items was a passion as much as painting a Rembrandt.

While waiters moved into the dining area and served the special appetizer, Starli slid onto the piano bench and began "Canon in D."

An hour later, Starli finished her last planned piece with a flourish and rose to a stirring round of applause. Smiling, she moved among the tables, nodding and commenting to different ones before approaching her friends. Caro and Toni huddled in a corner of the room.

"Stuffy. I can't believe Stroth has that boring Wallace speaking again this year. Even Professor Perrin would've been better." Caro gave Toni a sly teasing look.

"She's talking about my husband, Starli." Toni laughed and wrinkled her nose. "Stop it, Caro. You may think he's stuffy, but I happen to love him dearly."

"Well," Caro conceded. "He does have the most divine eyes of a man, and his hair encourages fingers to run through it."

"Crazy friend. If I didn't know you so well, I'd be jealous." Toni laughed. "What was going on with you and Mayor Stroth, Caro? I thought I was going to have to call in a referee."

Caro's lips twisted. "The invitations pompously requested we be on time. Could I help it if Undiscovered Treasures was inundated with last minute customers?"

Starli reached over and tucked a stray lock of Caro's brown hair behind her ear. "Of course, you couldn't help it."

"You should have called one of us. We'd covered for you." Toni's eyes shone, the golden flecks shimmered.

"Phooey, I'm not afraid of that bully.

A man rose from his seat and headed Starli's way.

"I see I'm about to be cornered into sitting at the mayor's table. I suppose that's why Stu made sure there was an empty seat." She sighed. "No getting out of it this time even—"

"Have you been avoiding him?" Toni's question interrupted her complaining.

"No, not exactly. We've both been so busy I haven't been able to accept most of his invitations lately. I'm afraid he's been a bit peeved at me."

"In spite of his dad's overbearing attitude, Stu is a good guy. You could do worse." Coming from Caro, that was saying a lot.

"You don't have to remind me of that. I know he is. It's that..." Starli hesitated. "...I'm not convinced he's the one for me..."

She allowed her quiet comment to flow behind her as she walked away, knowing her friends would hear and understand her sentiment. They'd heard it before.

"Have you eaten yet?" Stu reached for her hand and placed it on his arm, guiding her through the maze of tables. "I didn't think you'd want much, so have a sampling of several things waiting for you. I've saved you a seat."

She had no time to accept or refuse. They were at the table, and Stu was pulling out a chair to seat her.

For whatever reason, unlike his dislike of Caroline Gibson, Mayor Stroth was friendly and cordial every time she met him. He nodded a greeting now. "Excellent entertainment, my dear. I know I can always count on you to give us something besides the heavy beats or country twang so many enjoy today."

"Thank you."

Stroth's beady eyes studied her. "Too bad your business couldn't have come in first place this year, Starli."

Did the man really expect her to believe his statement? Everyone in their community knew who would be the recipient of the questionable "award." The same one who'd won the last two years.

Good thing her confidence didn't depend on the Mayor's business of the year award.

"Dad..."

Mayor Stroth flapped a hand and turned to the person seated beside him.

Stu leaned toward her. His beaming face warmed her heart even though a tiny bit of trepidation refused to allow the organ to overheat.

"Are you anticipating getting the award again?"

"I tried to tell Dad to leave the bank out of it this year, but he ran over top of my objections as always." The disapproval was heavy in his voice.

She patted his hand. "It's all right, Stu. We all know how proud your father is of you."

"Right." The frown remained for all of five seconds. "Let's not talk about that. Is your schedule a little less hectic after tonight? I really would like to spend more time with you."

"I'm always busy. You know that. We'll have to see how the weeks turn out."

"I suppose. Ah, here's dessert." Stu sampled a piece of the Crème Brule "Hmmm. Excellent.

That new chef of yours outdid himself tonight. If he cooks like this all the time, your plans to expand may be closer to happening than you thought."

"That's music to my ears."

"You like that?" Stu cocked his head at her. "I can make it happen."

"I appreciate how you've stood beside me through the years. The bank has been very generous."

"And I run the bank, my dear."

His tone was a little dry, and Starli knew very well what he conveyed. Love his bank, love him, to paraphrase the old saying a bit.

"I thought the speaker did a good job tonight. Even kept to the time limit." Changing the subject didn't always work with Stu, but it was worth a try.

"Not bad. At least he wasn't as bad as last year's long-winded essay." Stu leaned toward her and spoke in a low voice. "I couldn't quite focus on anyone but the pianist tonight. You've never looked better, My Dear."

Starli chuckled. "Well..."

Stu reached for her hand and squeezed it, his action speaking the words of affection he didn't say.

~*~

"Can you believe his son and the bank got the business of the year award? Again?" Caroline sniffed. "I know he's your friend Starli, but really?"

"Don't worry about it." Toni swiveled her head as she looked from Starli to Caroline. "We don't care if Stu gets it every year."

"And Stu spoke to his father about it.

Trouble is, Mayor Stroth has his agenda and refuses to budge from it." Starli added for good measure. Fair was fair. It wasn't Stu's fault his dad was one-sighted.

Her two best friends turned together and locked arms with Starli. Caro gave Starli's arm a little shake. "I haven't had a chance to tell you tonight, but your chef is a total knockout. Want to introduce me?"

What good friends she had, but she definitely wasn't interested in following up on Caro's curiosity with a comment. The farther she stayed away from that danger-topic, the better off she'd be.

As Toby, Perrin and Andy Carrington approached, Starli stepped back, listening as her friends bantered and teased each other good-naturedly. She'd almost decided to slip away when Caroline's eyes shifted and widened.

"What?" Starli turned to look. Joel had shed his work uniform. His casual pants and blue silk shirt, sent the blood pounding through her veins. He couldn't help it he was so dashing, could he? Maybe not, but he could help moving close behind her as if to mark her as his. She took a tiny step from him.

"You okay?"

His gaze skimmed her face—no physical touch—yet why did it feel as if each distinct feature had been heated with a hot fire?

"I wanted to meet your friends."

"Are you...?"

"All done. Camille and Juanita are cleaning up with the help of your new wash boy."

He grinned. He was obviously remembering

when she'd mistaken him for the same. "Well, do I get an introduction or are you going to slink away, ashamed of your chef?"

Reluctantly, Starli introduced him and watched as her friends wrapped him in friendliness and warmth. Was he that attractive, or were her friends pulling him into their group for her sake?

No need, but then how could she protest politely?

"Why don't you all come over to my house for an hour or so? We'll rehash the evening. And I'll show off my adoption letter." Toni beamed.

"Smashing. Starli can ride with me."

"No, I can't. I'm riding with Toni and Perrin."

"We've got the back seat filled with things for the baby." Toni's distress was obvious.

Starli turned to Caro who shook her head and jerked a thumb over her shoulder toward Toby.

"Toby insisted we pick up three of Andy's depressing works before we got here. I nearly cried all the way over." Caro glowered at her brother who'd wandered over to a different corner of the room and now flirted with a short redhead.

Good thing Andy had been drawn aside by a gentleman Starli had never seen or met before.

Too bad her friends didn't realize how desperately she was trying to avoid being alone with her chef. Starli drew in a deep breath. "I need to drive anyway. Besides I'll have to close up."

"Why? Manny is perfectly capable of doing that. Taking two vehicles is a waste of kero and makes for a lonely trip. We need to pool."

Anger surged through her. Who did Joel Peterman-Blair think he was? Her boss?

"Okay."

Okay? What kind of answer was that coming from a very angry person?

Seething, she went after her coat and justified her weakness to herself. She didn't want to make a scene. She didn't want to make her friends feel badly for not giving her a ride. She didn't want to be alone with a man as gorgeous as Joel in the intimate confines of that fast car of his.

She reached for her coat and stopped, her hand in mid-air. Her black leather gloves lay on the floor.

Frowning, she stooped and picked them up. Folding her coat over her arm, she walked to the door and gave it a shove.

It didn't budge. She shoved it again, stood back and stared at it a second, thinking, a trickle of panic tickling her insides. Jiggling the door knob, and with a vicious jab of her shoulder to the door, she shoved as hard as she could.

Nothing.

It didn't appear to be locked—at least the knob didn't feel like it. So why wouldn't the door open?

She pressed her forehead against the door and tried to relax. Toni or Caro would come looking for her—she reached up to rub her itching nose and coughed. Drew in a breath and coughed again. What was that smell? Smoke? Turning she saw it. Smoke was swirling from the metal trashcan that sat beside the settee.

The ugly monster of panic swarmed over her. Breathing hard, she pounded on the door. Listened. Pounded again.

A shout penetrated the heavy wooden door, then a scuffling. When the coatroom door swung open, Joel stood there, teasing in his tone, but worry in his eyes. "What took you so long? What's going on?"

Starli stumbled out the door, and Joel moved on into the coatroom. When he returned, he joked, but the look on his face said he thought the incident was anything but funny. "Your Majesty wouldn't be dawdling, would she?"

"I am not. The door wouldn't open." A sudden thought struck. "You didn't do—"

Real horror played across Joel's features. "You think I'd do that you?"

She adjusted her thoughts. Of course, he wouldn't. What was she thinking?

She grimaced. She wasn't thinking.

"Sorry, it gave me a fright for a few seconds there."

He took her hand and tucked it on his arm, patting gently. "Me too, especially when I saw that man moving away from the door."

"Which man?"

"The one the officer is talking with."

"Roland? Roland locked me in?"

"Is that man your brother-in-law? I didn't actually see him put the chair under the handle, but no one else was in the vicinity. Who else could it have been?"

"Are we the last to leave?"

"Yes, except for your friends and Manny

who's waiting on Juanita and Camille to finish clearing the kitchen. Let's slip out. If the policeman needs to talk with you, he can do it later."

"No. I need to find out what Roland says."

"Then let's get it over with. Can't see why you want to torture yourself with his presence."

As they approached the group, which included her friends, Officer Tope, a glowering Louis and smirking Roland, Joel called out. "Officer, Starli *was* in the coatroom and someone set a smoke bomb off in the trashcan."

"Are you all right?" The officer's gaze swept over her face. "Can you tell me what happened?"

"I'm fine. I went to pick up my coat and started to leave the coatroom, but the door wouldn't open."

"To be clear, are you saying it was locked?"

"I don't believe so. I tested the door knob, and it seemed to turn fine. The door wouldn't budge."

"I see. And, Mr. Peterman-Blair, you saw Roland beside the door? But not placing the chair there? Is that correct?" Officer Tope's brows drew down, but not in a displeased manner. Probably had a lot to do with having to deal with higher ranking, fellow-officer Stratton.

"Correct. I also saw no one else in the vicinity, and as I walked closer I distinctly heard Starli calling out."

The sigh Officer Tope exhaled would have knocked anyone under three feet over. He scowled at Roland Stratton. "You look awfully guilty, Stratton, and the only reason I'm not making a formal complaint against you with the captain, is because no one actually saw you place that chair. Otherwise..."

Roland smirked at first Starli then Tope. "Can't prove a thing. Why would I want to do such a silly thing?"

"Why indeed? You can go, but I'll be watching you." Officer Tope's gaze followed the man as he swaggered from the restaurant.

"Can we go now?" Joel asked in a low voice.

"If you insist." She sent him a grateful glance and allowed him to guide her from the building. "I do thank you for rescuing me."

"I'll always save you when you need me."

She stared at him as he walked around the front of the car. Was he serious or joking again?

He looked perfectly at home in his rented low slung sports car. She gave it the brunt of a withering glance. The mental image of her cheap plain car taunted her. She winced. It wasn't that she couldn't afford a much nicer car. She couldn't abide the show of pretense she'd lived with for the years she'd been married to Ryan.

"Blinding night." Joel settled into his seat and fastened his seatbelt.

"What does that mean?"

"Fantastic."

Starli stared through Joel's sunroof at the star-studded heaven. "Don't try to change the subject."

"Come again?" The engine purred to a start, and Joel pulled onto the road.

"I said, don't try to..."

"I know what you said. I don't know what you're talking about."

"Two things." She thrust two fingers in the air between them. "One. Don't ever presume to tell me what to do, especially in front of my friends. Two. Why did you prepare something different from the menu we'd decided upon?"

Defensive nitpicking, true. But a girl had to do what she had to do, right? Somehow that didn't make a lot of sense.

"You didn't like my surprise? I thought it was successful intervention. Saved your friend from being tossed out."

"Caroline would never be thrown out. It's my restaurant." Starli clenched her teeth. "And that's not the point."

"What is the point? That I created a dish that caught your mayor's attention and possibly gave your business another boost in popularity? Or that I failed to get your approval?"

The cold inside her spread. How could she explain her fear of losing her restaurant? Of not succeeding? The fear she'd lived with for years of another failure? "I want to know what you prepare. Don't you understand the restaurant is my life? I won't have it compromised. I have to keep on top of everything."

Silence.

Starli looked down at her shaking hands. Too intense. Why did she always come across as angry and anxious? She could blame it on the incident tonight. The truth was she was still way too uncomfortable with Joel

Peterman-Blair. She swallowed twice before she could speak. "Make a right at the next intersection. Toni's house is the third down on the left."

Joel nodded and took the curve fast. When he pulled in front of the house, he turned off the ignition and faced her in the dim interior light.

"I'm a chef. I create. That's my nature, and my career making a statement. The restaurant is your life, but cooking is mine. I would never—and I repeat—never do anything to harm my reputation. Regardless of whom I'm working for."

"But..." Starli couldn't go on.

"You hired me. You need to learn to trust your own judgment."

He slid out of the car and went around the front to open her door. As she stepped out, his gaze searched her face. Disappointment? Was he disappointed in her?

He spoke again. "Do you think one of your friends could take you home?"

Her lip stung from the pressure of her teeth. "Of course. Or I'll walk."

"Then if you'll make my excuses, I'll head for the flat."

Starli walked to the house door, but with her hand on the knob, looked back. The red sportster had zipped off, its taillights winking in the distance.

For the first time in six years, Starli wanted to cry.

Chapter Seven

The heavy wet snowflakes splattered against Starli's windshield as she drove. The houses were lit with homey lights, but the streets were empty. Thank God for Toby who'd generously dropped her off at Apple Blossoms so she'd have her car to drive home. He'd waved as he sped back to the Douglas's to pick up Caro.

In spite of the late hour, she was wide-awake, too keyed up to sleep.

Toni had asked her why Joel hadn't come and how he was doing as her new chef.

"The restaurant is busier than ever. Everyone vies for seats." Starli allowed a wry grin to widen her lips. "I think his reputation is spreading fast throughout the land."

"Sounds like Apple Blossoms has stepped up a notch. Joel will be good for Blossoms."

Starli had agreed as she thought of her beloved mountain people who enjoyed the soft music and low lights, and the excellent food Joel prepared. But how long would he stay? Days, even weeks or months was not an indication he would make Apple Blossoms his permanent job. In fact, she seriously doubted he'd be there a year. With his reputation and fame, could she blame him? What would happen if—no, when—he decided it was too boring, too laid back of a place for his talents—for him?

And would she have no one to blame but

herself for her pettiness with him that certainly didn't encourage him to stay?

Being locked in the coatroom and the smoke had shaken her. If someone—if Joel—hadn't checked on her, what would have happened? Asphyxiation from smoke caused more deaths than fires. Was that what someone wanted for her?

She shivered.

In a perverse sort of way, her mind switched to Joel again. She'd been too hard on him tonight, but was she wrong to insist on always knowing about his creations? She'd done so with her previous chef. She'd *always* done so, but even she had to admit, Joel was in a class above. What was it about the man, besides his obvious love of joking and teasing?

He was an artist. In his own field, with his talents, he had that sense of what was delectably divine. So far, she'd had no criticism of his creations. Still, it was early days.

She easily recognized that artistic trait in him. Hadn't she winced many a time when she'd listened to those being praised as the promising next pianist, by those less than masters at piano, and sensed the lack? The depth in their playing lacking the touch it needed to soar to the top?

Maybe, just maybe, she'd been a little too insistent, too hard on the man.

But she'd never admit it to him.

Starli pulled into her driveway and started to get out when a thought struck her. It was just late enough the park lake would be nearly empty. The spotlights were action-censored and on as long as there were skaters, and she knew they'd have the pond cleared of the recent snowfall. She had her skates in the trunk. Why not work out some of the kinks in her spirits? Forty-five minutes of skating would make her tired enough to sleep. Maybe keep the dreams at bay tonight.

The more she thought about it the better she liked the idea. There were a couple of park cops who'd be patrolling, so she didn't worry about attackers.

She restarted her car and headed to the lake, drumming on the steering wheel to the beat of one of her favorite skating songs.

The ice shone with perfection. Starli started out with a slow measured glide, gradually building her speed until the air stung her cheeks. Songs from the past resonated through her mind, guiding her moves, encouraging her executions.

She did a figure eight, executed a double axel, and focused on her moves. Mayor Stroth had begged her to put on a show for Appleton's Winter Festival, but she'd evaded an answer. The last time she'd had the confidence to do such a thing had been the year she and Ryan had performed at college.

She shivered and remembered a young Ryan. His rugged good looks and powerful body had been a temptation she'd not been able to resist. He'd been a perfect partner for her tall figure. Strong enough to lift her with ease, he'd been confident enough in himself so that even though his skating had lacked the professional finesse of her own, his enthusiasm made up for that lack.

Whirling, to retrace her way back to where

she'd started, she spotted a lone figure at the edge of the lake, moving toward her. Approaching her? A small sting of worry nibbled at her mind. A mugger? She studied the pond, then adjusted her path to give the figure a wide berth. He did likewise, seemingly determined to approach her.

Panic blazed through her. Blood pounded through her veins. Stories of women attacked in abandoned areas zipped through her mind. Where were the park cops?

Starli forgot about casualness. She lengthened her stride. He wouldn't catch her without some effort. Her heart rate changed into a frantic tom-tom.

She'd almost reached her starting place and prepared to unlace her skates when a hand, firm and strong, gripped her shoulder. A moan escaped her throat. Her nightmare exploded into real life with Roland chasing her instead of Ryan. She jerked away.

"Trying to outrun me again?"

Her knees went weak as she turned to see Joel behind her. "You scared me to death. Why didn't you call out?"

"Sorry. I thought you knew it was me."

"I didn't. What are you doing here? Why couldn't you visit with my friends earlier? I didn't know you could skate."

"That's a lot of observations and questions." Joel shrugged. "Called about renting skates at lunch today. Couldn't relax tonight, thought it'd be just the thing to put me to sleep. I've skated all my life, took a few lessons, but never was quite good enough to go professional, even if I'd wanted to."

He peered at her. "You're shaking. I know you're not afraid of me, so it has to be something else. Why are you here by yourself?"

"Not that it's any of your business," she snapped, "but the same thing with me. Needed something to help me relax."

Joel held out his hand. "Come on. Let's take a spin and get those shakes worked out of your system. You can tell me why a lovely lady like you can't sleep. You're safe with me."

Safe? She'd never be safe again. Mesmerized by his courtly manner, she stretched out a hand, placed it in his, and felt a jolt through her fingertips as they glided off. She liked the way Joel's long legs matched her own stride. She liked the way he kept quiet—after his teasing remark--and seemed to respect her wish not to talk.

They skated in unison for several minutes before Joel spoke.

"You're good. You've had lessons."

Starli's heart lightened. He was over his snit from earlier. She should apologize for her hatefulness. Her throat tightened. "I've always loved skating, and my parents made sure I had all and any lessons in whatever I expressed interest. When I was a kid I dreamed of being a professional, but my love for the piano overcame that."

"Ever do any competing?"

"A little."

"Let's try a few fancy things." His brows rose in question.

Starli hesitated but allowed Joel to slip a hand to her side. He pressed his chest against her back and cupped her other hand within his larger one.

With smooth movements they glided across the mirrored surface, the only sound the swishing of their skates and Joel's breath close to her ear. In a moment of weakness she allowed her eyes to close as he led her over the ice in spins and twirls. Once he even lifted her, then landed her back on her feet again so lightly she barely realized she was touching earth again. Though there was none, Starli was almost sure she could hear music to their swift, but graceful skating dance. In the depths of her being, her soul whispered for freedom and relished the feel of strong arms wrapped around her. She never wanted the moment to end.

When Joel twirled her for the last time, Starli's lungs heaved with exhaustion, but her spirit soared. She'd thought she'd never find a skating partner as good as Ryan had once been with her. A skating partner strong enough to match her stride for stride.

Joel peered down at her. "That's what I like to see. Rosy cheeks. Let's take a couple of quiet turns around the lake."

He held out an arm, and Starli took it.

"Want to tell me what's going on?"

Her spirit slammed the ice. Talk to him? No. Definitely not. "Tell me what it's like in England."

His look was a measured one. "A much higher level of expense, but beautiful country, rich history, moody weather. A wonderful place to live."

She felt her cheeks grow warm. "Have you ever considered living in the States?"

"No." His answer came slowly.

His tone was so matter-of-fact, his voice so convincing that Starli didn't have the courage to urge him to make West Virginia his permanent home. What had she thought? He'd give up his knighthood to come to a hillbilly state to cook forever? She felt her lips curl at her own stupidity. Ryan had been right. She was too stupid to be let loose in the world.

Her stomach clenched, and her eyes burned. From the past, Ryan's heavy voice boomed in her mind. *You're stupid. What a moron I married.*

Joel spoke. "Are you okay?"

Starli struggled to pay attention.

"Sometime I'll take you to England and give you the grand tour."

"I couldn't leave Blossoms." Starli shook her head. She would never leave her beloved restaurant, the one thing that had kept her sane through all these years after Ryan.

"You're really attached to that place. Everyone needs a vacation to relax."

"I haven't had time to relax. I spent several years learning the business, then getting my own up and running. It's the most prosperous in these parts. I don't want to take a chance on it going downhill if I'm away. Besides, I'm almost ready to branch out."

"Get a good manager."

"No one cares about a baby like the mother." Starli quoted her mother's favorite saying, remembering how often she'd used it.

Joel let go of her arm, spun in a circle and skated backward. "Your parents living?"

"Yes. I see them three, four times a year.

Dad retired early and now they travel extensively."

"Ah ha. So you're the poor little rich girl?"

Starli felt her ire rising. "I stand on my own two feet."

Joel nodded and returned to his place beside her. "You're a brilliant pianist. You should get serious about it and do some studying abroad."

"I can't—"

"I know. You can't leave Apple Blossoms." Joel stopped his spinning. "I've got another idea. Let's go back to the restaurant. You can play for me while I fix us a snack."

"It's two in the morning."

"So? We'll have the place to ourselves. Come on. Be adventurous."

She shook her head, studying the tall man beside her. She wished she didn't find him so attractive. Probably because he was so antithesis of Ryan. But though Joel wasn't football player-built, he was strong and muscled, giving every indication hard work was no stranger to him.

"I need to get up early tomorrow. Remember? We need to prepare for our Valentine's event, and we'll have tons of customers while the Winter Fest is going on."

"There's plenty of time. Want to skate together Monday?"

"I do need to get in some practice if I'm going to participate in the Winter Festival."

"Want a partner?"

"You?"

"Think we did a bully job tonight. We'd have them tossing the quid at us."

"You want to spend the time we'd have to, to get ready?"

"Yes."

Starli slid to a smooth stop and settled on the bench to unlace her skates. Joel dropped to one knee to help.

"Uncle Laurence thinks a lot of you."

The words were low. Starli bent closer to catch them. "He's a good friend."

Raising his head in a sudden move, Joel looked straight into her eyes. His tanned serious face, not six inches from hers, sent ripples of nervousness through her. Was he planning on...*kissing* her? Her mental voice screeched on the word.

She eased back an inch. "What?"

Joel stood and helped her to her feet. He slung his skates over his shoulder as they walked toward their cars where he opened her door and waited till she climbed in. Then he bent over.

"Uncle Laurence isn't the only one who thinks a lot of you. I...the whole town thinks the world of you. " He spun on his heels and trotted toward his sleek red sportster. The engine purred to life.

In the floodlights she could see his wave as he turned at the corner of the street.

~*~

Joel navigated the slushy street the next morning, wincing mentally at the thought of the dirt and salt caking the BMW's undersides. His image in the rearview mirror revealed the same face. Nothing had changed on the outside, but a volcano of emotions had erupted throughout his heart.

From the moment he'd laid eyes on Starli Cameron, he'd known she was the one for him. Weeks later, his feeling hadn't diminished. The impression of Starli's classic and beautiful face was forever tattooed in his mind. "You're mine, Miss Starli Cameron. You don't know it yet, but you will."

Joel swiped a hand through his hair and whistled under his breath. Uncle Laurence had refused to discuss Starli's past with him. His hand pounded the steering wheel. "Something extreme's given you that complex toward men. I mean to find out what it is and remedy that."

He hadn't had a chance to talk with that bloke, Rolly. But he would, the sooner the better. Was the man so bitter at his brother's death, he needed someone to blame it on? Or was there more going on than met the eye?

He spun into the parking lot of The Coffee House and braked. Starli had given him the impression she stopped here almost daily for her first cup of coffee—or tea—of the day. Would she be here? Could he talk his way into another few minutes with her?

As he walked into the shop, Rita Mae with her overblown beauty caught his attention, and Joel frowned. He remembered Starli's reaction and obvious dislike of the woman. Why?

"What's with the frown?" Rita ignored the other customers and sashayed toward Joel. She placed a hand on her hip.

Joel grinned, but avoided answering her question. "Give me a large Yukon to go. Busy this morning, aren't you?"

She cocked a sideways look at him and

pursed her lips. "Ah, good for the ole pocketbook."

Joel kept his smile intact, but turned away from her to scan the room, filled with the early morning people headed to work. No Starli. His gaze passed over each one, then returned to the far back corner where a girl sat, her head bowed, her blond hair shielding her face. And was that man sitting beside her...*Louis*?

He studied her. Something about her...Did he know her? She looked like...A white hand lifted a tissue and swiped at her cheeks.

As Rita set his espresso on the counter, Joel laid the money beside it. Like a streak, her hand shot out and covered his. His gaze lifted to her face.

"We haven't had that tour yet, good-looking."

"No, we haven't, have we?" Joel slid his hand out from under hers. He tilted his head toward the back of the room. "Who's the girl in the back booth? With Louis?"

Rita's gaze lingered on him for a moment then moved to study the dejected figure. She flicked her gaze back to him, her lips curled in scorn. "Don't know her? She works everyday with you."

"Camille?"

"Camille Findley. Your kitchen help."

"Our Apple Blossoms' Camille? Wonder why she's crying?"

"Who knows?" Rita shrugged and wiped at the counter with the rag she clutched. "I heard her mother's worse. Or could be she's upset her boyfriend just dumped her. Why she thought she could keep someone like Justin

Winters..."

Anger coursed through him. "Why shouldn't she have this Justin Winters? Isn't she just as good as he?"

Another shrug. "Hardly. The Winters own the Winter Sports and Fun stores. Big shots in these parts. Camille—well, not to cast allegations—but the Findleys are poor. Her father is useless, the mother sick and weak, the other kids lazy. Too bad she has so much going against her, even if she is a pretty enough girl."

Joel clenched his teeth. He picked up his coffee and headed toward the booth.

"Camille? Is that you?" He sent Louis a nod. "Louis."

The girl looked up, her face splotched red. For a second, her gaze remained unfocused, then she straightened and fidgeted with her coffee mug. Red crept into her cheeks, and she slid a look at the assistant chef.

"Mind if I join you?"

"Uh, I guess...of course, not, Mr. Peterman-Blair."

"I've got to go anyway. We'll talk later, Camille." The assistant chef patted the girl's arm, abruptly rose, and trotted away, not giving Joel another glance.

Well, so much for building a positive rapport with the man.

"Think we're getting more snow today?"

"I hope not. I have to get to work."

"You have trouble getting to work?" Joel sipped at his steaming cup and cocked a brow at her.

"Sometimes. That car of mine is as moody

as Mom's old cow 'bout to give birth." Camille coughed out an embarrassed laugh. "I'm going to have to look around for another one. As soon as I can."

"Can't have much fun without a car."

Lips drooping in a teenaged pout, she twisted her hands together. "I don't have time for fun. You know, something simple and clean, maybe low mileage. And cheap. Nothing fancy."

Of course, she wanted fancy. She was a kid.

"And I've talked to Starli about becoming an apprentice under her. You know, learn the ropes. If she'll just give me a chance—you know, promote me to manager—then someday I can start a restaurant of my own. I want that promotion so bad I could kill for it."

Hmmm. Obviously she seriously wanted the job. Hopefully, the last statement was an exaggeration. "What did Miss Starli say to your proposition?"

A bit of abashment crossed her face. "She didn't say no."

That said a lot. Starli wasn't convinced.

"Why don't you tell me what's wrong, Camille? I'm a good listener."

The moisture crawled down her cheeks. Her head moved back and forth. "It's Mother. The doctor called me last night and said her last tests came back bad. She has only months to live. I *can't* tell her. She wants to live so badly, has fought so hard."

"Can't your doctor tell her?"

"He left this morning on a trip and won't be back for two months. He wanted me to let another doctor tell her, but I don't want some stranger telling Mother she's going to die. What will I do without her?"

"You'll be the strong little soldier you always are." Joel swallowed. Platitudes. Couldn't he think of something comforting to say to this grieving child?

"I'm ashamed to say it, I've been so blessed with a good job, Louis and Juanita, and even Manny's friendship, but I don't feel very strong this morning. I'm shaking." She pulled her hand away from his and lifted it to demonstrate the fact.

"There is one who is stronger than we are. He'll be there for you."

"I know that, but I'm not keen on church much. I use to go when I was a kid." She sighed. "Maybe I should start back. Then I could talk with the preacher and have him tell Mother the bad news. But then, I've taken care of her for so long, it really should be me. If only I had someone to go with me."

She burst into fresh tears. "And I haven't had time to think about it, but when Justin and I went out for a hamburger last night, he said...he said it was over. Said he couldn't deal with all the drama in my life. When things get better, we'd review our options."

"Justin being your boyfriend?" Too bad he couldn't get his hands on the cold-hearted fellow right now.

Camille's head bobbed. "As if I'd take him back."

"Right." Joel leaned close. "Forget that cad. Move on, sweetheart. Concentrate on your mother. Would you like me to be with you when you talk to her?"

Her gaze lifted to his face. "You'd do that for me? You're serious, no kidding?"

"Of course, I'm serious. I'll be with you if you want me to."

"Mr. Peterman-Blair, you're the best. I love you." Camille jumped from her side of the table, the chair overturning and rushed to him, throwing her arms around his neck.

Joel returned her hug, and ignored the other customer's stares and Rita's questioning look. But it was a little harder to forget the cold scorn blazing from Starli's eyes glaring at him from outside the plate glass window.

Chapter Eight

Starli pressed down on the accelerator, and her car shot forward. She'd lost her taste for the delicious coffee Rita served.

Joel with Camille Findley. Wrapped in each other's arms for the whole restaurant to see. Her already tense stomach turned over.

"So much for the hours of skating practice he promised." Even as she muttered the bitter words, shame filled her. Not fair. Joel and she had no commitment to each other. She had insisted on nothing but a business relationship. He'd volunteered to be her skating partner, and she'd reluctantly agreed.

So what had she expected? That Joel would never look at other women? And why should she care anyway? She wasn't interested.

Was she?

Her heart ached. How could she please God with these unsettled emotions rioting inside her?

Jealousy—yes, she might as well admit it—of Joel and Camille. She wasn't interested in a romantic relationship with him, but she was attracted in spite of her denials.

Her own feelings of inferiority stemmed from Ryan's abuse. But no matter how much she worked at it, she seemed to never overcome it.

A car horn blared. Starli flinched and swerved. She slammed on her brake, but the other car failed to pass.

Caroline Gibson mouthed something at her.

Which meant nothing to Starli since she couldn't read her friend's lips. She gave her a brief nod and then slowed to allow her to lead.

After circling the block, Caro pulled into The Coffee House parking lot and stepped out of her compact car. Her freckled face creased, her wide mouth raised in a half-smile. "Where are you going like a swollen stream in the mountains?"

Spirit lifting, Starli laughed. Caro always had that effect on her. "I guess I was running away."

"From what? You forgot we were having coffee together this morning?"

"I think I did. Come on, I'll buy." Starli pushed at the heavy front door, her gaze scanning the seating area for any signs Joel and Camille still lingered there.

The two friends settled in a far corner with their double chocolate espressos.

"Okay. Spit it out. I want to know what's going on."

Was God punishing her for her foolishness by making her confess to Caro? "Nothing is going on."

A true enough statement.

"Starli." The warning note in her friend's voice told her that Caro wasn't going to let it go.

"You're worse than a terrier."

"I know." Caro grinned. "Give."

"Roland Stratton has been calling me."

"Roland? Ryan's brother? Why?"

"He makes snide remarks about mistreatment of his brother, and in particular, that I caused Ryan's death. He did allude once to the insurance Ryan had on himself."

"He said that? He's sniffing to see if there's any he can get his greedy hands on."

"I imagine. He's out of luck. I spent it all on the restaurant." Starli lifted her hands then dropped them back to the tabletop.

"And a good decision that was. When are you going to open the second Apple Blossoms?" Caro squirmed around in her seat, caught Rita Mae's attention and raised two fingers.

"I don't know. What if I'm pushing a good thing?"

Caro tapped the table with her fingers. "Do your research. You're the best businesswoman in these parts. I don't think you're going to do something foolish."

"Meaning I'm too cold, blunt, and ruthless to be foolish." Starli grinned to take the edge from her words.

"Meaning too smart, calm, and brave to be foolish." Caro tilted her head and gave her a measuring look as Rita Mae set their cups on the table.

"I'm not a waitress, you know." The woman glanced from one to the other. "I'm the owner, in case you've forgotten."

"Real-ly? Thanks for telling us." Caro eyed her with big innocent eyes.

Rita flounced off, but not before tossing back a taunt at Starli. "Shouldn't let your feelings show, dearie. It lets everyone know what a naiveté you are."

"What is she talking about?"

Starli cringed inside. Had everyone in the place seen her earlier and assumed she'd run because of Joel and Camille?

Well, she had, hadn't she?

She shrugged. "You know Rita Mae."

"Yeah." Caro giggled, then leaned forward. "Maybe you should call the police and report Roland's actions."

"And him a police officer? I'm sure they'll believe me. Besides, he's not hurt me. Much."

"The last time I heard, harassment is a crime."

As Starli started to slide into her car twenty minutes later, Caro called out, "Hey, did you ever ask Joel to go with us to the concert?"

Starli froze, then closed her car door. What Caro didn't know wouldn't hurt her.

~*~

A slender vase held a single creamy rose in the middle of the blotter on her desk. Near its center the rose turned a light pink. Starli stared, then walked slowly toward it. Gorgeous.

Where had it come from? Roland, playing a trick? No, he'd be more apt to send her a cactus. Caro? Toni? Bolstering her spirits? No doubt Caro would've already told Toni about Roland's harassment. But then they wouldn't have sent flowers. They'd either be on the phone or raiding the place with their presence and support.

Tied with a thin ribbon was an elegant embossed card. She lifted it and read the inscription.

Enjoyed our practice last night, Your Majesty. Looking forward to Monday. Want to ask me anything? Joel.

Caroline's crazy demand flashed into her

mind. Was that what Joel referred to? Heat from an overactive, traitorous heart shot a generous amount of warmth into her cheeks. What was with this man?

There was no time for a relationship. She needed to put all her energy into running her restaurant. Caro made some good points today. She was sensible. How hard was research? That was the place to begin.

Starli scooted the vase to the side, shoved away the mail and then turned on her computer. She grabbed a pen and paper and began a list. All thoughts of Roland and his annoyances, Joel, and her surroundings disappeared as she concentrated on gaining the facts on where she'd like to place a branch.

Would it work? Her fingers typed in rhythm to her thoughts.

Forty-five minutes later, she sat back and heaved a sigh. Yes. Sounded good, looked favorable. What was the next step?

The mail caught her attention, and she flipped through it. Nothing that couldn't wait...except, what was this?

A manila envelope with no return address had been addressed to her in a sloppy cursive hand. She reached for her letter opener, inserted it, and gasped as two pictures spilled out.

With trembling fingers, she lifted the top one. A smiling Ryan stared back at her dressed in his college football outfit, his posture confident of the admiration due him.

Had his smile always been so...slick? So smirky? So tight? His eyes so defiant and cruel?

Yes. Yes. And yes.

She'd just been too blind and in love with love to see it at twenty.

Her gaze shifted to study the second one. Ice formed in her body. Ryan, battered and broken from the car wreck. Where had Roland gotten this because, of course, it came from him. From the police files? Would they give him such a horrible picture? She shivered. He was blaming her yet again for his brother's death.

She dropped the pictures, fixed her gaze outside the large window, and clenched her fingers, the knot in her stomach growing. Without giving herself a chance to change her mind, she picked up the pictures and ripped them into bits, then reached for her trashcan to scrape them into it. Starli stared into the bottom of it and shook her head.

No. That wasn't enough. Not near good enough.

She scooted out of her chair and ran toward the back of her restaurant, the can held in both hands. She ignored the startled faces of Joel, Louis and Juanita, shoved at the big metal outside door. When it wouldn't budge, she slammed her fist against it. The trashcan fell from her grasp, the contents sifting to the floor in a disheveled mess. Dropping to her knees, she scooped at the bits of paper.

From the corners of her eyes, she saw feet approaching, then a knee touched the tiled floor beside her own. Clean, gentle hands gripped hers and stopped the frantic motion of her own.

Starli refused to lift her gaze, aware that Joel was scooping up every miniature piece of the shredded pictures and depositing them all back into the can. Then he set it aside and pulled her to her feet before he led her to a chair beside the counter.

"Sit here, Miss Starli."

She did as he told her.

Seconds later, he had a cup of hot tea in front of her.

"Drink this."

"I don't want..." She started to refuse, but he interrupted.

"Drink it."

It was only after she'd drunk more than half that he spoke again. "Now. Tell me what's going on. No lies."

"I don't lie." Starli snapped, heat suffusing her face.

Joel raised one brow. His eyes quizzed her.

"It's my brother-in-law. He's...He keeps reminding me I'm living while his older brother is dead."

"How is he reminding you?"

Starli shrugged and looked around the expansive kitchen. "Where is everyone?"

Joel waved a hand. "I sent them on errands. No one's here but the two of us."

Relief flooded through her. How embarrassing. This was so unlike her. How could she unfold like this, especially in front of her staff? She clutched her stomach until the wave of nausea eased.

"Are you all right?"

"Yes. I'm okay now." Starli nodded. "I...it just overwhelmed me for a few minutes."

"Is this brother-in-law phoning you?"

"What do you think?"

"And sending mail to you?" Joel nodded at the trashcan. "Threatening mail?"

"Not exactly." She looked away as shame nibbled at her body. "Pictures of...Ryan. Pictures of him after he wrecked his car."

Her chef's gaze focused on the silver trashcan. "Threats."

"No, not really."

"Yes. This person is trying to intimidate you. Frighten you into doing something he wants."

"He thinks I still have Ryan's insurance money. Too bad if he does. That's gone." She indicated the room around them.

"You used it to start Apple Blossoms?"

"I had to have some source of income."

"Good idea."

The swinging door banged. Manny stood there. "I'm sorry to intrude, Starli, but someone on the business phone insists on speaking with you. Can you take it?"

"Of course." Starli stood, knees wobbling, and eased her way to the phone on the wall. "This is Starli Cameron."

A low whisper came through the receiver and unnerved her. "Did you like the pictures? Remind you of something?"

Starli opened her numb fingers and let the receiver drop.

~*~

Joel sifted flour and measured oil, his thoughts on the woman who'd just left the kitchen. How to break through that reserve? How to help her?

She was so reserved that finding out any little detail about her was like digging in hard ground. Two things he knew for certain was a surprise.

Starli Cameron had been married, and Roland Stratton was harassing her.

That answered the question of what bothered her. But how serious were these threats? Why couldn't someone stop him?

He grimaced, then pursed his lips to whistle a silent tune. He'd picked up the fallen receiver Starli had dropped, to be greeted by dead silence. The Roland cad had hung up. The coward.

He'd meant to ask Starli about the concert Caroline had told him about. He wished Starli would just come out and ask him. Maybe he could get her to help him with Camille. She needed all the support she could get.

Uncle Laurence slipped into the kitchen and cleared his throat. Joel looked up.

"Starli has asked me to let you know she's having a small get together at her home Sunday evening. She would be honored for each one of you to be there." Manny's blue-eyed gaze searched each of the employees' face.

The maître de to the rescue. Starli was too overwhelmed to do it herself.

His uncle's gaze rested on himself just a fraction longer than the others.

He shot him his own silent response. *Who me? Of course, I'm going. Think I'd miss a chance to be with Her Majesty?*

Uncle Laurence gave a single nod as if he'd read the answer in Joel's eyes, turned and left the room.

Joel eyed Louis's work, offered a suggestion, then resumed his work on a new recipe. Should he add more nutmeg? Maybe a tad.

His thoughts returned to the stunning woman he worked for. Which would be harder? Deal with the Roland cad or crack that ice in Starli's heart?

More flowers Sunday night might serve as an ice pick.

Chapter Nine

Sunday evening, Starli walked through her home, straightened a cushion and adjusted the platters of finger foods, then turned on the fire in her gas fireplace. She eyed the pale pink candles, the stark white and ruby flower centerpiece that sat in the middle of her table. Was it too formal? No. Manny and Joel would expect the formality. Camille and Juanita would enjoy it. Louis and the bus boys would think only of the food.

She paused and listened to Caro and Toni's laughter coming from the guest bedroom. They'd offered to serve tonight, freeing her to enjoy the evening with her employees, and she'd jumped at the offer. They would be down any minute. She waltzed to her entertainment center and inserted one of the CDs she'd selected for tonight. She'd wanted to play something classical—maybe some Chopin—but Caro had convinced her that her guests would enjoy lighter music. Loosen up, had been her friend's words.

Loosen up? Her? She'd forgotten how to be casual and unworried. That is, until Joel had challenged her to that foolish race weeks ago. That had been fun.

She grimaced. Did she have any right to have fun when Ryan...

The doorbell rang at the same minute her friends' footsteps clattered down the staircase. Caro's lilting voice called out. "I'll get it. Toni, check on Starli. Make sure she's not in the kitchen."

Toni walked into the room and met Starli's gaze. "You look fantastic. I love that blue outfit."

"Are you sure it's not too formal? I wanted something simple, yet comfortable."

"And totally gorgeous on you. It's good for your employees to see some class, and lady, you have it." Toni's lips twisted. "You're being good, I hope? Caro will have both our hides if you're not."

"Of course, I am." Starli pouted, then turned as Caro entered the room.

Joel trailed behind her. In his hands he carried a huge bouquet of lilies, tiny blue flowers tucked among the snow white beauties. He held them out to Starli. "Flowers for a lovely lady."

His eyes coaxed her to accept the flowers, but there was a deeper persuasion in them for something more. Something he offered silently.

Her stomach churned. His magnetic drawing power tugged at her heart. She heard as from a long distance away Caro's squeal of delight, Toni's breathless ooh.

"You didn't have..."

"A thank you. For the party." Joel's eyes crinkled.

She studied him. He seemed not the least affected by her hesitation. Didn't anything ever bother the man? She knew her begrudging tone showed in her voice. "Then I guess I need to say 'thank you,' don't I?"

"Right you are."

Caro stared from one to the other, then

grabbed the flowers. "Oh, for pity's sake. Give them here. I wish some handsome man would bring me flowers. I'll have Toni make up a small corsage of them, then put the rest in a vase for you."

Her friend's bantering faded as she left the room, but Starli was barely aware. Joel sauntered across the room and examined the CD case. He turned and questioned her with a cocked eyebrow. "You don't have anything more lighthearted?"

"Something along the lines of bluegrass? Clogging music?" Tension knotted her shoulder muscles.

Joel inserted a CD, then nodded as the soft tune filled the room. He drummed fingers on his leg as he moved about the room, a deep hum spilling between his lips now and then. He studied the lone picture on her wall, then stopped at the patio doors for a moment. He turned. "Want to take a stroll outside?"

"I've company coming, remember? Besides it's terribly cold." A tiny spurt of interest nibbled at her. A walk in the cold was exactly what she needed.

He sat down on one of her loveseats, crossed long legs then patted the cushion. "Come sit down then. There's something I want to talk to you about."

Starli frowned but took the opposite loveseat. "I don't like that music. What do we need to talk about?"

"Camille Findley."

"What about her?" Was that really her obstinate voice? "I'm not ready to make a decision concerning her advancement."

"Since you're her employer, I assume you know what she's been going through."

"What do you mean? Her mother's been very sick with cancer. But they have so many new ways to conquer it today."

"Her mother is dying. She has about six months or less to live." Joel leaned forward.

She hadn't known the doctors had only given her mother months to live. Camille had said nothing to her. Would she though? Camille was a hard worker, but they weren't close friends. Lately Starli had been so consumed with the possibility of a second Apple Blossoms and Roland's harassment that she'd given little thought to anyone else's problems. "Why didn't she say something?"

"She did. To me. When I asked."

The emphasis he placed on his short sentences caused her to wince. Was there an accusatory tone in Joel's voice? What right did he have to accuse her of anything? She thought she'd been generous with the girl. Extra time off, a loan to tide her over, and up until the last month, concerned questions and sympathy.

She would not justify herself to her chef.

"Camille knows to come to me when she needs time off."

"She *needs* a friend. I let her unburden herself at The Coffee House one morning, then went with her to tell her mother she hasn't much longer to live. She's quite torn up over this." Joel's blue eyes sought Starli's and held her gaze.

"Oh, yes, the morning you held Camille wrapped in your arms." She could have bitten her tongue. Why had she let him know she remembered that morning?

"Ah, so you noticed."

Time to change the subject. "Why are you telling me this?"

"I want you to befriend her. She's hurting over losing her boyfriend besides the worry of her mother." His brows met over the bridge of his aquiline nose.

"I've always been her friend." Starli objected to Joel's familiar manner and automatic orders.

"You've been a friendly employer. She needs someone she can trust, someone to turn to. A female friend."

It was Starli's turn to raise her eyebrows. The sound of the pealing doorbell came from the front hall. "Are you a doctor? Besides a chef, sport enthusiast, and friend to the needy?"

Ouch. That was hitting pretty heavy. She turned as Toni appeared in the doorway, her face white.

"Starli..." Toni stretched out a hand.

"What? What's wrong?"

"It's..." Her friend heaved a sigh. "It's Roland Stratton at the door, asking for you."

"Oh, no." Starli gripped the sofa arm. What did he want? She'd hoped that he wouldn't find out about the party tonight and would leave her alone for one day.

"Shall I tell him you can't see him?" Toni stepped closer.

No doubt ready to do battle if she needed it.

"I can't talk to him, especially tonight. He just wants to make trouble."

"I'll tell him then." Toni started to move away, but Joel stood up as Caro led Manny and Louis into the room.

Joel touched Starli's shoulder. "Do you want him gone? Let me talk to him."

"Roland's on your front porch, Starli." Manny frowned.

"Shall I call the police?" Caro lifted her cell phone.

"He is the police, Caro." Toni's quiet correction reached Starli's ears.

And he was. There was no way to win.

"Starl-e-e, now is that anyway to treat a dear relative? Leave them on the doorstep? Shame on you." His deep gruff voice exploded into the room.

Starli stood up, then turned and wondered if she'd slipped into another nightmare. Roland, here, in her home? Her voice was cold when she spoke. "What are you doing here, Roland? I don't remember inviting you."

"Getting kind of high-minded, aren't you?" He wasn't quite as good-looking as Ryan had been. His thick arms strained at the sleeves of his plaid shirt. His fingers flexed and relaxed. "I had a call there were a lot of cars parking out front. Wanted to make sure nothing illegal was going on."

Gasps of shock and protest surrounded her like arms of love.

Those beefy fingers. Fingers like Ryan's. "I'm trying to entertain some friends tonight. Would you please leave?"

Ryan's brother ran his gaze over each of their faces, a sneer twisting his full lips. "I want to talk to you now. I'm tired of your weaseling."

Joel stepped closer. He was taller than Roland, and far slimmer. "Starli asked you to leave."

One side of Roland's lips tipped up. His nostrils flared. His gaze raked Joel's figure. "The knight from England? Why don't you toddle on home? You're asking for more trouble than I think a cook can handle."

Joel's fingers clenched, but he offered only a tight smile. "Do you think? Let me escort you out the door, Rolly."

Perrin, who'd volunteered to oversee the parking of cars, walked over to Joel. "I'll help."

Toni touched his arm. "Perrin, please be careful."

Roland's head jerked toward Toni. "Relax, Toni. I won't hurt your man."

"I'm not worried about *my* man, Roland." Toni's snappy comeback sent the blood to his face.

He scowled, then swiveled his gaze back to Joel. "I don't care too much for foreigners who interfere where they're not wanted. Watch your step, Brit."

Perrin and Joel moved closer, prepared to hustle him out of the house, but Roland stepped to the doorway and then stopped long enough to run his gaze over Starli. "I'm leaving, Starl-e-e. Wouldn't want to disrupt your social life. Take good care of that restaurant of yours. We'll talk later."

The group burst into excited—or was it nervous?—chatter as the door slammed behind him. Her ears rang from his last words.

We'll talk later. We'll talk later.

"A most disagreeable man." Manny frowned and shook his head.

"I've never cared for him or Ryan. He's a dangerous man." Toni took Starli's hand. "Are you all right, Starli?"

"I wish you would let me call the police." Caro rushed to the window.

Starli sank to her loveseat, her gaze fastened on the doorway where the man who'd worshipped his brother had disappeared.

He would be back. He'd promised.

~*~

The color had returned to Starli's cheeks. She'd been so pale after Roland had left, he'd insisted she take a sip or two of juice.

Rolly definitely needed warned off, and right now he was angry enough to be the man to do it. If the women hadn't been here...

Camille and Juanita showed up together and from their eager faces, Joel knew they were looking forward to the evening. Camielle hadn't wanted to leave her mother, but he'd talked her into it. It would do her good to get out for one evening.

The group clasped hands as Toni breathed a short blessing for their evening ahead and the food. Joel stood to the side and watched his co-workers as they filled their plates, enjoying their quiet conversation and happy moods.

"You're not eating? Not up to your high standards? I assure you that Toni is an excellent cook, even if I can't boil water."

"Have you never tried to cook?"

"I never had the time. From a child I've spent any extra time I've had on lessons, then later, practicing the piano. After that came college and marriage."

"Your husband didn't require any meals?"

The color rose in her cheeks. "He required a lot of things, but cooking wasn't one of them. He was seldom home in the daytime, and we had a cook for our evening dinners."

Joel leaned closer and murmured. "I'll tell you a secret. It's rather refreshing to know someone who's not trying to impress me with her cooking prowess. It gets quite tiresome to have to compliment a lady on a dish with too much salt."

"And being the perfect gentleman you wouldn't dream of doing that." Starli laughed.

His heart contracted at the sound. What kind of man had her husband been who couldn't appreciate her uncomplicated nature? How could anyone hurt her? He took her elbow. "Come show me what to sample."

Plates filled, Joel settled beside Starli in a corner of the room. After checking on her guests, she stared down at her plate.

"Camille seems to be having a good time." He observed.

"Why shouldn't she?" Starli crunched down on a celery stick, chewed.

"I'm glad she's here. Do you think you could help her?"

The frank green-eyed gaze resting on him was full of quizzical interest. "Help her? I have helped her. Over and over. I don't like to butt into other people's business."

He gave her a wide-eyed glance. "A nice sentiment. A very nice excuse for skipping out of your duty."

"Nice? Decent, is what I call it." Starli's eyes

were radiating 'don't trespass' warning signs.

Did he dare push her farther out of her comfort zone?

"Why do you talk about Camille every time we're together? If you have a crush on her, please don't inflict your emotions for her on me."

"I don't go in for 'crushes' as you describe it." Joel sampled a rolled up cream cheese, chive and turkey sampler tidbit. "We talk about her because she needs help. I'm asking you to help her."

"What do you want me to do? Hold her hand? Become a nurse? Counselor? I assure you, I'd be a failure. I can barely care for myself."

Her doubt nicked at his heart.

"There is something big you can do." He suggested.

"Big?" Startled green eyes flashed questions at him.

"I've talked to Uncle Laurence and your friends, and they all agree, so hear me out. Will you give a benefit concert for Camille and her mother?"

"Me? I'm not that good. No one will come."

Joel allowed his lips to twist into a taunt, broadcasting a challenge. Just enough to tease her. To push her to agree. "They'll come. They'll come for Camille and her mother. They'll come because they want to hear you. And the big shots will come because it's the right thing to do."

She bit her lip. At last she sighed. "I've got the skating exhibition to do."

"You can handle them both," Joel coaxed.

"I don't know..."

"You'd have two weeks to get ready. With your love of the piano, I'm sure you're always prepared. We'll advertise in the local paper and maybe a few surrounding ones. Maybe do a radio ad."

"You might be disappointed."

"You might be surprised." If she would only let go. Let go of the past and her fears, and trust. Trust God. Trust him.

Starli started to stand up, but Caro rushed up to them and tripped.

Joel jumped to his feet and caught her. "Whoa. You okay?"

"Sorry." With a sweet smile for Joel, she looked at Starli. "Have you taken care of what I wanted you to do?"

Cheeks red, Starli sneaked a look at him. Her voice sounded hollow when she spoke. "What you wanted me to do?"

"Starli Cameron, you're my dearest friend—well, you and Toni—but you're trying my patience. Pierre Markus' concert is next week." Caro crossed her arms. "You promised to ask him."

"Ask who what?" Joel inserted innocently, loving the confusion playing across Starli's face.

Pressed lips and angry eyes told him she didn't want to hear from him. "It's whom. And this is a private conversation. Would you mind?"

No way would he leave right now. "Don't mind me. I'll be a robin in a corner."

"More like a nosy jay." Starli scoffed, then beseeched Caro. "Can we talk about this later?"

"No, we can't." Caro tapped a foot. "Why do I get a feeling you're putting this off? Oh, that's right. Because I *know* you. Let's do it now."

"*Now?* I really don't want to."

Joel couldn't resist. "Would you like me to help you make up your mind?"

"I can't believe this." Starli jumped to her feet. "Badgered by my friend and annoyed by an employee. I'm going to go talk to Toni. At least she has some sense."

She moved off, then threw over her shoulder a parting remark. "Not like you two."

He laughed, delighted she could still tease even though she was provoked. "I think Starli is running from the obligatory request she promised to make."

Caro sank to Starli's vacated seat. "She is so-o-o man-avoidance. But then who can blame her, living with a mad man like Ryan?"

"Did he hurt her very badly?" Joel sobered at the thought.

"Yes. Mentally *and* physically. I'm afraid she'll never trust another man." She looked at him hopefully. "You haven't made any progress? I think she likes you."

"I certainly hope so." Joel smiled.

"Thankfully, Ryan didn't hurt her face. For a long time after they were married, Toni or I would notice bruises here and there on her arms and legs. She always shied away from a direct answer, and we stupidly believed her because believing anything else would have ruined her life. Which it did anyway." Caro shook her head, her face dark with anger.

"Then when she showed up with that broken

finger, we both knew something was wrong. We insisted she tell us. We wouldn't let her get by with the excuse of falling. She kept blaming herself for Ryan's anger at her."

"Why didn't you talk to her?" A coldness settled in his heart.

"Oh, we tried. We begged her. But by then, Ryan had psychologically threatened her so much she was afraid to leave. He vowed to drag her back if she did, to kill her if she said anything. Said he'd get away with it being a cop. The bully."

Tears welled in the woman's eyes.

"His family was well known. No one suspected anything. The whole town grieved when he died in a car wreck driving drunk."

"Everyone but you and Toni."

Caro tossed her head. "I only attended the funeral because of Starli."

"Sad."

"It's been almost seven years since Ryan's death and that long for Starli to heal as much as she has." Caro shifted in her seat. "You know what I've wanted Starli to ask you. We talked about it. Would you go as Starli's partner?"

"My pleasure, Caroline. By the way, why do they shorten your lovely name to Caro?"

Caro wrinkled her nose at him before jumping to her feet. "Caroline is too prestigious for me. I'm just plain Caro."

With a quick conspiratorial wink at him, she rushed across the room.

Well, he had the invitation, even though Starli hadn't issued it.

Camille stood by herself holding a glass in

her hand.

With a lazy stride he headed toward her, but before he took five steps, she set her glass down and hurried over to where Starli stood with Louis.

He hesitated, debating on invading their territory—at least Starli's—but what did he have to lose? If the girl was begging again for the manager's position, he could lend his support--at the risk of displeasing The Queen.

He'd take his chances.

He was just in time to hear Camille's passionate declaration. "That's not fair, Starli. You'll be sorry. I'll make sure of that."

With stormy eyes and stomping feet, she headed to the front door, Louis following the girl.

He felt obligated to talk to Camille, but his own heart demanded he check on Starli even if she didn't need—or want—his help.

Chapter Ten

Her life was a mess.

Should she? Or not? Why not tell Joel that she didn't want him for a skating partner Friday night? That would solve his disruption to her sense of complacency. Wouldn't it?

Wouldn't it?

Or was she fooling herself? Would she ever feel peaceful again? She shook her head. That wasn't right. God promised peace in her heart. Pastor Haag said so. And she believed it, didn't she?

Why then couldn't she turn these feelings over to God? She felt like an outnumbered dog surrounded by an angry group of wolves. Had she backed herself into a corner by her refusal to trust anyone—any man—again? Her refusal to face the rushing torrential fear of abuse?

The blood pounded in her cheeks. She knew her friends didn't know the depth of her weakness. They, and the whole town, for that matter, thought her strong and independent. And she supposed she was in some areas of her life.

Starli winced as the truth hammered at her.

Joel's sporty red car seemed to be tossing an amused question at her as she pulled into the skating pond's parking lot. Why shouldn't Joel have Camille and—Starli swallowed—Rita Mae as a friend? She'd made it clear their relationship was purely a business one.

And it's what she wanted. She straightened

her shoulders and stepped out of her car. Unlocking the trunk, she picked up her skates and moved out to the lake.

"I say, perfect weather. Think it'll hold for Friday night?" Joel reclined on one of the pond-side benches, his skates lying askew beside him.

Starli sat, unzipped her boots and kicked them off. She pulled on one skate, laced it, then looked up. "Forecast calls for cold weather, but no storms."

"Bully." He dropped to one knee. "Here, let me help you finish that."

Starli pulled her foot away and avoided looking at him by checking her watch. "Go ahead and get ready. I'm fine. We need to get started."

She could sense his hesitation, his study of her face, but he said nothing more. Sitting beside her, he kicked off his own boots. He shoved his feet into black skates, then bent over to lace them.

Uneasy, Starli finished her skates and stood. "I'm going to warm up."

Without waiting for his ascent, she moved out onto the ice and executed a few basic turns. Perfect.

Joel joined her, and they worked for two hours on their routine. Unlike the other evening, Starli reined in her feelings. She concentrated on her movements and tried to ignore the man beside her.

When they'd finished, she headed for the bench, but Joel stopped her. "Let's take ten to cool down. Come on, race you to that pier."

"That's not cooling down." Starli argued,

even as her gaze measured the distance. Could she beat him as tired as she was?

"Tell you what. You beat me last time. This time whoever beats can ask a question from the other."

"What kind of proposition is that?" What information was he after?

A teasing light shone from his blue eyes. "Afraid, Miss Starli?"

"I'm not afraid of anything." The words came too quickly, and she regretted them as soon as they were spoken. She was afraid, all right. Afraid of the past, afraid of what Roland had in mind, afraid of failing again.

"Then?"

"That is so childish. If we have to race, let's do it for something important."

"You have something in mind?" That teasing light brightened, and he edged closer.

She puffed out an exasperated sigh. "What kind of things would we ask?"

"Anything we want." Joel shrugged. His half-smile belied the casualness he portrayed. "I thought that was an easy prize."

"All right." She whirled and took off, striding as fast as she could. Starli risked a glance over her shoulder, then pushed herself harder. He was catching her. How could anyone go any faster? The wind bit into her cheeks, and forced the tears to blur her vision.

Ten yards to go. Joel's tall figure caught up with her. He raced beside her for another two yards, hilarity bubbling out of him, then pulled away, and Starli wanted to stomp the ice in frustration. She slowed her pace.

He flew past the pier, did a quick

roundabout turn and skated back toward her. He looked relaxed, but was he hiding the telltale rise and fall of his chest? Good. At least she wasn't the only one worn out.

"Want to shake my hand?"

Starli skated beside him, her breath coming in heaves. Her body sagged. "No, I don't. I can't believe you won."

"I had plenty of motivation." He peered at her. "I wanted to ask my question right badly."

"I can imagine. But that can wait. I need to rest." She ignored his stare and sank on a nearby bench, too tired to pull off her skates.

"You all right?"

She nodded.

"You're not going to try to weasel out of answering my question? I assure you, it's an easy one."

"That really comforts me." Starli bent over to begin unlacing her boots. Her fingers fumbled with the lace, pulling it into a knot. She yanked at it, then sat back.

"I really will help you if you like." Joel offered, stomping his foot into his own shoe.

"Thanks. My fingers are numb." She stretched out a leg.

Joel knelt in front of her and undid the knot, pulled off her skate, and reached for her boot. "I really like your friends. Caroline is a lot of fun."

"She considers herself awkward and homely, but she's loyal and a beautiful person. So-o-o funny when she wants to be."

"She mentioned a concert performance Saturday evening that a bunch of you are attending. Sounds like fun."

Suspicion reared its ugly head. Did he know Caro had made her promise to ask him to go? With studied indifference she issued the invitation. "You're welcome to come along, if you'd like."

"Sure. How's everyone traveling?"

"Perrin's renting a limousine for the evening. He and Toni, Caroline, Toby and his friend, Amy George, me, and now you." Starli flashed him a broad smile. "Toby wants to ask Andy Carrington, but Caro's having a fit, so I'm not sure if Toby will be brave enough to face her wrath."

"I take it she's not too fond of the gentleman."

"I think she protests far too much about him for her dislike to be genuine."

"Want to go with Camille and me this afternoon? We're looking for cars."

Does he have to talk about her every time we're together? "Is that your question?"

"Hardly. Want to help us pick out a car for her?"

A threesome? Didn't sound appealing to her. "I don't think..."

"I thought you were going to try to befriend her?" Joel interrupted.

"I am her friend although after her Sunday night temper tantrum I'm not sure she'll claim me. But I know nothing about cars. It's a waste of my time. Besides, I have more research to do."

"Research?"

Why had she let that slip? Maybe it'd be simpler to just go. As a threesome. She grimaced, and Joel laughed.

"Is it that distasteful to be in my presence? Or is it Camille?"

"Joel, I don't care who you see. You and Camille can go out every day for all I care."

"Really? That's a relief that I don't have to worry your feelings."

Unreasonable ire rose. He didn't have to be so blasé about it.

"But I want you to go, and I know Camille would be delighted."

How would he know how Camille felt? And why was she being so obstinate? She'd never been like this as a child growing up. Spoiled by her doting parents, yes. But she'd been a happy, well-adjusted person. Or at least she'd always thought so. That's what marriage to the wrong man did to you.

"Okay. If you insist on my inexperienced help, you've got it. But I warn you, I know nothing, absolutely nothing about cars. I don't know a Ford from a Chevrolet."

"Trust me, you'll have fun." Joel rose to his feet.

They headed for their individual vehicles. As Starli settled in her seat, she called to Joel through her open window. "Hey, you didn't ask your question."

"I've decided not to ask it."

Relief flooded through Starli. Escape. Then curiosity reined in her relief. "Why not?"

"You already answered it, Your Majesty." Joel shut his door.

~*~

Joel pulled up in front of Camille Findlay's box-like frame home, honked and started to get out as the front door flew open. Camille bounced down the sidewalk, her burnished blond ponytail bobbing with every step. Before he could open the passenger door, she flung it open.

"I'm so thrilled. I can't believe I'm going to get a different car. Isn't this exciting?" She pulled the seatbelt around her thin body.

"Blooming right."

"Where are we going?"

"I asked Starli to join us. I figured she'd have some good ideas of where to go."

His peripheral vision caught her quick glance. She shifted in her seat, then spoke casually. Too casually?

"I thought *you* were going to help me."

Joel shot her an inquiring look. "I am."

"I mean, I thought it would be you and me. Do we really have to take *her*?" Camille's cheeks bloomed crimson.

"You don't want her to go?"

"I'm thinking of quitting the restaurant." Camille shook her head. "She's—"

"You remember where she lives?"

~*~

Ten minutes later, Starli walked out to Joel's car, dreading the afternoon. How would Camille respond after their altercation Sunday night? By the way she was moving her hands, Starli suspected Camille might be objecting to her presence at this excursion.

All Joel's fault, kiddo. Starli chuckled at the thought of Joel on the receiving end of Camille's displeasure.

"I'll sit in back," she called when the front door swung open, and Camille started to get out.

"That's okay. I'm younger." Gracious words yet the tone implied otherwise.

Was Camille being snippy? She wasn't *that* old that she needed special consideration.

"I think I can manage it." Starli tried and failed to keep the sarcasm from her voice

"Are you sure? I'd love to sit in front with Joel." Camille chortled, then in a lower voice said, "He did promise to help *me* today, you know."

Perversely, the front seat suddenly seemed the most desirable. Starli bit her lip. Why hadn't she just accepted?

Joel leaned over and peered up at both of them. "Camille's right, Starli. Let her sit in the back."

Starli looked at Camille, a sudden surge of triumph speed bumping its way through her heart. Camille's face fell for just an instant, then she scrambled into the back.

"Hang on, lovely ladies. We'll give this beauty a real blow-out."

"There are speed limits." Starli's sharp reply cut through Camille's laughing squeal.

"I'll be careful."

Starli clutched at the door handle. "What gives you any special privileges? Laws are laws in America."

"Right-o. Just a second or two to clear its head."

"You'll land us all in jail."

~*~

The urge to show off just a little in front of his ice maiden was too much to resist. Joel pressed the gas accelerator hard. The little sports car responded as though she was panting for the command. He laughed. The heady exhilaration of a powerful machine in his control shot through him.

The sound of the siren overtook the whine of his engine. In the rearview mirror, he caught sight of the blue and white flashing lights.

Coppers.

On the way to a burglary? A homicide? Sighing, he slowed, but they stayed on his tail. Joel signaled, pulled off the road then reached for his identification. "No problem, ladies. This'll only take a minute."

"Yeah. Camille and I'll make sure to take time out to visit you in your cell." Starli's sarcasm bit into him like a winter storm.

The uniformed cop pecked on the window. Joel obligingly pressed the button, and the man bent over to talk to them.

"Starli Cameron? What are you doing riding with a guy who's trying to break the sound barrier?"

"You know him?"

"Of course I know him. Detective Eddie and I attended high school together." She sent him a withering glare. "Hi, Eddie. That's a good question. I've been wondering what I'm doing riding with this maniac ever since I climbed in his car."

"Is he a friend of yours or did he kidnap you?"

The bloke was making fun of him, but what could he do? Sounded as if Starli was having a smidgen of fun at his expense too. "What's a detective doing making traffic stops?"

The detective spoke to Starli. "He wants to know why *I* stopped him. Seems pretty obvious to me."

"I thought so too, Eddie." Her sigh was drawn out.

Yeah, that was smugness in her voice. She was enjoying this.

"We're a small community, Joel. That means our police force is limited. Our chief, one detective, two basic cops, a couple of temporaries. Eddie does what needs done when it needs done."

It was his turn to puff out an exasperated sigh. "You want my identification?"

Eddie ignored Joel's question and directed another one at Starli. "What's this wise guy's name, Starli?"

"This is *Sir* Joel Peterman-Blair, come clear from Britain to honor us hillbilly West Virginians." Starli's voice dripped so much West Virginia syrupy twang, Joel could have scooped it up with a spoon.

"You don't say. He should have some special treatment then, wouldn't you think?" Tone for tone, Eddie matched hers. He straightened. "Would you please step out of the car, Sir Peterman-Blair?"

Joel caught Starli's sly grin and spoke in a low voice. "You called him, didn't you?"

"No, I did not. Why would I?"

He slid reluctantly out of the car, but not before he laid a frown on her. Maybe she needed some of her own medicine for a change.

Camille leaned forward and whispered, "Mr. Peterman-Blair, you're not in serious trouble, are you?"

"Of course not. I'll be fine."

"Eddie's just teasing him a bit, Camille.

Don't worry. It's good for him."

"Not sure I care for that kind of teasing." Camille reached forward and patted Joel's hand still resting on the door frame, then tossed her a disapproving frown.

"Please lean against the car, Mr.—excuse me, Sir Peterman-Blair. We hillbillies want you to have some special treatment."

Great. Just great. Wry amusement spread through him as Joel placed his hands on the top of the car. This is what he got for showing off at his age.

~*~

Great. This was hilarious. The funniest thing she'd witnessed in a long time. Starli wanted to laugh aloud. A sudden spurt of mischief nudged her. She leaned across the seat and pleaded. "Eddie, please go easy with this lawbreaker. I'm in serious need of a good chef, and he has done a wonderful job. Can I bribe you with a complimentary dinner for you and your family?"

"Are you recommending I let this criminal go, Starli?" Eddie pursed his lips as if in deep concentration.

"What about just a fine?"

Joel sputtered, but if she wasn't mistaken, there was a shade of mirth in that sputter.

Eddie stroked his round chin. "Well, since it's you, I suppose I could go easy."

"Think about that steak dinner you like." Starli promised the teasing man who was her friend. "And for free too."

"Done." Eddie whipped out his ticket pad and scribbled furiously on it, then handed it over to Joel for his signature.

"Do you mean to tell me you just took a bribe?" Joel demanded. "Is that allowed?"

Eddie lowered his head and glared at him. "No, it's not allowed. You would have gotten the ticket regardless of what Starli offered. She's just being her usual generous self to a cop who's been cut back on his work hours and has a wife and two kids to feed."

Joel stared at him for a few minutes before glancing down at Starli. She lowered her eyes. Now was probably not the best time to reveal the triumph she felt.

He raised his hands. "Right. Sorry about that, sir. I'll cut the kid stuff and drive like I've got some sense."

The detective took the pad, tore off the ticket and handed it over. A wide grin spread across his broad face. "See that you do. You've got some precious cargo sitting in there with you. Starli means a lot to Appleton. We couldn't do without her Apple Blossoms. Put us on the map."

Five minutes later, Joel put the car in gear and took off. He looked over at Starli, and she met his steady gaze. Laughter bubbled up inside her.

Then without warning, his lips twitched. He burst into a guffaw.

Starli fought to hold in her laughter, but couldn't. Her stomach ached as she gasped for breath.

"Why are you two laughing?" No laughter was coming from the back seat. "Starli, you could have been easier on Joel. He was showing us a good time, that's all."

Camille's huffy words hit her full in the face

as her chuckles subsided. Now she was getting the blame for Joel's antics?

"That ticket was well worth seeing you laugh like that." Joel added.

Did Joel always have that effect on everyone he was around?

Or just her?

Chapter Eleven

Exhibition night. Ten hours to go.

"**Y**ou and Joel are going to be the hit of the evening. I promise you." Toni hugged Starli.

"Thanks for the vote of confidence. I'm not sure we'll be in sync the way Ryan and I once were."

"Trust me, dear friend, Joel will be with you every step of the way. He'll judge your moves before you do them. And he won't try to hog the limelight." She shifted the sleeping baby in her arms, then bent her head to kiss her forehead.

Starli's fears eased a little, and she nodded.

"He's good for you, Starli, in more ways than one."

Sobered, Starli watched her friend leave the restaurant. Whether her friend's observation was on target was yet to be seen. One thing for sure, motherhood looked good on Toni. She'd really enjoyed having both mama and adopted baby daughter for lunch. Too bad Caro hadn't been able to make it.

Her cell phone rang, and Starli checked the caller. Hmmm. Why would the cleaners be calling now when they should be getting ready to deliver her costume for tonight?

"Starli, something awful's happened." The babbling voice rushed over Starli's tentative greeting.

"Janine? What are you talking about?"

A wail echoed through the receiver. "Y-o-u-r dress is m-i-s-s-ing." Another anguished sob, a sniff and hiccup.

What on earth? "Calm down. Now tell me what happened."

"I came in to work at eleven."

Okay. That was simple enough. "Then what?"

"Had some customers. Finished up some work left over from yesterday. Then I began getting the orders together that needed delivered this afternoon. And your's was g-o-n-e."

"Shhh. Don't cry. That won't help. What do you mean 'gone'?"

"Gone. Disappeared. Not here."

"But—"

"I know, I know." Janine broke in with another frenzied denial. "I can't figure it out. It was my last cleaning last night, and I wrapped it especially carefully, ready to go to you first thing this afternoon. I knew you needed it for tonight, but it's not here."

Starli frowned. She'd never ever known Janine, the magnificent—as she was known because of her power to get *any* stain out—to fail. "Do you think one of the employees—"

"No. I was the last one out, and it was safely hanging where it should be. I'd be more apt to believe I did something."

"Well, then. What can the explanation be? It didn't just disappear on its own."

"I know, but I've looked everywhere." The laundress seemed on the verge of breaking into tears again.

"Is anything else missing? Any doors left

open? Windows broken?"

"No-o-o. Wait!" A pause. "The back door lock always sticks when I first open it in the mornings, but this morning it opened right away. I didn't pay attention because my cell began ringing."

That was interesting. Had someone picked the lock?

"Do you suppose someone broke in and stole your costume, leaving the door unlocked when they left? But why would they do that?"

"I don't know, Janine, but it sounds like that's exactly what happened."

"I'm so sorry."

"Don't worry about it. I have other outfits I can wear." But not her favorite.

Minutes later, Starli hung up and stood staring out her office window. Had someone stolen her outfit? It was the craziest thought she'd ever had, yet what other answer was there? Janine had enough faith in her workers to vouch for them. Her thoughts circled back to the question.

Who would steal her outfit, and more confusing still, why?

Her stomach knotted. Roland?

Annoying her again would be right up his alley, but verbal threats had been more his style lately. So what was she going to do? Stew and fret the rest of the day? Well...

She laughed at her own thoughts. She had way too much to do. Good thing too.

When the phone rang again, she was humming the song she and Joel would skate to tonight.

Stu Stroth's enthusiastic voice came

through bright and cheerful. "Afternoon, Starli. Ready for tonight? This is a tremendous thing you're doing for the Findleys. I hope they appreciate it."

The way Camille was acting, she'd wondered that herself.

"Why don't I swing by and pick you up? You'll be too tightly strung beforehand, but afterwards, we could stroll around and grab a bite. Sound good?"

What would it hurt? She'd ignored him long enough. "Sounds good. I'll see you at seven."

As it turned out the weather was just as the weatherman had promised. Clear, cold—but not too much so as to keep the town people at home.

Starli's stomach jumped with nervousness as she and Stu pulled into the reserved parking place the mayor had arranged for her.

"Nervous?"

"A little."

"I want to talk seriously with you, Starli. I've admired and stood by you for years when Ryan abused you. I've supported you when you wanted to open Apple Blossoms."

Oh, no. Another speech. But he *had* been wonderful through the years, backing her projects, listening to her complaints and comforting her when she literally sobbed on his shoulder. He was a good man. Maybe Caro was right, and she could do worse. "You certainly have, Stu. What would I have done without your support?"

"Dad's after me to settle down, and I know we could go far together. You and I both love our town, we're a lot alike in our business skills, and I think we have a mutual affection for the other."

Starli nodded. All true.

He took both her hands in his. "I know you need to go get changed and ready, but promise me you'll think about us. Promise, Starli."

She stared into his intense—too much so?—blue eyes for seconds, then nodded. "I promise, Stu. I will think about it."

"Good. Then I'll see you afterwards."

She could see the crowds, bundled up and wandering around the park, in high spirits, by the sound of the laughter and noise. Music blared from the overhead speakers. Couples linked arms and strolled together, greeting friends and family with boisterous "hellos." The more adventurous skated, sleds overflowed with rosy-cheeked children as they slid down the park hill.

Scents of roasting hotdogs, hamburgers, and venison floated through the air. Tempting smells of soups galore enticed the attendees to stop and sample. Cornbread, muffins, candy and cookies beckoned to young and old alike.

Starli had purposely avoided the park all day. She'd put in a full day at the restaurant to keep her mind off the evening. It wasn't as if she'd never performed in front of this many or more, but it had been years and only with Ryan.

Tonight, her partner was agile and handsome Joel Peterman-Blair, and as much as they'd practiced, she was still nervous. Would he sense her mood and respond, proving strong where she was weak? Would they move in harmony, each reaching out to the other in their every whirl and jump? Or would their performance be judged as awkward and ugly?

Whereas Joel was tall and a well-muscled trim, Ryan had been shorter, muscular and solid, swinging her around with an ease that...

The memory of Ryan's brute strength used against her slithered into her mind as easily as a wily snake.

Starli shook off the thought and headed toward the dressing room set aside for her. She'd already sent her substitute outfit ahead with Caro who should be waiting. She wound her way through the crowd, spoke and nodded at random. Nerves made it impossible for her to focus on faces.

The door swung open as she approached the room, and Caro peered out. "You're here. I thought you were going to be late."

A glance at her watch told her she was right on time.

Caro pulled her in and gushed. "Look what came for you."

Starli gazed at the velvety nosegay of purple violets that lay on airy white tissue paper. She reached out a hand and lifted the corsage to her cheek. "Who sent them? You? Toni?"

"Not from me." Caro shook her head till her hair fanned out around her face. "I totally forgot you love violets when you skate. And I called Toni. Not her either. I don't know where they came from."

Happiness surged through her even as she searched in vain for a card. The flowers had done the trick. It didn't matter who sent them. Confidence zipped through her. She could do this. Tonight she could perform for the town like she used to.

Caro helped her slip into her old white skating outfit with the sparkling silver trim. With trembling fingers Starli tried to pin on the violets, but Caro pushed her hand away and did it herself. Then she held Starli at arm's length.

"You're our beautiful snow princess again. Now plaster a big smile on that face and keep it. Forget everything else but that you love to skate and will wow the crowd. Remember, you've got Toni and me, and a whole bunch of others out there who care about you and who'll be cheering you on."

"I'll do my best."

"You and Joel." Caro's words floated behind her as she walked toward the pond.

Where was Joel? She hadn't seen his car when she'd pulled in. Would he stand her up or get busy and forget like Ryan had done more times than she cared to remember? Nervousness clutched at her stomach again. Dear God, what had she gotten herself into? Could she perform without Joel? Impossible with the moves they'd planned together.

But when she stepped out on the edge of the ice, there he was, resplendent in a blue and silver figure-hugging outfit, his gaze on the shoreline crowd, as if searching for someone.

Her breath caught in her throat. He looked fantastic—a Greek god with his chiseled facial bones and blond hair. His lean body, firm and muscled, stood out against the colorful crowd.

He turned and a light brightened his blue eyes. His gaze dropped to the violets on her shoulder, then returned to her face. "This is it, My Love. Let's go out there and show them what skating is all about."

"I'm ready." Shaky, but said with a willingness that bolstered her courage.

They stood arm in arm, and when at last the announcer began his spiel, Starli felt the muscles under Joel's sleeve tense. Her own body responded to the excitement. *This* was it.

"...Ladies and gentlemen, our own lovely and tal-ent-ed...Starli Cameron, a-n-d her partner—all the way from Great Britain—Sir Jo-el Peter-man Blair!"

Starli stepped out, with Joel beside her, and they spread out, their fingers touching, the spotlight focused on them. The crowd cheered, but the cheers faded as she wrapped herself in the small world of performance she'd always loved.

Then as the music began their introduction, she slid into position, facing Joel, his gaze riveted on her. They paused then broke into their beginning moves.

As she waltzed into her routine, Starli forgot the crowd, forgot the past, and forgot everything but the moment with Joel. He never faltered and never sought the limelight for himself. Every movement served to complement and enhance her own.

His strong hands lifted her, and Starli's brain counted one, two, three, before he settled her back on her feet, and they moved on to execute their flying spins in unison. Her spirit exalted with the breathtaking, exhilarating world she and Joel were creating. If her heart hadn't already been pounding from the excitement, she could have soared into the icy heavens.

When at last the music exploded into its grand finale—as one, they finished with a spiral, moved back into their ice skating waltz, and Starli floated into a hydro-blade.

The crowd erupted into a roar. Joel lifted her to her feet and raised her hand to the people in the stands and at the lakeshore. Then he dropped her hand and flung out an arm in preference to her. Starli gave them a bow, a curtsy, waved, and clasped hands with Joel once again as he pulled her close. She heard his words—his mouth near her ear—over the drowning sound of the ecstatic clapping and cheering.

"Thanks for wearing my violets."

~*~

Rita Mae stood beside Joel, her head bent toward his, her fingers digging into his arm. Her little-girlish voice whispered in his ear her enthusiasm over his ice-skating talents.

He listened, but his gaze searched the crowd. He didn't want to miss Starli.

"And I don't think you've heard one word I've said."

He flashed a quick grin at her. "That's where you're wrong. I quote, 'and the way you lifted Starli—as big as she is—why, that shows how strong you are. I admire a man who's strong.'"

She pouted, and Joel was ashamed of the unkind thought that flickered at the edge of his mind. Rita was much too old to pout effectively. Leave that to the younger ladies. "She's not big; she's tall."

"You are so-o-o kind to everyone, dear Joel.

Let's go for some espresso. My treat." Rita gushed and patted his arm.

Joel wanted to jerk away from the clinging woman, her pats and effusive compliments. Instead, he eyed the two women approaching. He couldn't take his gaze from the one. "If you'll excuse me, perhaps another time?"

Starli's long, floating stride slowed. A queen in a fur-lined parka suddenly displeased at her subject's supposed wrong.

She'd seen Rita Mae. Starli said something to Caro, and they both laughed, but Starli's eyes didn't laugh when she looked at him.

"How's my ice skating queen doing?" Joel tried a light note.

Rita snickered beside him.

"I'm not *your* ice skating anything." Starli's eyes shot green shards at him.

"True, but you are the ice queen—or princess, if you prefer—of Appleton. And if I'm not mistaken, I'm still a part of Appleton." Joel folded his arms and leaned against the back of a bleacher.

Starli cocked her head. "Maybe. Maybe not."

"Oh, so smart." Rita muttered under her breath.

The wisecrack was deliberately pointed, and Joel frowned. He needed to get rid of her. Starli would bristle until he did. He turned to Rita. "I think Starli and I did a fantastic job of wowing the crowd, wouldn't you say?"

Unfortunately, the lady in address refused an answer and only rolled her eyes as if she found his question ridiculous.

"You were both fantastic. Starli's great at anything she sets her mind to." Caro crowed.

Joel took a step closer. "Starli, will you let me take you home?"

"I'm not leaving yet."

"Then let's stroll together, and we'll get supper. Aren't you hungry?"

"I am starving. Caro?"

"You two go." Caro waved a hand. "Rita, how about lending me a hand to put away Starli's skating things?"

A look of annoyance crossed Rita's face, and a huff of impatience escaped her lips. "Sorry, but I've got things to do. No time to wait on queens."

Joel gave Starli no time to think up any more reasons to refuse. He placed a hand on the small of her back and guided her away, the involuntary flinch from her body stinging his fingertips even through her parka.

A low voice halted their exit. "Starli."

~*~

Starli turned. Stu Stroth stood watching them.

"Stu." Oh, no. She wanted to slap her forehead. How could she have forgotten she'd sort of promised him time after her skating routine? "I'm so sorry. I forgot we were going to meet."

"Yes, I see that. But I'm here now."

"Not so quick. She also agreed to go with me." Joel's mild tone didn't defuse his possessive clasp of her arm even when she tugged at it.

"Starli?"

They wanted her to choose? How on earth did she get herself in these messes? One more remark from either of them, and she'd go help

Caro restore order to her changing room. Or go home. By herself.

And really, if she chose, which man would it be? Joel? Stu?

Her heart said there wasn't any choice to make.

"Really? I have to *choose*? I—"

Stu's cell rang, and he withdrew it from a pocket, his unwavering gaze fastened on Starli. He spoke only a few words, then slowly hung up the receiver.

"I have to go. But it doesn't matter. I can see the answer in your eyes."

She wanted to deny his statement, argue she wasn't making a choice, that it didn't matter to her which man she spent the rest of the evening with.

But it would have been a lie. Her heart—traitorous organ it was—had already spoken.

"Stu, please. Don't be like that. What about—"

He waved a hand and walked off, never looking back. But the reproach from his words dampened her spirit.

"I see the best man won." Joel's jovial words fanned the burning embers of annoyance inside her.

"Is that all you can say?" If her tone was a trifle savage, she hoped he didn't try to blame her. There was only so much a woman could endure.

"What else is there to say? You chose the one you wanted to spend time with tonight, and he conceded the choice."

"I did no such thing."

Joel captured her hand and linked his

fingers with hers. "I think you did."

She would not answer his insistence.

"Your Majesty, when a woman agrees to meet a man later in the evening, and for whatever reason, forgets about that appointment, then the meeting was not that important or interesting to her."

"But—"

He held up a hand and went on. "Especially when a man is issuing an ultimatum with his tone."

"He wasn't."

"Oh, but he was."

"How could you know that?"

He cast her a that's-not-even-worth-answering look. "Because if I'd been on the losing end, I'd fought a little harder. *I* wouldn't have given up so easily. You'd have known I meant business."

He said that emphatically enough. Just like he meant it.

Was that her heart beating so erratically? Felt an awfully lot like it was stuck in her throat. She had to take a couple deep breaths before she could speak again.

"I see. Perhaps the victory won't be so sweet if I turn out to be as cantankerous as you think I am for the rest of the evening."

"I like a stiff battle."

She laughed. He was totally and completely incorrigible. There was no reasoning with the man. So why not try to forget Stu's hurt until she could soothe it, and enjoy the rest of the evening with her chef?

~*~

They took their time walking the path

around the lake, stopping long enough to watch the antics of the children on the ice, and to sample blue cotton candy on a stick. At a booth selling jewelry, key chains and other odds and ends, Starli hesitated, but he took her hand and led her toward the samples.

He rummaged, not particularly interested in anything, but definitely interested in anything Starli paused to eye. His gaze dropped, and he leaned over the counter, his attention caught. Tiny crystal figures shone, glittered, and reflected colored light rays on the first shelf of the glass countertop. Not quite an inch high, they were the most expensive item in the booth, and probably the only item worth wasting money upon.

He looked up, motioned to the clerk and said in a low voice as he pointed. "Let me see that one."

The clerk lifted out the tiny ice skater figurine and offered it to him for his inspection. "It's a lovely figurine."

He was reminded of the lithe figure Starli made on the ice. He made up his mind. "I'll take it. Don't bother with a box. I want it like it is."

Ten minutes later, they were outside again walking the last few feet to the parking lot. In front of his car, he paused.

"Let me have your hand."

"What?"

"I want your hand, your left hand." Joel insisted, his gaze on hers, holding it. "Don't ask questions."

Her cheeks were rosy from the cold air, but now they paled a little. She pulled her left hand from her pocket and edged it toward him. "Why?"

Joel hadn't realized he was holding his breath until then. His muscles relaxed, and before she could change her mind, clasped her hand, transferring the tiny charm from his palm to hers. Then he let go. S-l-o-w-l-y.

She didn't immediately check to see what he'd deposited in her palm, although her fingers clenched around the charm. She continued to stare at him. After a moment, she opened her fingers and looked down.

Her stare lasted so long he began to think she hated the charm, then with utmost care she lifted it and held it up toward one of the pole lights. The crystal sparkled, and her face softened with a warm light.

Nothing, absolutely nothing had ever been as beautiful as the sight of this woman smiling her shy, happy smile. He wanted to ask, was oh, so eager to ask, 'Do you like it?' but he didn't.

And she didn't verbally answer his unspoken question, only looked at him, the answer in those usually cool eyes, now lit with happiness.

When a child's ball flew past, missing them, the spell was broken, but Joel noticed how carefully she tucked the charm into an inside pocket.

"Ready for a hotdog?"

Starli propped a long thin finger against her lips. "No, not tonight."

"Then may I propose an escapade? Let's vacate these grounds and find a fine pub to feast within." He deepened his accent.

Starli laughed again, and how he loved the sound.

"Why must everything you say and do be so dramatic? Life with you would..." Her voice trailed off.

What had she meant to say? Her face flushed and, for just a second, he caught a glimpse of the shock in her eyes.

"Life is short, and we're here but once. Let's enjoy it while we can. And together would be even better."

She frowned, her chin lifted. "I'm going to pretend I didn't hear that last sentence."

"You don't want to spend our lives together?" The thought appealed to him. Wasn't that what he was working toward?

"Stop, or we'll go our separate ways right this minute." She tapped one foot.

He'd teased enough. Joel capitulated to her demand. "Okay. You're the boss. Where shall we go?"

They left in his car and chose a well-lit, small diner off the main road.

"Next to ours, it has very good fried chicken." Starli assured him.

When Joel saw that Starli ordered chicken strips, he insisted on ordering steak.

"I just told you their chicken is divine."

"So you did. But this way we can sample each other's plates."

"I don't eat red meat much."

Joel pretended shock. "You don't eat real meat?"

"Much."

"Tonight, I want you to be adventuresome."

"I think I've heard that before." Starli

propped her chin on her clasped hands.

"You know what your trouble is?" Joel leaned closer.

"Why do I have the feeling that whether I want to know or not you're going tell me?"

Joel wished Starli had a strand of hair falling into her face so he could reach over and tuck it behind her small ears. Perfect ears as far as he could see.

"Because you need to know this. From me."

"Right. And what does Sir Peterman-Blair deem is necessary to broaden my education?"

He wanted to laugh. "You need to lighten up a little and quit worrying so much about what's going on around you. Stick with me, and I'll show you a good time."

"That's my lesson for today?" Her smirk showed him what she thought of his advice.

The waitress approached and set down small platters with their orders. After the blessing, Starli lifted a French fry and nibbled at one end.

Joel mock-scowled at her. "You don't eat beef, yet you'll eat a grease-laden French fry?"

"One of the comfort foods I allow myself." She lifted another one and offered it to him.

He leaned forward, and she stuck it in his mouth.

"Hmmm. It is good. Now try this."

He fed her a small piece of steak and watched her chew it. The steak was delicious, and she must have enjoyed it for she asked for another bite. He watched her white teeth sink into the steak. She had a way of tilting her head back, her gaze fastened on the ceiling as if afraid of being disturbed while savoring the food. Her pleasure in the little things of life was a simple reaction, yet endearing because of the unconscious portrayal of it.

As they left the restaurant he tucked her hand inside his. When she didn't pull away, he relaxed. They strolled toward his car.

Was that a light on inside it? He slowed and pulled back on Starli to halt her. "Wait here. I didn't leave a light on. Let me check it out."

He sprinted to his car. The passenger side door was open just enough to keep the light on. He peered in at the broken pieces of some object lying on the floorboard, then reached in to pick up one small piece of glass. He straightened, turned it over and heard the gasp behind him.

"I thought I told you to wait."

"That's my figurine." Starli pointed a shaking finger at the shard of glass.

She sounded on the verge of tears. The tiny piece of glass *was* an ice skate. He held it up to the outside security lights.

Reaching for the ice skate, she fingered it, turning it over and over. "Isabella's Dollar Store here in town sells the cheap version made with a cheap plastic. She stocks tons of those kinds of items. In the winter, it's hockey, ski, or skating figurines. They're a big favorite among those who like bargain items. I ran in there to get an emergency supply of paper one day this week. She had them on the discounted table I passed." Starli leaned in the car to pick up another small sliver of glass and stared down at it.

"You left it in the car."

"Yes." The sadness in her voice hurt him. "I

didn't want it to get broken. My pockets aren't that deep."

"I see."

"Roland smashed my figurine, trying to hurt me and telling me what he plans for me."

"You think Roland did this? He wants to break you?" Anger and disbelief battled for control in his voice.

She shrugged and turned away from him, staring into the nearby trees. "Perhaps not physically, but mentally and emotionally, he's letting me know he'll try to."

He turned her to face him and lifted her chin with one finger. "Starli, how can you be certain it didn't just fall? Why wouldn't he take something more valuable from you?"

"Believe it or not as you wish. I lived with the Strattons. I know what they're capable of. I know them." Her voice trailed off.

Joel's gaze drifted to the palm of her left hand where the head of the figurine rested, glittering in the street light. Mocking? Threatening this beautiful woman?

Was it time for him to have a talk with this man?

Or was all this a figment of her imagination?

Chapter Twelve

Starli stared at the clothes hanging in her walk-in closet. What to wear? She flipped through each plastic sheeted garment and discarded one after the other. Greens and blues of all shades, hot reds, an occasional light pink, and numerous whites and blacks.

No. That's not right. Not that one either. I have to look perfect tonight.

Why?

Starli slammed her mind-door on the question.

She paused at the sight of the black dress with the bright red flowers emblazoned over it. She'd seen and bought that dress the year before Ryan had died. It'd caught her eye, and in her naiveté, she'd hoped it would rekindle Ryan's love.

But the time had never been right. He'd died, and she'd never worn it.

Slowly, she pulled off the plastic wrap and fingered the soft, flimsy material. If she wore her black velvet bolero jacket with it, no one would guess she'd owned it forever. Starli whirled to hold it in front of her in the mirror.

Perfect.

When the knock on her door came, Starli was ready and went to open the door. Her breath caught, and she gripped the doorknob tighter. Her legs weakened as if they'd suddenly turned into water-soaked spaghetti straws. The man in the tux standing in front of her looked like an important aristocrat.

But then, he was.

"My Lady, your carriage awaits." Joel held her black fake-fur coat as she slipped into it. He inclined his head and held out one arm.

Her cell rang, and she fumbled for it. Janine's voice was so excited she could barely make out what the woman was saying.

"I found out who took your dress. At least, partly."

"You mean my skating outfit?"

"Yes. The lady who does our nightly cleaning? She has a daughter, just out of high school, who helps her most nights to help pay school expenses at the junior college in Charleston."

"Okay. Why on earth would she steal my outfit?"

"She didn't. Seems a school friend approached her and coaxed her to give it to her. Said it was a joke she was playing on a good friend. Said the school friend promised to get it to you." Janine tched, tched.

She could just see the woman shaking her head in annoyance.

"You can bet I told her a thing or two. She was in tears and begged me not to call the cops."

"But who was this friend?"

"She couldn't remember her name for sure. Said she wasn't ever good friends with her in school and was surprised she even approached her. I remember now. She thought her name was Cari or maybe Camy."

Camille? It took a few minutes to convince Janine not to call the cops, that she didn't want to press charges. When she at last shut down her phone, Joel questioned her with a raised brow.

"I'll tell you about it in the car. That way I don't have to repeat it a dozen times." She grinned.

"Right-o."

The stars glittered bright in the dark blue sky. Perfect. Perfect sky. Perfect dress. Perfect man.

Her face warmed. She was glad of the dusky night to hide her confusion. When had she started thinking like this about him? Since that night she and Joel had skated together for Appleton's winter fest.

No, to be truthful, it was way before then. But she didn't want to acknowledge it. Didn't want to think about her growing admiration and attraction to this man who might pack his bags any moment and move out of her life.

It wasn't worth it. Was it? And if so, why?

Why? Because she *felt* like it. Joel was always telling her to live, to try something new and different. Tonight...well, tonight, she was going to forget the past and enjoy the present. Enjoy being with her friends and the evening. Enjoy the perfect gift Caro had given her. Enjoy having an escort like Joel.

Joel opened the passenger door of the limo, and a chorus of hellos greeted her as she ducked her head to take one of the middle seats. She caught a glimpse of Andrew Carrington beside a scowling Caro and wanted to laugh at her friend's blatant attempt to ignore the man who adored her.

"Hi, there, Andy. I'm so glad you came."

Starli spoke a delighted welcome to the quiet man. She didn't care what Caro said. He was a jewel. "Glad to be along, Starli. This is a real treat. I'm always so busy exercising my own talent that I seldom take time to enjoy someone else's."

Starli heard Caroline's grunt of disapproval but ignored it. "You'll enjoy Pierre Markus. He is the best. His concerts are always sold out."

The warm glow inside herself kept her quiet on the ride to the Charleston Performing Arts Center. Her ears were attuned to the low murmur of her friends' voices. She was quick to voice a comment now and then, but her mind flittered from thought to thought.

She sensed Joel's strong presence, the occasional brushes of his arm, and heard the rustle of his pants as he adjusted his long legs. Once he flung his arm on the back of the seat as he turned to talk with Andy, and his breath grazed her cheek as he spoke. She clasped her hands together, reining in the growing warmth inside her.

When Caro lost an argument with her brother, Starli laughed, but all the time her conscious mind reamed in on Joel and his every move.

She asked Toni where baby Danica was.

"Scott's daughter is watching her tonight. Blake's with his buddy Sidney."

"I need to stop at Dolly's Babies and pick up that doll that's all the rave. You don't think she's too young for it, do you?"

"I certainly do." Toni laughed. "And no more stuffed animals for a long time. Her room's overflowing with them. You and Caro are going to spoil her terribly if this keeps up. I'm right, aren't I, Perrin?"

"Whatever you say, Sweetheart."

"Hmmm. That's what aunts are for." Starli sniffed but allowed Toni to see her smile.

"You promised to fill me in on your phone call. You feel like sharing now?"

Joel's quiet comment reminded her of her promise to relate all.

"Not really, but I do want to let everyone know at once so I don't have to repeat myself." She cleared her throat. "I need to tell you all something so you'll be up-to-date on the ongoing drama of my life."

Voices hushed. Faces morphed into worried expressions.

"What's wrong?" Toni leaned forward a bit to lay her hand on Starli's knee.

"The day Joel and I did the skating exhibition for the Winter Fest, Janine called me and said my outfit was missing. She was frantic."

"How could that be? She's always so conscientious." Toni's expression turned into puzzlement.

"That's why you wore your older white outfit, isn't it?" Caro leaned forward. "I wondered why you switched at the last minute, but didn't have time to ask."

"Janine called right before you picked me up tonight. Said she'd sort of found the culprit. The daughter of her cleaning lady had been coerced into allowing an old school friend to pick up my outfit. She told her it was a joke on an old friend."

"That's the craziest thing I've heard this

week," Caro shook her head. "I hope Janine got the name of that jokester."

"Sort of."

"What do you mean?" Toni's puzzled eyes searched her's.

"She said the girl wasn't close to this 'friend,' but that she thought her name was Cari or maybe Camy."

Silence. No one spoke. She could feel Joel's gaze resting on her, studying, probably deciding if she'd put two and two together as he must have already done.

"Do you suppose—I'd hate for what I'm suggesting to be true since I'm the one who pushed you to hire her—but could she have been talking about Camille Findley, Starli? I know no one else in town who goes by the nickname of 'Camy.'"

Drawing, in a long breath, Starli responded. "I have no proof, Caro. None whatsoever."

And this time she met Joel's gaze.

~*~

When the chauffeur stopped in front of the center to allow them to disembark, Joel took her arm and led her aside. "Let's check out the gardens. We've got plenty of time."

Starli nodded. "Ten minutes. We'll freeze if we're out too long. We're not dressed warm enough."

"I'll keep you warm."

It'd been a long time since she'd felt what she was feeling now. Cozy. Warm. Happy.

They walked silently and studied the white lights and exhibits the center had used to decorate for their winter display. Joel patted her hand once but didn't let go. He looked thoughtful, almost...was it gaunt? As if he was worried about something.

"Starli, I wanted to ask you..."

Sudden panic shot through her body. What if he wanted more than...friendship? No, she couldn't. Not yet.

Maybe not ever.

She turned toward the entrance steps, and Joel followed. Perrin met them at the door.

"Five minutes till Pierre's first piece."

Saved. The relief washing over her forced her to admit to being a coward. She didn't want him to persist in forcing an unwanted conversation at her about something she wasn't willing to talk about yet. And maybe never.

Starli hurried to check her coat, then, knowing Joel wouldn't voice any intimate topic in front of Toni's husband, relaxed and allowed the two men to lead her to their reserved seats.

Caroline had chosen well. They were some of the best in the center section. She sat down between Andy and Joel.

When the famous pianist at last strode onto the stage, Starli leaned forward, her gaze riveted on the small man who produced such powerful music. She allowed the music to wash over her and absorb every nuance of her being.

What seemed as minutes later, the little man stood to his feet and bowed elegantly to the enthusiastic crowd, Starli reached around Joel and hugged her friend. "Thank you so much, Caro. It's been wonderful. I loved every minute."

"A little high-toned, but I liked it."

As Starli and her friends made their way slowly up the aisle to the foyer and into the vestibule, Joel's cell phone beeped. He checked the number, stepping away from the others.

Starli buttoned her coat, her gaze fastened on him.

When at last he faced them again, he said nothing.

"What's wrong?"

His gaze met hers. "It was Camille. Her mother is bad, and she asked me to come be with her."

"Why you?" Caro's forehead wrinkled. "What can you do? What about Pastor Haag or Pastor Scott? Text her back and tell her to call one of them; that you're out of town and can't get there. That you'll see her early in the morning."

"She knows I'm not home, but I was there when she told her mother she was terminal and promised I'd be there when she was passing if I could." Joel paced, his fingers clicking as he thought. "I don't want to let her down, but I don't want to cut our evening short."

Then don't. Starli pressed a hand to her mouth. Had she spoken aloud? How could she be so callous? Joel didn't know Camille like she did.

Or did he? The little demon of suspicion reared its ugly head.

"I don't mean to speak out of turn," Perrin offered, his blue-green eyes showing the concern he was feeling, "but *how* did she know you weren't home? And if she did know, why would she call *you* when you had special plans this evening? It's not as if she doesn't have other friends in town to call on."

Joel paused his pacing, his brows lifted. "*I* didn't tell her."

"Then?" Toni cocked her head at him.

"I hate to break it to you, but Camille is a bit of an exhibitionist with her emotions." Caro looked every bit as determined as her words sounded. "Almost everyone in our town has tried to help that family. *In spite* of her family, Camille's done well for herself, but that doesn't take away the fact that she thinks the world owes her."

"Are you serious?"

"She was playing you."

"Easy, Caro." Toby pulled his sister close. "We don't spread rumors, remember?"

She knew as well as everyone here—except perhaps for Joel—of Caro's too caring heart. She might be one of the first to know what happened in Appleton, but no one could ever accuse her of being a gossip.

"Sorry, didn't mean to come across as crass. It's just that—"

"Your friends know what you meant. That's why we love you." Starli gave her a hug.

"I don't understand where you're coming from, but let me call her back and make sure she's found someone to be with her for the evening."

Heads nodded, and Joel walked a few steps away. He was back within a couple minutes. Joel answered their question. "She's called Pastor Scott. And Justin's there."

"I heard she'd beckoned, and he came running."

"Where do you get all your information,

Caro?" Toni's perplexity at Caro's comment echoed Starli's own question. If you needed answers, Caro was usually the one to go to.

"It's not like I haven't tried..."

No one said a word, but Starli knew what Caro had stopped herself from saying. She'd been the one on the forefront for years, encouraging Camille, leading the drives for food for the family, pushing Starli to hire her. Caro ought to know. She'd practically lived there for months at a time.

"I'm glad we don't have to cut Starli's evening short." The quiet comment from Caro was accompanied with a shrug.

"Why would she take that cad Justin back after he walked out on her?"

"There's more to it than that, Joel." Toni slid her hand onto her husband's arm. "He didn't walk out on her. It was the other way around."

Joel was shaking his head. "She seemed crushed when I talked with her. I can't believe she lied about it."

"It's not our business unless, of course, it hurts our friends. Don't worry about Camille. She's a strong person. She'll make up her own mind and probably have Justin tying the knot before spring."

Coming from Toni that was saying a lot.

The chef shrugged. "Well, I'm sure you all know more about her than I do."

Was Joel, like Caro, a champion of the underdog, or was he attracted to the blond kitchen help?

Starli straightened. She'd been patient with Camille over and over again, because despite excuses for late arrivals to work, her family problems and her own flirtatious actions, she wanted to be fair to the girl. But Camille would have to shape up if she thought there was any chance of her becoming a manager at Starli's restaurant.

But she wouldn't be any man's second fiddle. Never again. She'd been foolish to allow herself to dream—albeit, privately—about Joel. How could she? *God, where are you when I need some wisdom?*

When they were ushered into the ritzy Seven Brothers Restaurant, Joel whispered in her ear. "Hold up. Give me five minutes. I want to explain something to you."

Starli stared at him. Really? After his subtle wish to run to Camille? She pulled her arm away. A tiny despicable desire to hurt him swelled inside. "No, thanks. I want to talk with my *friends.*"

She'd accented "friends" on purpose. She knew she had, but hadn't been able to stop herself. It was a horrible action, and despising herself for it, she spun on her heel, and followed the rest, tears stinging her eyes. Why did she have to allow him to ruin her evening? He meant nothing to her.

Another lie.

Joel ambled behind her—she could hear the lazy tap of his dress shoes—and by the time she'd squeezed in between Toni and Caro, Joel strolled up, his hands stuck deep within his pockets.

Toni scooted over so Joel could sit beside Starli.

She started to protest then stopped. No need to spoil everyone else's fun just because she was angry with Joel.

Forcing herself to laugh at their jokes and laughter was hard. She enjoyed watching Caro's confusion when Andy Carrington insisted on paying for her meal in spite of her protest. Hearing Toni spin the latest accomplishment of her daughter created a longing deep inside her. But Ryan had insisted it was *her* fault they had no children.

She ignored Joel and refused to answer when he whispered to her. It was only when Caro's brother, Toby, spoke to Joel that her attention focused on him.

"You okay? You look pretty pale."

He hadn't eaten anything. A glass of cranberry juice sat in front of him, but only a little was gone. Was he taking her anger that seriously? Surely not. Not him.

"Are you okay?" Starli started to ask, the concern overriding the hurt inside her, but she had no time to think any more about Joel. A face caught her attention. Roland Stratton sat three tables over, gaze fastened on her like glue, his mouth set in a grim grimace. Now and then he lifted a glass and gulped his drink. He was dressed to the nines, so he'd been somewhere classy. At the concert center? Had he sat close beyond her watching and laughing at the emotions rolling across her features?

Her heart fluttered, and as if a giant hand clutched her throat choking off the air, her head spun. She licked dry lips. When she set her spoon on the dessert plate, her fingers shook until the utensil clattered.

How had he known she'd be here?

~*~

The pain had intensified, although it still wasn't as bad as he'd had at times. Kidney stones were nothing to sneeze at, which he knew to his own sorrow. But between that and the phone call from Camille, he'd managed to make a mess of things between himself and Starli. She didn't know about the kidney stone pain, but she knew he'd been trying to help the girl.

He'd wanted to tell Starli about his kidney stone attacks, but naturally she'd only thought of one thing. Camille and him.

In spite of Starli's judgment of him and her coldness, he was rather pleased. If she was jealous of Camille, that proved something, didn't it? Surely she thought more of him than just an employee.

His contemplation was broken when he caught sight of her shaking hand trying to set down her spoon. He read the fear on her face. Joel followed her stare and caught sight of a big man glaring at their table. Roland Stratton sitting with a table of three others. Had they been at the concert too?

"So the Rolly bloke's here." Joel kept his voice low.

"I'm afraid so."

The man had cleaned up nice, his tuxedo fit him well, the dark stubbled cheeks that looked as if he never shaved—fashionably so, but the smirk on his lips and the heavy lidded eyes that harbored threats detracted from his looks. Joel wanted to jump in front of Starli and shield her from his view. For two bits he'd...

Roland Stratton stood when the others at his table rose. His chair almost overturned, but one heavy hand reached out, caught it and shoved it gently against the table. His deliberate, but quiet motions caused Joel to narrow his eyes. What was he up to?

The man strutted closer, just a step behind the others. Joel heard the silence as the others caught a glimpse of Roland walking closer to their table. Roland's gaze never left Starli's white face.

Joel stood as he approached, prepared to send him on his way, but the man only paused a second. His lips widened in a knowing leer. He let his gaze roam over all their faces, then returned to Starli's. With a mock salute, he moved away, and Joel heard the collective sigh from the group.

"I think you should get a restraining order to keep him away from you." Caro's babbling overpowered the rest's murmuring.

Would it work? Could a restraining order keep Roland away from her? Could she even get one?

"I'm positive he has lost his senses. I think I will let him know his scheme won't work." Toni crossed her arms and glared at Roland's retreating back.

Perrin wrapped his arm around his wife. Patted her shoulder. "Easy, Sweetheart. He knows what he's doing. Makes him feel in control."

That was certainly true enough.

The man swaggered across the room. When he disappeared through the doorway, Joel hesitated, then looked at the other men. "I'm going to see what, if anything, he's up to."

"I'll go with you." Toby stood.

"Please be careful. Roland is ruthless."

Fear for her chef had replaced Starli's earlier annoyance. The concern in her eyes was worth any potential danger from the man. He covered her hand with his own. "I'll be fine."

As the two men headed into the foyer, Roland's heavy frame was exiting the building. Joel moved toward him, but Roland turned and glared at him.

Joel stopped. Follow him, or not? He could see nothing amiss, but to be sure...Joel asked the coat room attendant for Starli's coat. When the man handed him her coat, he thrust his hand into a pocket, and pulled out a small dollar-store box of sparklers. Wrapped around it was strip of white paper.

He looked at Toby. "Are you thinking what I'm thinking?"

"I don't think it's a good idea for Starli to see anything from that man. It can't be good."

But had Roland placed this inside her pocket? Unlike the incident at the town council dinner at Apple Blossoms, where he was almost certain Roland had been the culprit pinning Starli inside the smoky coatroom, he'd not been anywhere near this one. He hadn't had the time for any mischief.

"You think she'd be too upset if we take a look at the paper—just in case?"

"We're doing it for her." Toby gave him a long look, and Joel could see where Caroline got her act-first-consider-the-consequences-later personality.

"Right-o." Joel unfolded the plain piece of paper, and they both read it. *See you at the fireworks.*

Joel refolded and tucked it in his inside jacket pocket. "I'll get rid of it later. It's already been enough of a shock just seeing him."

"What are you guys doing?"

Starli stood near the door, her green eyes wide and glinting. Were they tears?

He felt rather than saw Toby shift his weight. No need to let her ask any more questions. "Here's your coat."

He held it out, but her brows lifted.

"Why do you have only *my* coat?"

Joel shrugged and shook his head. "Checking to make sure Rolly hadn't tampered with it."

She searched their faces. "I don't believe you. Where's Roland?"

Chapter Thirteen

Joel eyed the crowded restaurant at the doorway to the kitchen. Pride surged through him. Even at $250 a plate—a dear price for a small town—they'd had to turn people away who wanted to attend the benefit dinner for Camille Findley and her mother. He suspected they'd demanded tickets as much to hear their hometown success—Starli Cameron—as anything else.

Apple Blossoms had definitely put small-time Appleton, West Virginia on the map. And her talent as a pianist didn't hurt the popularity of the place either.

Uncle Laurence stepped up beside him, his tanned face wreathed in smiles. "Are you feeling better?"

He'd fought two days with the pain before passing the stone. Agony. Fortunately, Louis had stepped in and taken most of the load from him. Grudgingly, for sure. The man's mutters were enough to almost make him decide to suffer through the pain and do the work himself.

"Back on top."

"A great success tonight, nephew. You did well."

"Couldn't have done it without Starli's consent." He spotted Perrin, Toby, and Andy sitting at one of the larger tables. Camille Findley sat at a table of honor near the front, a good-looking young man beside her, gazing at her as if he couldn't believe his luck. She looked flushed with excitement. Her friends, just a tad bit too loud, but young and excusable, laughed beside her.

"It's almost time."

Uncle Laurence nodded. "I'll let her know."

He placed a hand on his uncle's arm. "Allow me, please."

When Manny nodded his consent, Joel walked down the hall, tapped on the office door, and Toni beckoned him to enter. He stepped inside and shut the door behind him, eyeing her two best friends who'd so warmly welcomed him into their circle.

"Do you mind if I have a few minutes alone with Starli?"

"Of course not." They chorused together. Giving Starli a hug, Toni said, "You'll be fine. It's not like you're a novice at this."

With a teasing nod at him, they left.

"Uncle Laurence says it's time, and I've got to get back to the kitchen in a few minutes. But I wanted to thank you for doing this. Camille seems overwhelmed with gratefulness. She cried when I told her what you agreed to do."

Starli shrugged, but Joel saw her swallow. Passing it off, she was.

"Whether Camille appreciates your time and giving, I want you to know, it means a lot to me that you are helping."

"I'm not altogether sure of the worth of it, but I promised you I'd play, and I do what I say."

Red rosebuds amid the cloudy white baby's breath lay on top of her desk as if discarded.

"Aren't you wearing the flowers?"

"Why do you insist on buying me flowers?"

"Don't you know why?" He strode to the door and flung it open. He allowed his eyes to reflect a hint of the emotion he felt. "Cheers, My Dear."

~*~

Starli stood in the dining area doorway a second and took in the crowded room. She couldn't believe it when Joel had told her with smug satisfaction in his voice that they'd sold out completely and at an outrageous price for such a small town. He'd insisted on the high price even though she'd warned him he'd be disappointed at the turnout because of it. Why would anyone pay out that kind of money to hear her play? Especially for two hours.

But it wasn't for her. The benefit was for Camille, and she was determined to give them their money's worth. But not only for Camille. Her behavior at Pierre Markus's event over Joel's high-handedness was inexcusable.

Starli plastered a pleasant expression on her face and began the walk to her piano. She nodded and smiled at those seated at individual tables, but didn't speak. Only when she passed Camille's table did she pause.

"Are you having a good time, Camille?"

"Oh, yes." The girl leaned into Justin's embrace and laughed—or was it a smirk? She lowered her voice. "There's only one thing that would make me happier."

Starli leaned down to catch her next words.

"If you'd trust me enough to make me a manager. I couldn't ever be as good as you, but I am a hard worker. You have to admit that. I want that job badly."

Amidst Justin's half-hearted protest at the girl's obvious badgering, Starli straightened, feeling as if she'd been slugged in the stomach. Really? Now, of all times? She'd never had an employee badger her like Camille did. She acted like a kid who'd never grown up, a relative who felt they deserved the best.

The problem was, Camille really did work hard.

Her problem was, she hated being badgered. She wasn't sure Camille was ready for such a responsible position, and the more she pushed, the more Starli was apt to pull back. It wasn't professional if nothing else. Worse, she had a sneaking feeling Camille could possibly be behind the random acts of mischief.

Smiling, she moved away. All of a sudden she knew she'd be glad when the evening was over.

Settling on the bench, she spread the white skirt of her dress, calming herself, forcing thoughts of the childish girl out of her mind. As she pressed the keys to begin Beethoven's Moonlight Sonata, she forgot everyone. Only the music mattered.

When the first half was over, she rose, pleasure washing through her as the clapping began. They'd enjoyed the music, and that was enough for her. Her fingertips rested on the glossy surface of the piano, even as her mind replayed the melodies she'd finished.

Once the applause abated, she walked, hoping to take the minutes to sip her favorite drink and spend them in quiet. But the people at each table reached for her. Their words and praise demanded a response. She forgot her plans to escape to her office and glided about the room. Her heart warmed at their lavish and sincere enjoyment.

Another ten feet, and she'd reached the hallway door. Joel appeared beside her. "I've been waiting for you. You need to eat a little."

"No, not now. Later. If you will, send Juanita with a glass of juice. I'll take a breather for ten minutes. Don't let anyone disturb me." Starli turned away and hurried down the hallway to her office and straight to her comfy chair, not bothering to turn on the light.

She'd no more than settled in, when the sight of a lounging dark silhouette in the corner caught her peripheral vision. Heart pounding, she froze, then her fingers fumbled for the switch on her desk lamp.

A caustic lazy voice reproached her. "Howdy, Starle-e-e. What took you so long?"

"How did you get in here?"

"Now is that anyway to talk to your dead husband's brother?" Roland's toothy grin was particularly disgusting when he clicked his tongue. "Shame on you."

"What do you want, Roland? I've already told you I spent all of the insurance money." Was that really pleading from her voice? Why couldn't she get over this family?

"Yeah, that's what you said. But what about all the money you're raking in from this joint?"

"I have expenses. You know that." Where was everyone? Why hadn't Juanita come with her juice?

Crossing the room, Roland flattened his big hands on her desktop and leaned toward her.

"Listen to me. You got away with killing Ryan—"

"I didn't—"

His response was rapid and unexpected. His hand rose, slapped the side of her head, snapping it back with the vicious swat. Ignoring her interruption, Roland plowed right over her words. "—and then wasted his money on this place. Never thought to share, did you? Starli's always been number one in your book, hasn't she?"

Her head spun from the slap. For a second, Starli was sure she would pass out. Drawing in a deep breath, she pulled from deep inside her the strength she'd relied on for so long. She would not pass out in front of Roland Stratton. She would not.

"I'm leaving." Starli drew back and rose.

"Not until I'm good and ready for you to leave." Roland lunged and gripped her slight wrist, his beefy fingers digging into her skin.

"Don't, you're hurting me. Stop." Not her hands. Not the part of her that provided healing and peace through her music.

The pressure didn't let up, then with deliberate cruelty, he stroked her little finger. Her crooked finger. The finger Ryan had broken in a fit of rage.

Starli whimpered, fear eating at her insides.

Like a mesmerizing snake, Roland glared at her.

"Roland, please. I have to finish this benefit tonight."

"You're begging? How does it feel to be on the receiving end of pain?"

When hadn't she been with the Strattons?

She gasped as Roland bent her finger another fraction.

The sound of hurrying footsteps penetrated her pain and fright. Roland tilted his head and scowled. Then he flung her hand away and hissed. "Don't you forget it. That's only a touch of what I've got planned for you."

Starli staggered back and caught herself on the back of her chair.

The door flew open, and Juanita stood there. As Roland shoved past her, he knocked the glass from her hand.

His rapid footsteps echoed in her ears. The sound of the heavy back door as it was slammed shut reverberated down the hall.

"I thought I heard a man's voice." Joel stuck his head in. "What's wrong?"

Manny stepped in the room. "Are you all right, Starli?"

Their voices blended into background noise. Juanita babbled, but Starli paid no attention. All she could hear was Roland's parting shot, "What I've got planned for you."

She averted her face and shivered as Juanita clucked and fussed. Manny sent for another glass of juice and instructed one of the janitors to clean up the broken glass.

Joel knelt in front of her and picked up her hand. He held it so long that Starli was drawn from the fog of fear that surrounded her. What was he doing?

His gaze was on her wrist. He'd turned her hand over, and there...was the beginning of a large purple bruise. He lifted his gaze to hers, and she saw the shadow pass across his features. The question. The hurt. The anger.

And then his hand was cupping her face, gently turning it. "Who did this to you, Starli? Was it...?"

His voice was so low that she had to lean forward to catch the words. She swallowed before she could choke out the one word. "Roland."

Joel turned to Louis standing at the door, his voice a growl. "How did that cad get in here?"

"Must I be a guard too? With all I have to do?" He scowled and backed from the room.

"I don't want this to ever happen again. Uncle Laurence, hire a guard."

"No."

Starli flinched as faces turned toward her. "I can't afford it right now. Anyhow, he didn't hurt me."

Much.

"What do you think this is?" Joel growled, his angry glance raking her face and wrist. "Have you gotten that restraining order yet?"

"I'm all right. I bruise easy." She moved to the door.

"Where are you going?" His voice was almost savage.

She steeled herself, willed her voice to steadiness, although her insides were melting. "I'm going to the restroom to repair the damages, and then I'll finish entertaining our guests."

Her neck tingled. Starli knew their gazes followed her as she walked down the hall, but she didn't look back. She wanted to get this over as quickly as she could. She just hoped her numb hand could play.

~*~

Starli resumed her piano seat forcing herself to present a calm and at ease persona, but inside her body emotions were raging. Angry at herself for not standing up to the present Stratton bully, shamefully afraid of Roland's threats, and fearful he was Ryan's nemesis coming back to finish her off, Starli tossed aside her plan to play something soothing and soft. Instead, she poured herself into Chopin Ballade No. 2, knowing the softer beginning would give her fingers time to regain their feeling.

Though they fumbled slightly at first, by the time she'd finished the piece, her body had energized. The passionate, intense music pulled her away from what had happened and flowed from her, zapped away the fear and anger and enabled her to courageously pause only seconds before beginning the second of Chopin's Ballades. She wrapped the triumphal music around her snugly and reveled in the strength and power of the songs.

Giving herself only seconds to recover from the intensity, she finished with Mozart's "Piano Sonata No. 11" and Brahms' "Piano concerto No. 1 in D minor" and sat with bowed head. Her mind whirled with the music, and the musical euphoria drifted through and around her...until a roar filled her ears. She lifted her head.

The standing people were radiant. It took a moment to realize that the applause—the roar—was for her. They thought, no, they judged her as an overwhelming success. She felt a flush creep up her cheeks.

She acknowledged their approval with a slight bow, her chest heaving. Her gaze looked for and found Joel and Manny.

Manny nodded to her, his pride for her shining in his eyes.

Joel lifted one hand and kissed his fingertips, tossing the victory kiss her way. She wanted to reach up and catch it in a childish gesture.

~*~

Joel's soft whistle of a measure of "Rhapsody in Blue" reached her ears as she closed and locked the restaurant door. When she turned around, he leaned against the building, his legs crossed, his pursed lips breathing out puffy white clouds in the crisp air.

Her heart thumped at the sight of Joel's casualness, but she also breathed out a sigh or relief. Roland wouldn't wait around with Joel here.

Yet she'd needed to be alone and half wished he'd not waited. Starli glanced at her car.

"What?" Oh, dear. She did sound disagreeable, but it'd been a long evening.

"Come along. I'm stopping by Uncle Laurence's."

"No."

"Oui. You've gone and hurt my feelings. Must you always be so abrupt with me? I assure you I'm perfectly harmless."

"Must I always remind you that I'm not interested in anything to do with you except in a business way?" Starli returned his question with one of her own, but she couldn't keep a smile from her voice. He was so ridiculously attractive.

"I told Uncle Laurence I might bring a woman friend. Why not you?"

"Go ask someone else." Camille's name was on the tip of her tongue, but she held it back. Looked like the girl was back with Justin.

Joel stepped closer and stretched out an arm. Two fingers touched and smoothed her cheek. "I prefer you."

Her breath caught as Starli gazed into his intense eyes. He was too...close, too...too dangerous. She took a half-step back. "You are the most aggravating person I've ever seen."

"Everyone else just gives in to Your Majesty's desires. I stand up to you."

The skin at the corners of his teasing blue eyes wrinkled. Why couldn't she breathe evenly when she needed to? "Why me?"

"I want to see you home."

"I've got my car. I'll be fine once I'm in it." Why was she being so obstinate?

"I don't trust Rolly Stratton."

His shortened version of her brother-in-law's name was hilarious, but the shiver that ran up her spine wasn't. Roland's threats weren't idle ones.

"Your Majesty, if you won't go with me to Manny's, how about letting me see you home?"

Manny lived only minutes from Apple Blossoms. Why not go? The night air would clear her head, and truth to be told, she wasn't ready to say goodnight to this handsome man.

Reaching for her hand, he drew her closer. "It's nippy tonight. You do know I was over the moon at your performance?"

"Over the moon? I haven't heard that one."

"Pleased. After expenses, we'll be able to give Camille around $15,000."

"I still can't believe we sold out." Starli stared up at the silvery moon.

"Are you tired?"

"Some. This nippy air's reviving me."

He rubbed her wrist. "How's the bruise?"

"I'll be okay." The round purplish-blue spot on her wrist belied her words. "I've had..."

He growled and his sharp glance told her he knew what she'd left unfinished.

"You should pursue more training if you really are interested in being a professional pianist. As our young people say at home, you were wicked tonight." Joel led her across a street.

"I think you meant that as a compliment, didn't you? I don't have time and besides, I'm too old now to do serious studying."

"Tosh." Joel knocked lightly on the door and opened it a crack. "Uncle Lawrence?"

"I knew you would be peckish." Manny grinned at them as he swung open the door. "Neither one of you had a bite all evening."

"I'm as hungry as a bear."

"Then you'll enjoy my cucumber sandwiches, won't you" Manny placed the tray on his coffee table and arranged their drinks as if it was the event of the year.

"What a whopping success tonight was. Wasn't Starli cracking tonight?" Joel picked up one of the sandwiches and examined it. He raised an eyebrow at his uncle.

Manny grinned. "It has your special sauce on it."

"Nice one." Joel popped it into his mouth,

chewed.

"Thought you might enjoy seeing some photos of Joel as a youngster."

"She doesn't want to see those ridiculous pictures of me."

His pettish tone whetted her appetite to see the pictures. Starli laughed when Joel shifted in his seat. Let him be the uncomfortable one for a change.

"Of course, I do." What fun to tease him.

"If you bring those things in here, I'm nipping out of here."

His threat didn't faze Manny. The maître de waved a hand. "Go pester Vera, then. Starli and I'll reminisce over my pictures."

"I don't want to talk to your housekeeper."

Joel's woe-be-gone expression sent her into a gale of laughter. She could hear the smugness in her voice and wouldn't have changed it for anything. "I'm looking forward to it, Manny."

Joel rose, scowling, but he touched her shoulder as he left the room. Starli watched him go and touched the spot that felt as if fire had seared her skin.

She *was* playing with fire, and if she didn't want to get burned, she'd better be careful around good-looking knights.

Chapter Fourteen

The windows in each storefront were strung with lights, Valentine Day enticements, toys and clothing. Sleds and shovels stood in the hardware window for those who still might do some late winter shopping.

Starli raised her face to the sunshine that brightened the town. The air nipped at her nose and bit into her cheeks. She loved it. The weatherman predicted snow this weekend. She had half a notion to take a day and head for Beckley to get in a couple of skiing lessons.

But. The big but. The middle of February was only days away. She still had the marketing research to finish and hadn't made up her mind where to begin another Apple Blossoms. Beckley or Charleston?

January was the month she shopped for all the birthdays coming up in the current year. Toni and Caro thought she was crazy, but she loved doing it then. She got them all out of the way and could anticipate the special gifts she'd purchased for the special people in her life. And this year, baby Danica was on the list. Yeah!

Only this year, she hadn't finished in January. She'd promised herself to get this shopping done today. And she would.

Two hours later, she passed The Coffee House and hesitated. She'd love to have an espresso. She hated to see the woman, but why let her get to her? Surely five minutes wouldn't kill her.

Starli shoved at the door. Surprised that Rita wasn't there, she placed her order and left, her cup in a firm grip. Relief flooded her she wouldn't have to deal with facing Rita again. Yet deep inside an uneasiness refused to leave her at peace.

She had only one more gift to buy. Caro's. After those wonderful tickets to hear Pierre Markus Caro had given her for her upcoming birthday, she wanted something very special for her friend.

She was fingering the silk scarves in Appleton's only finer store, Sharon's Favorites, when she heard the whispering and giggling from behind her. She turned.

Rita Mae held one hand to her mouth to smother the giggles erupting from her ruby lips. She clutched at the rack of coats as if she was overcome with mirth. Worse, Joel lounged beside her. Starli frowned and any resolves she'd harbored at forgiveness hoisted sail and floated away.

"What are you two doing?" Starli hoped she didn't sound as crabby as she felt.

"Following you." Rita gushed and giggled again. She cast a coy look at Joel.

"Why would you two follow me?" Were they laughing at her? Did she have mud splashed on her boots? She refused to look down and check.

"You didn't suspect a thing." Rita Mae laughed again.

Starli pressed her lips together, her teeth nipping at her tongue. How irritating Rita Mae was.

"And why would I suspect you're following

me? I've been busy, minding my own business. Which is what you should have been doing."

"Oh, it's been fun finding out what you've been buying for everyone. Let's see..." Rita ticked the items off on her fingers "...that expensive satchel for Toni. Hand knit sweaters for Toby and Perrin. The latest electronic game for Blake, and a dozen toys for Toni's kid."

Dear Lord, am I ever going to be able to get over this woman? She sent the wordless prayer swirling toward heaven even as she studied Rita Mae. What pleasure did she derive out of spoiling everyone's peace?

"So? You know what I've bought." Starli shrugged and turned away. "Are you happy now?"

"Starli..." Joel began.

"Miss Starli, to you." She snapped over her shoulder as she headed toward the handbags.

Joel followed her. He must have asked Rita to give him a few minutes alone with her, because the other woman moseyed toward the jewelry counter.

"It's not exactly as Rita Mae portrayed it."

"Oh, really? Who cares?" Starli picked up a handbag then tossed it down.

"Will you listen? I'm trying to tell you what happened."

Enough was enough. Starli whipped around. "No, I won't listen. I don't care. Get that? Please, go back to your girlfriend."

"She's not my girlfriend."

She refused to answer that objection, although her heart gave a traitorous leap. She cast him a scathing look for good measure. *Sure.*

"*She* followed me and insisted on helping me pick out a couple gifts." He looked like a little boy pleading for his way. "I assure you I did not want her with me. I had an important gift to buy, and I sure didn't need her help."

Drops of moisture beaded his forehead. Good. He was sweating. The perfect man was sweating. Starli suddenly wanted to laugh. How ridiculous this whole scene was. She had a sudden vision of herself as the Biblical brawling woman on the rooftop arguing with her neighbor.

"Fine. She was helping you whether you wanted her to or not. I hope you had fun."

He blocked her way. "I had fun picking yours."

She went quiet. "Mine? Why would you buy me a gift?"

"Right in here." Joel patted the bag he lifted. "I heard you're a Valentine baby."

"I am." She squinted at the bag. "Did she pick it out?"

"Nope, the decision was mine. Actually, she wasn't much help with anything."

"Really?"

"I'd rather had you."

Then why didn't you ask me? The words popped into her mind so quickly she was afraid she'd spoken them aloud. "I didn't buy you anything." Yet.

"But you don't know when my birthday is, do you?" Joel laughed. "You've still got time. Two whole days."

"You've a February birthday too? I can't accept a gift from you. You're my employee."

"And you're my employer *and* my friend."

Joel countered.

She was silent, studying him. True, he was the most aggravating man she'd ever met, but an adorable aggravation.

"Let's take a ride this afternoon and see where we end up. There's a drama department in Charleston that's putting on a winter play. Suppose to be funny, but meaningful. Juanita said the college kids do a great job. We could see it."

Starli opened her mouth to refuse. She had no business socializing with him if she wasn't interested in a relationship with him.

"Sounds good."

Really? How fickle was that when she had no clue how she really felt about the man?

~*~

Starli stared at Joel's strong hands as he guided his car. He did it with expertise, but then she suspected whatever he did, he gave it all he had.

Her gaze took in his chiseled cheeks, his long nose and rather heavy brows.

A tingle began in the pit of her stomach. She laid an arm across it and frowned. Was she attracted to him? Seriously?

No.

Yes.

Maybe. Starli shook her head. What kind of judge of men was she? Her only choice of a husband had been a total flop. She flipped down the visor.

Who finds a good woman, finds a good thing. The proverb popped into her mind. What about the woman who found a good man? Was Joel a good man?

Had God sent a good man into her life?

She'd vowed never to have a relationship with a man again. But Joel...

"What's wrong with you? Relax. No frowning today. We're going to have fun."

Why not? Why not enjoy herself? Again. With him.

"Where are we going?"

"I looked over the map and picked out a few back roads that sound interesting. There's a couple of quaint shops. Thought we'd check them out. Maybe we could find a few things to brighten up that stark house of yours."

"Stark? I like it simple."

"It's not simple. It's stark. We'll look at some old pieces that can liven that place." Joel stretched out a hand toward her and when she didn't respond, moved it up and down in emphatic waves.

Starli stared at his hand. The urge to place her hand in his, to trust him, to forget her past swept over her. Her insides trembled, her bones warmed as soft as mush.

He who has begun a good work in you will perform it.

Pastor Haag had drilled that into her when he'd counseled her. God, he'd said, wouldn't leave her distressed. He would make her strong again.

As if in a dream, Starli stretched out her own hand and touched Joel's with her fingertips. His fingers closed around hers, pulled it snuggly into the palm of his hand, no timidity in his firm, but gentle grip. He exuded strength and confidence.

She tugged once, but he didn't let go. She

forced herself to take several deep breaths and relaxed. The soft sound of classical music and the peace of the afternoon seeped into her soul.

"Tell me about yourself."

Her mind blanked out. What did he want to know? About her marriage? About the abuse?

"What about?" Her question was a croak, and she cleared her voice.

"Anything will do, but if you want specific, tell me about when you first learned to drive. That should be interesting."

Starli told him about her first car that had been the pride of her life. "Daddy believed in making your own way—to a certain degree, so I wasn't given a brand new car. But I did get to pick out what I wanted from the local used car lot." Starli chuckled. "Of course, I wanted the fanciest, coolest car I could find, against Daddy's advice. It turned out to be a nightmare. The first time I drove it to school, it stopped in the middle of the street—in front of all my high school friends—and refused to budge. I was humiliated. Refused to drive it again."

Joel laughed.

Their first stop at one of the antique shops had yielded nothing of interest. Once Starli stopped before a darling end table and lifted an eyebrow at Joel. He scowled and shook his head. "They're asking too much," he whispered.

The second shop overflowed with treasures. Joel enthusiastically went from object to object.

"We can't buy everything. There's no room in that minuscule car of yours." Starli objected as

Joel placed an antique cream pitcher on the delighted owner's countertop.

In the end they chose a painting—of questionable value, but one that Joel argued had presence and would give any of her visitors pause. Since she'd already decided she liked it, she gave in. She watched him drag a heavy brocaded chair to the front of the store.

"That will really go with my stuff." She teased.

He crossed his arms, one hand stroking his chin, and peered at the dusty relic. "I'd say a king sat in this chair."

"Right." Starli laughed. "In the U.S., no doubt. And which king would that have been?"

"George Washington?" His lips tilted in a crooked smile. His British accent thickened. Even the shop owner grinned at his foolishness.

"Sold." Starli pounded the counter top with one fist.

When they loaded their purchases, but found they had no room to put the chair, Joel coaxed a promise from the owner to hold it for him till he could return to get it.

Starli fastened her seat belt as they took off and adjusted herself to escape the claw foot of an end table digging into her neck. "I feel like a real hillbilly with this car stuffed to the gills.

"This makes us hillbillies?" Joel looked in the mirror at the full back seat.

"Haven't you ever seen pictures of mountain people in cars and trucks overloaded with their belongings? Where are we eating?"

"Are you hungry?" He grinned at her quick change of topic. "We've got just enough time for a relaxing meal, and I know the place. Rita Mae told me all about it and how to get to it. Look in the dash for the map she drew."

Starli did as he bid, but her heart sank. The beauty of the day had dimmed. Why did he mention that woman? "Rita Mae gave you directions for you to take *me* there?"

He cocked his head at her and smirked. "Well, I don't think it was in her plans for me to bring *you* exactly."

She laughed and read the directions as he drove. Thirty minutes later, he pulled up in front of The Fisherman's Wharf hanging out over the bank of the Kanawha River.

"How did you know I love fish?" Starli enthused.

Joel unfastened his seat belt, climbed out, then went around to open Starli's door. He reached for her hand and intertwined his fingers with hers as they walked the plank toward the weathered gray building. "I know only a little about you."

"Then that should be enough." She eyed the long line of noisy people.

"No, I want to know everything about you." He squeezed her hand lightly. "Every single detail. What you like and what you hate. Your favorite food, your thoughts, all the songs you love. I want to know about the dreams you dream and the hopes you have. I want to know what makes you cry and how to make you laugh."

She was caught in a web of...what? Love? The tenderness in his voice, the soft caressing thumb that slid across her palm—all of him lured and drew her fast into the web he was spinning.

And she didn't want to struggle out of it.

"I knew you'd hate to wait to be seated, so called ahead and booked a table. We've got exactly two hours to eat before we head to the church."

His calm, matter-of-fact voice released her from the daze. She blinked, unsure whether she was glad or sad. "They don't book tables."

"Are you sure?" He chuckled, and she wondered how much he'd offered to get a reserved table.

Once seated at their corner table, Starli opened her menu. "Oysters. Yes. I love them."

"Clam soup. Let's try that."

"Shrimp."

"Squid."

Starli looked up. "They don't have squid."

"Joshing you."

In the end, they ordered a sampler plate. When the waiter placed their orders on the table, Joel reached for her hand again, and his voice was low and serious as he bowed his head and asked the blessing.

Starli listened to the resonance of his reverent voice, the rich low tones, and swallowed. Dear Lord, she loved his voice. This wasn't good. She had better get a barrier erected pretty fast.

~*~

Joel didn't want to let go of her hand. He'd like to pull her close and snuggle her within his arms. He didn't have the right. Not yet, but soon.

"You're greedy." He teased as she swallowed a luscious looking oyster.

"I know." Starli grinned and plopped another one into her mouth.

"Hey. I want one."

"Then you'd better hurry up." Starli aimed her fork at a particularly juicy one. "Or I will eat them all."

Too late. He stabbed at the same one and lifted it to his lips.

"Hey." Her gaze was on him as he pretended to study each of the oysters left.

"I'll take that one too."

"That's the biggest."

"Nope. You already ate the biggest." Joel smacked his lips.

When they arrived at the church forty-five minutes later, it was packed. An usher found seats in the second row. Joel felt like an excited teenager on his first date with the woman of his dreams.

He loved how she blossomed when she was with him. The tightness in her beautiful face eased, her laughter came easily.

Tears clung to her lashes when the lead actor reached the spot of forgiveness in the play. Joel swallowed the lump that rose in his throat and silently prayed that Starli would reach out for the same kind of help.

He took her elbow as they left, and they both tossed twenties into the donation basket. The sky had clouded. Soft flurries floated to the ground, icing their bit of West Virginia.

Joel edged onto the main road.

Starli reached for the armrest as the car's wheels spun on the road. "Slippery?"

"Right. I'm going to take it slow."

"That play was totally beautiful. I've never

been here before, although I'd heard they were good."

Joel adjusted his rearview mirror. "I was impressed. For amateurs, they did a jolly good job. Shall we stop for a drink?"

"I'm fine."

"What is that truck...?"

The force of a blow sent Joel's head almost against the steering wheel. The car shot forward and slid. Joel brought it under control. His gaze flew to the mirror again as he fought to keep the small car on the road. A big pickup truck stayed just feet behind them.

Starli grabbed at the dashboard. "What's going on?"

"Someone's trying to push us off the road." Joel gritted out between clenched teeth.

"What? Why? Can we outrun them?"

"This car's pretty fast, but with all the deer and the slippery road, it's dangerous. How soon before a gas station?"

"I don't know." Starli's body jerked as the truck rear-ended them again.

"Then call 911. Tell them what's going on. See if they can send a sheriff. Hold on, I'm going to speed up."

Starli clutched the armrest as Joel stomped the gas pedal, and the car did its best to deliver. She shifted to cast a peek between the furniture in the back seat. "We're pulling away."

Joel's lips formed a thin line. "Let's hope we can keep away from him and still stay on the road in one piece. Make that call."

Starli punched in 911, then looked at Joel.

"What?"

She bit her lip. "No reception."

"Keep trying until you can get through.". He had to get away from this madman. What if he caused them to wreck and Starli was hurt? No. He wouldn't let that happen.

Starli twisted to stare out the back glass again. "He's gaining on us."

"Is that the lights of a gas station ahead? Hold on, I'm going to swerve into their car lot.

Joel flew off the road and bumped across the rough patches, the shocks protesting as the red car bounced and skidded. Joel did a 180-degree turn and faced back the way they'd come. He leaned forward and pounded the dash when all they caught was a glimpse of the rear end of a large pickup as it flew past the station. "Did you get anything?"

"Part of the license. STU29 something"

"You know anyone with a black pickup?"

"Dark green, I think." Starli objected.

"Black with silver trim, I'm pretty sure."

Starli shook her head. "Makes no difference. I know no one with that kind of truck."

Joel rubbed his forehead and looked at his fingers damp with sweat. "What about Roland? The car was in too good of shape to be used on a farm, but what about a business owner in town? Any friends who own a dark truck?"

"I refuse to believe any of my friends would want us to wreck." Starli's head whipped toward him, her brow furrowed. Her voice lowered to a whisper. "Roland? I-I don't know what kind of truck he has. Do you think it was him?"

"No idea." Determination steeled inside him. "But I'm jolly well going to find out."

Chapter Fifteen

Starli was halfway up her walk before she realized what her subconscious was screaming. She stopped and stared.

"What's wrong?"

"I left the outside light on."

"Are you sure? You didn't forget? Could the light have burned out?"

She shook her head. "I never forget."

"Let's go check it out then. Follow me."

She allowed him to lead as he headed toward her porch, lagging behind and, at the bottom of the steps, she waited. He reached up, fiddled with the modern white light attached to her house and then twisted the spiral shaped bulb. When it lit, he turned to her, a frown on his face.

"You were right. Someone unscrewed the bulb."

She didn't answer him. Her gaze fastened on the second step as she climbed, the step she'd promised herself forever she'd have fixed, the one she knew to not step on, and the one she warned her friends to avoid.

The step was broken, as if someone in haste, or unknowing of its weakness, had broken through. At the side of the step lay an object. Bending, she picked up a black scarf.

"What is it?"

"A scarf."

"I see that. Yours?"

"No, it's not mine." She brushed her fingers

over the soft material, then turned it over to study the distinctive label. "It's cashmere, and though you might not believe it, I haven't wanted to pay the outrageous price for it. Hence I don't own one. Plus..." she looked up "...I own dozens and couldn't justify buying yet again, another one."

"Really? I wouldn't have thought—"

"No, you wouldn't have." She grinned at him. "It's locally made and the only place who sells them is Sharon's Favorites. Everyone loves them, but few town people actually buy one. See the label. The apple blossom logo w/the name of the town is all the rage with the tourists."

Joel reached out and took the scarf from her. "The big question is: who left it on your doorstep?"

"The same person who unscrewed my light bulb? The same person who broke through my step—the step all my close friends knew was weak and needed repaired."

"Someone unfamiliar with it then. Quite sure you're right."

Joel's grim tone sent her gaze to his face.

"And pretty sure I know who I'm talking with first."

"I have a better idea. Perhaps we can check with Sharon. She might happen to have receipts of who bought one."

"Hmmm. Long shot, but I can try."

"We."

"What?"

"We can try."

"You're too busy with the restaurant."

"And you're too busy with being the best

chef around."

"True." He eyed her. "Agreed then. We go together."

Relieved he'd given in so easily, she nodded.

"You need to go in. It's cold out here."

"Come on in. I need a hot cup of tea." Starli hung her coat on the hall tree and walked to the kitchen. She dug in her cabinet till she found her specialty teas.

Joel took them from her. "Sit. I'll fix the tea."

With confident moves, Joel moved around her kitchen as if he'd done it all his life. He scooped the tea into the delicate-looking tea pot, opened two cabinet doors, and the muscles in his back strained against his shirt. She lifted her gaze to his neck and studied his hair. Trim. Had he had it cut today?

Ten minutes later he set down a steaming cup. "Tell me a little about the Strattons."

She cupped her hands around it as a shiver crept up her body. Should she? Her head throbbed from all the excitement of the evening. "I just can't seem to get rid of my past, no matter what I do."

"Your past? You mean your brother-in-law?" Joel eyed her over the rim of his own cup.

"My past. The wrong decisions I made. The price I've had to pay because of them."

"No one should have to pay forever."

Starli grimaced. "Maybe. But sometimes the consequences never end."

"Isn't there anyone who would believe your story? After all, you grew up around here, didn't you?"

"You mean in the police division? There were a few who did, but they couldn't get any concrete proof. I didn't make any medical claims. No one heard anything, but they wouldn't. We seldom had company, and when we did, it was Ryan's buddies from the force for a game of cards."

She sipped her tea. "The truth is, I was a coward then, and I reckon I still am."

Eyes troubled, Joel met her gaze. "I can't accept that. You've done such amazing things. You stand on your own feet. You're quite awesome."

"Roland is a cop. You think they're going to take me serious when I tell them he's calling me and sending notes? I don't think so. He received the "cop of the year" award last year. He's the darling of Appleton station." She stood and walked to the sink. "I'm glad you think nice things about me, but the best thing to do now is ride this out. Hopefully, Roland will eventually move on to someone more interesting to vie his threats upon."

Joel scowled, and in an instant, Starli's heartache lightened.

He drummed his fingers on the tabletop, his gaze on the window behind her. She watched the stillness in his face and the flickers of emotion rippling across it. Thoughtfulness, worry, distress, anger, resolution.

His gaze flicked to her face. "I'll have a talk with the cops."

Fear flooded through her. "Roland is mean. Please be careful, Joel. I'd hate to see you hurt because of my problems."

He sent her a crooked grin. "Will you visit me if I end up in the hospital?"

She knew he was joking, but no laughter

bubbled inside her. Ryan's brutality from the past had been too real, and Roland, from the same blood as his brother, threatened because he was prepared and willing to carry out his threats.

The realization that she couldn't bear it if Joel was hurt hit her. It was so unlike the feeling of...relief she'd experienced when Ryan had died in that horrible car wreck. Had she wanted it to happen? Prayed for it?

No. Not that. She shook her head.

But had the desire for freedom from his hateful personality lived in her subconscious so long she'd unknowingly brought it to pass? Had God given her, in a facetious manner, her desire? Had she been wicked for wanting him...gone?

What a terrible person she was. What uncovered sins lived in her heart?

Swallowing, she fought down the urge to cry.

"I'd better go." Joel stood. "Will you be okay?"

Starli blinked away the tears and saw the hesitation in his eyes.

"We've got a long day tomorrow. It's past time to find the answers you need." At the door, Joel stretched out a hand and cupped her cheek. "Goodnight. Don't let Roland spoil our day. Remember the good times, Starli."

For an instant—for only an instant, Starli swayed, wanting him to take her in his arms and soothe away the hurt. Instead, he stared into her eyes for a moment longer, then turned away. The dread in her heart lent heaviness to the door as she closed it. She pressed her forehead against the paneled oak door, the wood grain cool against her heated skin. She lifted a hand and touched her cheek.

The endless night stretched before her like eternity. She'd softened her attitude, accepted and enjoyed his presence way too much.

Joel had forgotten again to add the "Miss" to her name she'd foolishly insisted he use. She didn't mind. It'd been a ludicrous demand. He'd called her Starli—when he wasn't calling her, Her Majesty—as if it was a natural thing. Her name on his lips was music, not like the ugly, whining sound on Roland's snarling ones.

The lights in the house were dim. They'd not turned any on but the kitchen ceiling light, and now she walked there to stare at the phone, which seemed to take on a life of its own. Was Roland waiting somewhere in town to call again? Planning his next move of harassment in defense of his dead brother? Determined to make her pay?

She flipped the light switch off, then moved down the dark hallway to her bedroom.

Something nagged at her memory. Something about today. Something that was very wrong.

~*~

Golden sunlight peeked through her flimsy curtains when Starli opened her eyes. She yawned, stretched and sat up. Why did she feel so lighthearted? Oh, yes. Tomorrow was Valentine's Day and her birthday. Today, Toni and she were lunching together at Blossoms. Hopefully, Caro would be able to make it, but her business was booming with winter shoppers looking for close-out deals.

Starli threw back the covers, then slid from the bed. She mentally ticked off what needed done today. An early meeting with her employees to pass out the appreciation gift certificates she'd bought for them, spend a couple hours at the soup kitchen around eleven to help the women of the church serve lunch to the needy, an hour at the church to finalize preparation for the Easter Cantata in April, and she still needed to find the perfect gift for Caro's April birthday.

She frowned as she stared in the mirror at herself.

Joel. What was she going to do with him? Morning had cleared her mind. She bit her lip and pulled the comb through her hair. She might as well admit she was attracted to Joel. He was a handsome man, but just because she was attracted to his good looks, didn't mean she was...

Starli saw her mirror image's cheeks redden. She tossed down her comb and twisted her hair into a knot at the top of her head, the shorter strands free-falling against her neck.

That nagging something in her conscious still remained hidden in her brain. As much as she'd pondered over the whole of yesterday, that little bit of bother wasn't coming out of hiding anytime soon. It wasn't the scarf. That was odd, because why would someone leave behind an expensive item like that? Of course, they hadn't on purpose. So *why* had they left it? Scared off? And it was even crazier to think they knew she and Joel were coming and had tried to get away before they arrived. Weird. She might as well put it on the back-burner of her mind.

And, yes, it was probably Roland. Again. Would he never get enough of harassing her? Rita might have done it, but Starli doubted it. In spite of her silly insults, she had learned her lesson with sabotaging Toni's business. She sighed. Or Camille, resorting to random acts of mischief to obtain the manager's position. Honestly, she couldn't think of another person in Appleton with any justifiable reason to annoy her.

When she entered the foyer of Apple Blossoms minutes later, Starli sniffed at the tantalizing smells. She peeked into the kitchen. "Everyone here?"

Louis wiped his hands on a white cloth and growled. "Dining room."

Was she imagining it to think Louis was grumpy again this morning? Perhaps the gift cards she was giving them might cheer him up a little.

It took only minutes to thank her staff for their hard work at making Apple Blossoms a continued success. As she passed out gift cards to all but Manny and Joel, she enjoyed the expressions of pleasure and appreciation they portrayed.

The only one who disappointed her was Camille, and although the girl said nothing, her downcast—it wasn't anger—features were a giveaway.

Would she eventually have to let the girl go? Best to ignore it and move on for now.

As the employees filed away, Joel stepped up to her. "That was a nice display of generosity."

Her back stiffened. "I wasn't trying to be generous. My employees earned it fair and square. I believe it's only right to reward them for that."

"Your duty then?"

"You make it sound as if I have no generosity in me."

He smiled at her. "I want to make sure *why* you're doing what you do."

"As if that's any of your business."

His smile broadened. "Shall I tell you why it's my business?"

Her heart couldn't afford to listen to him. "No, I don't want to hear your foolishness."

His laughter followed her as she sped down the hall, his words ringing in her ears. "You can't run from it, Miss Starli. Might as well face it now."

Shoving at her office door, she let it slam behind her none too gently. That man. How could he be so aggravating when his uncle was such a dear? And especially after last night when she'd almost—almost—forgotten about his aggravating tendencies.

That didn't mean she wanted to hear any ardent declarations today.

Minutes later, when Starli walked into the soup kitchen, she stopped dead. Joel, engulfed in a large, somewhat stained apron, stood among beaming ladies of all ages. He lifted the fork he held in a salute. "Saved a place right beside myself, just for the lady of the season."

"What are you doing here?" Her too-loud question caused several ladies to turn to her, eyebrows lifted.

"He's so-o-o helpful." Rita Mae cooed. "We

love having a professional here. Don't we, ladies?"

Heads nodded their agreement.

Mrs. Stroth, the mayor's wife, eyed Starli as if she was a mischievous child in need of a reprimand. "Dear, you must learn to tone down that voice. You're turning into a shrew before your time. Stu doesn't deserve that."

Starli bit her lip and picked up the proffered ladle. What was the matter with her? When Mrs. Stroth and, worse, Rita Mae, turned away, to greet the first diners, she demanded. "Are you following me?"

He tilted his head in her direction. "Following you?"

Infuriating heat burned her cheeks. "You know what I mean."

"Do I?"

She shot him a glare, but he spoke before she could whisper a retort.

"I was invited to help out today. Since we're closed, I thought I'd do a good deed. Thought you would approve."

His smugness had her wishing she could take him down a notch. But how irritatingly adorable he was. Not that she was about to let him know it. He was altogether too confident.

"Of course, when I heard you'd be here, that was the extra incentive I needed to agree."

"I knew it." Satisfaction spread through her.

Joel lowered his voice. "I love those twinkles in your eyes when you decide to smile at the world."

"You do?" Starli's gaze dropped to the mashed potatoes in the steaming bin before her. Sweet words. Her heart contracted. Did he really mean them? Or were they the words he cast at any and every woman crossing his path?

"Will you let me pick you up tomorrow?"

Ah, ha. He wanted something. "Buttering me up to get what you want?"

Joel speared a moist slice of turkey then transferred it to the tray held out in front of him. He nodded at the man. "I'd love those twinkles whether I ever saw you again or not."

Starli spooned a portion of potatoes onto the tray then seeing the man's longing glance at them, gave him an extra scoop.

"I think those words run off your tongue like melted butter." Starli whispered, but smiled at the woman juggling a baby and young child through the line.

"I never say what I don't mean. Don't you know that by now?"

Best to ignore that one. "Are you planning to join our church's Easter cantata?"

"No, but Pastor asked me to give the benediction."

"You?" Starli's free hand flew to her mouth.

"I worked with the youth in my church at home. Quite an active group. And I've been known to speak a time or two."

The line of people was forgotten. The glow on Joel's face was for real and full of sincerity.

She had no chance to speak. At that moment, the door swung open again. Roland stood there in uniform, his stance, self-confident, bordering on cockiness. He swaggered across the room.

The workers responded with a warm welcome. When he tried to apologize for being late, they shooed away his excuses. Rita Mae, beside Starli, waved her gravy spoon. "Over here, Rolly, dear. You can take my job."

The sour taste of bile seeped up from her stomach. Were they all so blind? Did they not see him for what he was?

He made straight for the offered job, gave Rita Mae an untoward pat, then squeezed in beside Starli and managed an unnecessary bump that almost sent her face-first into the mashed potatoes.

Starli pressed closer to Joel and tried to ignore Roland. When Roland pressed his shoulder against her, she shot him a glare and hissed. "Will you stop it?"

His brows shot up. "Am I bothering you, Miss Starl-e-e-e? I'm just trying to do my job. Too bad you don't know how to do yours."

Joel leaned across her. "Didn't you hear? She wants you to stop touching her."

An unpleasant red crept up Roland's face.

"Mind your own business. Or better yet, go back from where you come."

"Oh, I'm bully well going to do that." Joel lips stretched into a taunt. He paused and let the silence thicken. "When I get ready, Roll-e-e-e, my man."

Roland's big hands clenched. "Why, you..."

"You know, Roll-e-e-e, it's an awfully weak man who would bully a woman."

"Are you blaming me for something, Brit?"

"Are you guilty?" Joel snapped at him.

Roland slopped a spoonful of gravy onto the tray in front of him, and ignored the surprised look on the woman's face when it landed on top of her bread.

"We West Virginians don't cater to highfaluting people. In fact, we don't even like them."

"That's odd. I'm finding a few West Virginians who are quite distasteful. You know what the good book says, don't you, Roll-e-e-e, my man?"

The man's lips curled. "And what would that be since you're so set on telling me?"

"Why, it says God spews the lukewarm from his mouth. I suppose that's a reason for us to do the same. Especially those who are disgusting versions of manhood."

"Why you—" Tossing down his gravy spoon, it landed, handle and all, in the thick, hot liquid, splashing a drop onto Starli's hand. The policeman turned away, then swung back. "You better watch your back, Sir Smart Mouth. I'll be watching *you*." With that, he stormed off, ignoring the female voices calling after him.

"Joel," Fear crept up her spine as Starli gazed after the man who'd done his best to make her life miserable. "I appreciate your...attempt at standing up for me, but I wish you wouldn't have."

"What? You aren't swooning at my valor?" Joel's eyes laughed at her.

"No, I'm not swooning." He didn't need to know how much she wanted to cry at his words. "I'm too afraid for you. The Stratton Family is no one to mess with. They're vengeful and make it their business to get even."

"I'm not worried. I can hold my own."

"I hope so. He meant what he said."

Chapter Sixteen

By the time Joel had finished his volunteer serving at the soup kitchen, he'd changed his mind. A face-to-face with Roland Stratton wouldn't get him anywhere and only end up badly. Better to keep an eye on the man—when he could, and that wasn't saying he'd learn anything useful. But if he could keep him from frightening Starli even one more time, it would be worth a loss of sleep.

He parked his flashy red car away from the police station but close enough he could keep an eye out for when Stratton left the station. He chuckled at the thought of the man's sudden realization he was being tailed.

He hoped Roland wouldn't, but tailing a cop? He wouldn't get away with it for long. But, maybe—long enough.

The thought no more than entered in his mind when his passenger door pulled open, and Camille settled into the seat beside him.

"Guess what." She simpered at him.

"I'm not crazy about guessing games."

"The doctor said Mom might make a recovery after all." She squealed the news.

"Are you kidding?" How could that be?

It couldn't. Not that quick. Something wasn't adding up right.

"Why would I kid about that?"

"I'm happy for you. I'm surprised that the doctor made such a mistake. It's neither logical nor ethical."

"Whatever." She waved a hand at him and pouted. "I don't care about that. Mom's going to get better, we have money, thanks to the benefit you gave us, and I'm on top of the world. I thought you'd be happy for me."

"I—" Joel watched as the girl scooted out of his car again and bounced down the street.

He'd seldom been taken in by swindlers, but he'd been hooked, line and sinker, with this one.

~*~

Starli slipped into the church early that evening. Dim lights illuminated the interior, softening the blue of the cushioned seats, shadowing the dark wood of the altar rail and pulpit. She hesitated then knelt and bowed her head.

From somewhere else in the church muted music escaped into the halls and floated into the sanctuary. Though the worship leader favored many of the more modern songs, Pastor Haag, made sure a number of the beloved older ones were included too.

Eyes closed, she mouthed the words of the beloved hymn. "...let me hide..."

Her throat choked up. She'd been hiding for years. Ever since Ryan had died? When she'd gotten married? No farther back than that.

She knew the exact moment. When she'd forsaken her dream and calling to study music, to accept Ryan's offer of marriage. She'd known when she'd done so—although she'd never admitted it to anyone, let alone to herself—that the decision was the wrong one for her, but she'd never guessed how wrong until she'd experienced the abuse.

She'd longed for a child so much when Ryan had been alive, but somehow that dream had never materialized, along with many others. Ryan had constantly accused her of being the cause of their childless state. But had she been? She'd never been checked by a doctor, never had the courage to go against Ryan's overbearing ridicule and demands.

The music flowed on, drenching her in emotion. "Helpless..."

Oh, yeah. How many times had that emotion passed through her heart? No, not passed. Dwelt. Taken root and flourished.

She'd been helpless, all right. Her whole married life, from the first time Ryan had slammed his meaty fist into her jaw and knocked her out. Her protests had grown weaker as his threats and abuse became more severe.

Yet, Pastor Haag had counseled her that part of the problem had been herself. She'd consciously-or unconsciously—allowed Ryan to take control of her mentally and physically. Pastor urged her to yield to Christ, to call upon the Savior to make her strong and anew.

She remembered how she'd followed his prayer, the words easy on her lips. But deep in her heart she'd held something back. She'd coddled those deep, deep feelings.

Tears streamed down her cheeks as she came face to face with the knowledge she'd held hate and bitterness deep within her. She'd not wanted to forgive.

Forgive Ryan for all he'd done to her?

Never, she'd vowed.

In her own way, she'd rejoiced at his death

and gloated about it secretly, feeding on the sympathy from her dearest friends.

How could she have been so wicked?

As the song played to the end, Starli wept. At last, she felt she'd come to rest in the source of strength and hope. When the last words of the hymn floated to her, she felt a tissue being tucked into her hand. She looked up to see Pastor Haag's serious dark eyes probing her face.

"Is everything all right, Starli?"

Starli swiped at her face, stood, took his outstretched hand, and nodded. She drew in a deep breath. "Yes. For the first time in a long time, I feel like I've come home."

~*~

Hours later, the choir finished their first Easter cantata practice and the whole group of singers mingled and chatted as they slowly headed toward the vestibule.

Starli's fingers glided softly over the piano keys, going over the harder sections. Her heart warmed as she listened to her friends laugh and socialize their way down the aisle.

Pastor Haag, his thin shoulders bent, greeted each one on their way out the door. Toni and Perrin looked as much in love as the day they'd married. Caro and Toby, her brother, with his newest girlfriend, chatted and joked together. Starli smiled when Andy Carrington, his hungry eyes fastened on Caro, followed them out.

When the last person had gone, Starli closed the lid of the piano and ran her fingers over the smooth wood. She drew in a long breath.

"Let me get my coat, and I'll walk you home,

Starli." Pastor Haag strode his way up the aisle.

"Oh, no. There's plenty of light. I'll be fine. You must be tired." In truth she wanted the solace of her own company. She should be afraid. Roland could pop up anywhere. It would be foolish not to be. But the terror was gone.

After another assurance to the elderly man that there was no need in him accompanying her, she gathered her coat and tucked the soft pink woolen scarf about her neck. She stepped outside and stopped in dismay as a lounging figure straightened.

"I was beginning to think you'd given me the slip out another way."

"Joel? Why are you here?"

"I wanted to walk home with you. It's not safe for you to be out this late by yourself." Joel took her arm and threaded her fingers through his own.

His hand was strong and firm. How right it felt. Life *was* good. She would enjoy the moment and be thankful he'd cared enough to see her home.

The silence stretched, but Starli didn't mind. Joel seemed to enjoy the crisp night. His gaze fastened on the trees that surrounded them. She enjoyed the feel of his hand against her own. One spot on his palm felt rough, and she ran the tip of her finger over it. Had he burned himself?

"The woods are lovely, dark and deep, but I have promises I must keep, and miles to go before I sleep, and..."

"...and miles to go before I sleep." Starli

whispered the words with him.

"You read Frost?"

"I read any poetry to do with winter."

Joel straightened his shoulders and stretched out a hand in theatrical abandonment. "Burns really let himself go in this one: 'Blow, blow, ye winds, with heavier gust! And freeze, thou bitter-biting frost! Descend, ye chilly, smothering snows! Not all your rage, as now united, shows more hard unkindness unrelenting, vengeful malice unrepenting than heaven-illumined. Man on brother Man bestows!'"

Starli clapped. "Wonderful. I didn't think there was anyone else locally who could appreciate those heartless sounding words."

Clasping her hand in his again, he amended, "I'm not local."

The torrent of sadness that flooded over her caused her to gasp. Why did he have to remind her his days were numbered here in West Virginia?

"Don't frown. Wipe that look...ah, is it sadness I see in those lovely eyes?" Joel bent lower to peer into her face.

Deny, deny. Don't let him see. Starli opened her mouth to refute his question, then closed it. Her free hand crept up and settled on her chest. That peace she'd received tonight was too precious to do anything to sabotage it. Why not be honest? Let him see what was really in her heart?

Her nod was a slow one. She whispered the words. "I think it might be."

"You're sad, perhaps, at the thought of my leaving?" Joel's eyes weren't laughing now.

Serious and blue and searching, his gaze never left her face. What was he looking for?

She didn't answer.

"And why would the prettiest girl in Appleton be telling a British citizen this?"

"Perhaps she doesn't want him to leave because she just might need his chef-services." Starli cocked her head and tried to infuse some teasing in her voice.

"You'd better be careful." Joel gave her arm a squeeze. "I *might* think you like me."

Biting her lip, she took the plunge. "It could be she *might* miss him too, if he left."

Joel stopped walking and turned toward her. "You never cease to amaze me, My Princess. Life with you would be a never-ending, delightful surprise." Then he leaned forward and lightly touched the tip of her nose with his lips.

He strode on and said nothing else for several seconds.

Hoping to break through his silence, Starli spoke again. "What about this from Shakespeare? 'Poor naked wretches, wheresoe'er you are, that bide the pelting of this pitiless storm! How shall your houseless heads, and unfed sides, your loop'd and window'd raggedness, defend you from seasons such as these?'"

She could feel his gaze on her but ignored it. Her sigh came from the heart. "It's such a breathtaking description of humans' endurance of winter. There's something about the classics that stirs the heart, don't you think?"

"It's a striking passage." Once again, he

turned her toward himself and studied her face. "I don't know what's happened, but you're different tonight. I like it. Tell me."

Should she? The overwhelming feeling of confessing to him what had happened tonight at the church swept over her. And why not? Joel would understand.

But then she wanted to keep this miracle to herself just a little longer, to soak in her joy, to enjoy the wonder and freedom from the burden she'd carried for so long.

"Perhaps I'm beginning to like you. A lot." She tossed her head and walked away.

Joel touched her shoulder and pulled her close to his side as they strolled around the pond. The area was deserted, but Starli didn't mind. Tonight Joel was company enough, and for the first time in a long, long time, she felt protected and at ease with his arm surrounding her.

Would it last? Was it the real thing? She very much hoped so.

Chapter Seventeen

Starli counted her packages again. One, two, three...eleven. That wasn't right. There should have been ten, but she'd definitely counted eleven birthday packages. Her hand ran over each one as her gaze studied them.

She lifted a small square one. What was this? She didn't remember...she didn't even have paper like this. Was it a gift from someone? Well, she'd soon find out.

The edges undid without tearing as she pulled at the tape. She slipped the paper off and let it fall back to the table. With care she lifted the lid. Inside was...a heart-shaped chocolate with the words 'You're mine' engraved on the top.

From Joel? She lifted the paper again and searched, but there was no card, no indication who had sent it. A winter chill ran through her. Could it have been from...

Or even a worse thought, someone had invaded her home. Violated her space. What had he—or she—touched while here?

The peace of last evening wavered inside her, the threatening wind of terror trying to blow out her candle. The doubts beat at her newfound faith while memories from the past replayed in her mind.

Ryan and his abuse. Roland and his serious harassment.

Her own weakness and fear.

Her hand shook as she replaced the tiny box

on the tabletop.

I will trust the Lord. He is my rock and my shelter.

Determination swept back.

I won't listen to the doubts. I will be strong.

With both hands, she carried it to the kitchen and tossed it into the trash. There.

She wouldn't let anyone interfere with her newfound joy. She wanted this evening with her friends to be perfect. She'd determined last night to forget the past. If this—this *person*—wasn't happy with that, too bad.

Hurriedly, she carried her offering of a cheesecake—one she'd ordered and had especially made in Charleston to her car. She eyed the creamy delight nestled in the big box she'd reserved for it. Then she locked her door and drove to Toni and Perrin's home.

As Starli staggered her way up the walk, her arms full of the dessert and a couple presents for Danni, she could hear the muffled laughter inside Toni's home. She was late which never happened. Now, if it'd been Caro they were talking about...

Her heart leaped as she used one finger to press on the doorbell. She didn't see his car, but surely Joel was here.

"Hey, friend, you're late. You okay?" The relief in Toni's voice as she swung open the door warmed Starli.

"I know." Starli nodded and thrust the armload of gifts at her. "Here take these, I'm going back out after one more."

"Let me call the guys to help you. You come on in."

"I've got it." Starli hurried to her car and

crawled halfway in to gather the last gift. When she backed out, Joel stood there, his arms outstretched.

"No, thanks." Starli tucked it securely under her arm.

"That wouldn't be for me, would it?"

His wistful tone sent a smile to her lips.

"Why would you think that?" She wrinkled her nose at him and headed toward the house. "Remember? I don't like you."

"That's not what I heard from your lips last night."

He *had* heard. Her body warmed as if July had suddenly nudged February out of the way.

"I was ready to go after you."

"Are you my watchdog now?"

He pulled on her arm to stop her advance, and when she turned, tweaked her nose. "No. Your protector and friend."

"I see."

Inside Starli scooped up baby Danni from her swing and hugged the child close. "You are such a darling. Toni, she gets more beautiful every day."

Toni smoothed her baby's cheek with two fingers. "She does, doesn't she? She makes us so happy."

Perrin slipped an arm about his wife's shoulders and pulled her tight against him. "And you're the best thing that ever happened to me."

Starli looked up in time to see the look that passed between them, the way Perrin wrapped his arms around Toni, the way she buried her face in his shoulder for just an instant before she pulled away.

Waves of sorrow dashed over Starli's spirit and receded back into her heart. Toni and Perrin were so deliriously happy and in love. Why couldn't it have been that way in her life? Maybe not with Ryan, but what about...Starli caught her breath, and her gaze swept to Joel's face.

He'd flung off his coat and stood talking with Toby and Andy, his hands moving to match the pace of his talk. What about Joel?

What about him? Her gaze fixed on those hands—creative, supple hands. And his face. He wasn't beautiful. No, anyone describing him would have used the term distinguished with his wide mouth, and a nose that would have dominated his face had it not been for his gorgeous eyes—so alight with fun, laughter and life.

A sense of wonder and anticipation hung over Starli as she clasped hands with her friends. Perrin intoned the blessing on the feast Toni had prepared. Chairs scraped as they took their places, the carved ham was passed from hand to hand, and the pile of whipped potatoes devoured.

No matter how many times she and her friends gathered, her heart warmed at their simple love for each other. She *was* blest.

Joel's fingers touched her own as they passed each dish. She loved the teasing light in his eyes and tore her gaze away more than once. When she'd met his questioning one for what seemed like a dozen times, she smiled, and his lopsided grin answered hers.

Starli cleared her throat and looked at each of her friends surrounding the table. "I'd like to tell you all something." Faces turned in her direction. Questioning, friendly, and curious. Heat rose in her face. How hard could this be sharing with her friends? After all, they loved her. She steeled her determination.

"I...I need—no, want to tell you all something. I know Valentine's Day is for sweethearts and couples, but it's also about love. I've recently had some alone—time with God, and have addressed several issues in my life. I'm not saying I've arrived or can forget, let alone really forgive the Strattons from my heart, but I'm working on it. It's the only way I'll truly be free of their...oppression. "

Encouragement rode Toni's features with a soft glow. Caro stared as if she was ready to shout a rousing cheer.

"After almost six and half years, I've finally found peace in my heart." She lifted a hand to touch her chest.

Their supportive expressions gave her the courage to finish.

"Last night I faced up to the fact that the bitterness and hatred I had in my heart against Ryan and his family was my fault. For years I justified my feelings—who wouldn't have felt that way after what Ryan did, I said to myself. But God finally got my attention, and I accepted that only I could allow those feelings to reign inside me. I couldn't forgive myself until I'd forgiven Ryan—as hard as it was."

She let out her breath, then laughed. "There. I'm done."

For a moment no one said anything. Then Toni jumped up and ran around the table to hug her. By the time she was done, the rest were in line demanding hugs.

Joel took her by the shoulders. His whispered words drifted to her ears, his breath fanned her heated cheeks. "I'm proud of you, Your Majesty."

Later, Starli tucked her feet under her on one of Toni's love seats. Joel sat close, but he didn't touch her. His serious expression as Perrin read to them from his latest book caught Starli's attention.

When Perrin finally closed the book and laughed at their urging for more, he said, "No. If you want to know what happens, go buy it."

Soon paper was knee deep around Starli's chair as she opened the pile of birthday packages her friends had given her, but there was no package from Joel. Had she mistaken him at the store two days ago? He'd clearly held up the bag and indicated her gift was in there.

Happiness warmed her heart that her friends had taken her hint about Joel's birthday coming up soon, and had included him in the Valentine's Day/birthday celebration.

He pulled out the set of books she'd gotten for him. A local cookbook that was a favorite of the tourists and another one she'd ordered online. She'd searched for a rare book on poetry she was positive he wouldn't own, and finally, one of Perrin Douglas's own romantic adventure books.

The approval in his eyes was thank you enough. He liked them.

Joel stood up, walked to the French doors and looked out. "Anyone up for a walk? I'm still stuffed from dinner and need to work off some of these calories."

"Not me." Caro stretched and shivered. "I'm too lazy, and it's cold outside. How much snow is there?"

"Lazy bones." Toby drawled at his sister. "Andy looks antsy. Get up and take him for a walk, Caro. It's the least you can do for the man."

"Sorry, I'm not moving until I have to. Besides, I want to keep reading Perrin's new novel, and now's the perfect time to start it."

Toni shook her head and patted Perrin's head. "I want to stay with Blake and Dani.

Perrin, stretched out on the sofa, his legs dangling over the edge, his head in Toni's lap, yawned. "I've done all the exercising I'm going to do tonight. Take Starli. She loves the cold."

Joel's gaze went to Starli, one brow cocked in question. "Come go with me."

"I'd love to. Let me help put up the leftovers first."

Toni waved a hand at her. "Don't worry about it. Caro, Amy, and I'll get it later. Go, before it gets too late."

Starli slipped into her coat, then stepped outside with Joel. The earlier snowstorm had tapered off with only a few lazy flakes drifting earthward.

"When I see a world as beautiful as this is tonight, I can't empathize with King Solomon and his writing that everything was vanity. I've always felt he must have surely been in a deep slough of despondency." Joel strolled with his gaze on the cloudy sky, his hands shoved deep within the pockets of his leather jacket.

"Exactly. I'm ashamed to say that I've never liked that passage of scripture. I don't like thinking everything is useless. Yet I've been near enough to that slough that I've almost slipped into it many times." Why was it so easy to confess her weaknesses to this man?

Joel pulled a hand from his pocket and took her arm. "Here hold on to my arm, My Lady. I want to clear up something. Do you remember when we went to Markus's concert, and I didn't eat? I wanted to talk to you about something?"

"The night you were smitten with Camille."

"Really? Is that what thought?" He didn't look at her, only stared down at the ground, an unusual expression—was it...shyness?—rolling across his face.

"I remember."

"I had a bout of kidney stones."

"Joel, why didn't you tell me?"

"I couldn't."

"Why on earth not?"

Starli was almost sure, Joel's tongue was in his cheek when he spoke again.

"Would you have taken pity of me?

"Certainly not." Her lips twitched.

"Alas, I'm taken with a heartless woman."

"You're the craziest man I've ever met." Starli gave in and laughed.

"But lots of fun."

He hit the nail on the head with that one.

"I wish you would have told me sooner. I might have been—"

"Kinder?"

"Don't you wish? More understanding."

"So you say. Let's move on. I've got important things to say."

"You do?" Starli's heart skipped as if it was a five-year-old child.

"I've been here almost two months." He stopped. "But it seems I've known you forever."

"Is that the important item you wanted me to know?" Starli teased, fear of what he would say making her stomach tighten.

"Partly. I want you to marry me."

His words reverberating in her head, Starli pulled away from him. "What did you say?"

"You want to hear it again?" The laugh crinkles at the corner of his eyes deepened.

Was he serious or was this another of his jokes? Starli strode off, but Joel grabbed her arm and turned her around. His hands gripped her upper arms.

"Do you remember where we first met?"

"In the Apple Blossom kitchen."

"I was soaked from doing the unfamiliar task of washing dishes, and you were on your typical high horse. I fell in love with you right then in the kitchen of the sweetest named restaurant in the world. I adored your shiny blond hair, your wide-open green eyes, that little mannerism you have of tilting your chin in arrogance, and your straight regal back."

He'd noticed all that about her? Still..."I don't know. This is a surprise. I didn't think..."

"Think what? That I loved you? Be honest, Starli."

"I'm trying to be. I didn't expect a proposal...tonight." A gift, yes. A proposal? No.

"Why not? Why wait? I know you're the one for me."

Joel has decided to stay in West Virginia and help me with Apple Blossoms. She looked up at him wondering but afraid to blurt out the thought. "And Apple Blossoms? You're willing to stay here—with me—and..."

Joel was shaking his head. His fingertips tightened a little on her arms. "I want to help you continue to make it a success, yes. We'll find an excellent manager to care for it. But we'll be spending quite a bit of time in England."

"I can't leave Apple Blossoms." Starli's heart thumped. Her hands trembled. "It's my..."

"It's your security blanket." Joel's words, soft and low but quite definite, had the impact of a fist.

"It's *not* my security blanket. It's *my* business." Starli snapped and pulled away from him. Didn't he understand anything? Didn't he understand her? What this restaurant meant to her?

For the first time, she realized Joel wanted her to leave Blossoms. Leave. How could she? It was *her* business. *Her* project. *Her* success.

"Starli. Listen to me. I can't give up my citizenship of England. I have projects that need completed. There are commitments I have that I can't get out of. But I want you with me, by my side. I can help you find the right manager and an excellent chef. We'll keep our hands on the business. Hopefully I can help you open a couple more branches."

She turned away. There was no way she'd turn Blossoms over to someone else. How could anyone care for it like she did?

Shaking her head, she struggled to keep the trembling from her voice. "I can't, Joel. I've built Blossoms up from nothing. I've sweated tears over this business. It's my life. This business *saved* my life."

Joel hands moved to her shoulders. "You care for a business more than me?"

He's the strong magnet, and I'm a lowly pin. Her heart sank to her feet. A bleakness like she'd never experienced twisted her stomach into a knot. Fear as if she stood on a yawning chasm gripped her. If she jumped, she feared she'd never have another chance. She whispered. "I can't."

For a moment Starli held her breath. Joel's stillness as if he realized the bridge neither one of them would or could cross lay between them. Then the corner of his mouth lifted.

"Your Majesty, you are still the same arrogant sweetheart I fell in love with, aren't you? You can't make it easy for me, can you?" His hand lifted as if to touch her cheek, then dropped.

Would that lump in her throat go away if she swallowed enough? "I have to have time to think."

"About what? Whether you can be brave enough to loosen your hold on Blossoms? You've already decided without any real reasoning or thought. Of something to keep me here? Of why I should give up my citizenship? I can't, Your Majesty. That's not doable even if I wished it." He lifted her hand and ran his lips over her fingers, pausing to kiss one of them. Then he tucked her hand in the crook of his arm and turned her around.

Her gaze lifted to Joel's face more than once on their silent walk back to Toni's. Once she started to speak, but the sadness in his eyes he turned on her, closed her mouth.

The sidewalk to Toni's front porch had never seemed so short. Starli placed one foot in front of the other, but she wanted to halt their death-like march and reason with the tall man beside her. His spoken words from minutes ago echoed in her mind. She'd made her decision. What could change? She wouldn't leave Blossoms. Joel wouldn't leave England.

After he opened the door for her, he turned away but Starli clutched his arm, panic like a monster at her heels. "Where are you going?"

He winked and pointed a finger at her as if giving her orders. "I'm going to my flat. You go on in and have a wonderful night. Tell the others I'll catch up with them later."

His long legs strode down the sidewalk, until the darkness prevented her from any further sight of him.

Shoving her hands into the pockets of her coat, she drew one out again and gazed at the object in her hand. A tiny crystal ice skater glittered at her from the light of the porch.

He hadn't forgotten. Joel must have sneaked it into her pocket earlier to replace the broken one. His birthday present to her? Tears blurred the sight of the figurine as a feeling of dé·jà vu swarmed over her like bees.

She lifted her hand and stared at her pinkie finger with the slight crook.

The one Joel had kissed.

Chapter Eighteen

Can I take it back? Can I change my mind?
A month had passed since Valentine's, and day after day slugged by until Starli thought she'd scream.

I am not a man-chaser, she chanted, but at work, she made excuses to visit the kitchen. She planned her lunchtime around Joel's, but he either left the restaurant—assumedly to run errands—or there was always someone else with him.

Joel, as polite as always, willingly discussed with her anything to do with the menu. But that was all he talked about. The restaurant had morphed into a funeral parlor. The fun, the teasing, the lightness of spirit gone.

Permanently? For her—probably.

The sadness she'd felt Valentine's night when they'd last been together, clung to her, trying to drown the peace in her heart. She clutched at it, fearful of losing the ground she'd made spiritually. That tenuous hold was the only encouragement she could squeeze from her life right now.

She'd had a total about face. She'd dallied with the most precious earthly thing ever offered her. Admittedly, she'd wanted her way. The restaurant *and* Joel. Now at the risk of losing the one, the other seemed not so valuable. Feckless heart. What was she to do now?

Caro bounced into her office around eleven one frigid morning. A hand propped on her hip, her face screwed into concern, she demanded, "What is going on? You've refused Toni's invitation to Sunday dinner, you claimed work when I wanted you to go into Charleston shopping, and you left church so quickly Sunday morning, we knew you were avoiding us."

Dropping her gaze, Starli fiddled with the papers on her desk. A second later, a tanned hand slid into view and touched the papers.

"You were in seventh heaven at our Valentine's dinner. I thought you and Joel were doing great. What gives, Starli?"

A twinge of anger nibbled at Starli. "It would be nice not to be the object of everyone's speculation."

"When one makes oneself a spectacle, others can't help but speculate."

Starli bit her lip, amused at Caro's feeble attempt of philosophizing. "I guess you thought wrong. Mr. Peterman-Blair has no plans of living in West Virginia." She could hear the ice in her voice and made an effort to soften it. "He made that very clear."

Caro's hand withdrew. "Toni is coming at 11:30 to eat lunch with us. We won't take no for an answer. You can do that, can't you? You don't have something better to do?"

That hurt. Starli winced. "You know I love our luncheon dates."

"We'll see you then." Caro lifted a brow, nodded and left the room.

At eleven thirty, Starli left her office and stood in the doorway to the dining area. Toni and Caro huddled together at their favorite table, their expressions serious. As she approached them, they both ceased talking and turned toward her. Just as she thought. They were discussing her. And probably Joel. As much as she valued these two friends, she wished they'd let this one go. With one hand on a chair, Starli asked, "How's Danni?"

The light of motherhood broke over Toni's features. "She's wonderful, but fussy this week. I think she might be cutting her first tooth."

When Starli sat, Toni asked her. "I'm having a small dinner party at home tonight. Will you come? I won't listen to any excuses."

"Who's going..." Starli's suspicions roused.

"It doesn't matter." Caro puffed out an exasperated breath. "Since when do you have to know who'll be at one of our gatherings?"

"All right. All right. I'll come." Starli gave in rather than cause any more outbursts from her friend. Caro had a kind heart, but she didn't mind speaking her mind.

"Great. Have you heard any more from Roland? Has he backed off?" Toni's concerned gaze rested on Starli.

Starli pressed two fingers against her forehead. "Actually, I haven't heard from him since February when I received that package from him."

"I'm almost afraid to ask what you mean."

"I didn't see him. Just the gift."

"What was it?" Caro asked.

"A heart-shaped chocolate, engraved with the words, 'You're Mine.'"

"That's downright spooky." Caro's eyes were

as big as fifty-cent pieces.

"He was in your home?" Toni's incredulous voice bordered on panic. "How could he have done that? He doesn't have a key, does he?"

"I don't know for sure if it was him in my home. It wasn't very pleasant thinking about the possibility." Starli shivered. "I have no idea how he or anyone else could have gotten into my house. But perhaps being a policeman, gives Roland the ability."

"Did you change the locks?"

"Yes." She hesitated.

"What?"

"I don't know, but I can't see Roland doing that."

"What on earth do you mean? You can't be serious." Toni's shocked voice rose louder than normally.

"Actually, I think I know what she means." Caro sat forward and nodded.

"Well then, one of you had better clue me in."

"Don't get me wrong, I'm not taking up for the man or feel any warm fuzzy feelings for him of a sudden." Starli had no idea if she was making sense or not. "But up-to-date, he's never used cards and packages to convey his anger at me. So why start now? Voicing and physically acting on the threats are far more powerful and scary, as far as I'm concerned."

"Exactly what I was thinking." Caro nodded.

"If you are right, Starli, then you've got an even scarier thought: *who* sent the candy, and why? What do they want?"

Starli looked at her friends as they stared back at her. She didn't have an answer, but she didn't think they expected one.

"Have you noticed anything else odd lately?" Caro asked. "How's Camille doing, by the way?"

"If you mean, Camille acting like a spoiled child, then yes. I'm hoping she straightens up her act soon, or I may have to let her go."

"That's too bad. I was so hoping she'd buckle down and make something of herself." Caro shook her head.

"The thing is, she's a good worker when she's there. But at times she'll miss a day and forget to call in, or she'll be late. Not by a lot. Fifteen minutes or twenty, and it makes me feel like a Scrooge to take her to task about it. Worse, her new aim is to be 'like me' if I'll give her a manager's position. And if I don't, I'll be sorry."

"Seriously?" Caro laughed but sobered. "That sounds like a threat. Could be youth speaking, or—"

Toni's brow wrinkled. "Either way, you shouldn't feel badly. You need to do what you feel is right and not worry about it. That's good business sense."

"Toni's right. No matter how much my bleeding heart aches for the Findleys, you need to do what is the right thing for Apple Blossoms."

"I believe her threat was a childish one. I paid it little mind, other than being annoyed." Starli lifted her hands. "But she's making little impression on me as good manager material. It's hard for me to imagine she'd go this far though."

"I think you should move in with us." Toni

bit her lip.

"No, I won't be run out of my own home. I wouldn't think of putting you guys in danger, if there is any."

"We're kind of cramped, but you could share my room." Caro offered.

"Same answer. Besides, I've been in that apartment of yours. It's barely big enough for you and Toby, alone trying to find a nail to hang me on."

"Toby can move in with Andy for a few weeks until this is resolved."

"No. How long will that take? Ryan bullied me for years. Now Roland's got it into his head to do the same. I'll have to toughen it out."

"If he hurts you, I'll tear him apart myself." Caro's cheekbones were two flags of red.

Starli's heart expanded at their protectiveness. "I'll be okay. Hey, we haven't ordered lunch."

After their orders were taken, Caro whispered. "Now. It's time. Give it to us. What's going on with you and Joel?"

These two friends were much too precious to her to tell them it was none of their business. Truth be told, she reckoned they did have a right to know. They'd seen her through her struggles with Ryan and had put up with enough of her miserable life. They deserved to have some answers.

"Remember when Joel and I took that walk on Valentine's night? He asked me to marry him."

If she'd wanted responses, she couldn't have asked for better ones.

"Joel asked you to marry him?" Toni's gasp

of pleasure made Starli want to cringe.

Caro pumped the air then bombarded her with the question. "And you said what?"

"I said no. Sort of."

"You actually told that gorgeous hunk of a man no?" Caro frowned and lowered her head as if she'd plow into her friend.

"I'm afraid I did. He wanted me to leave Apple Blossoms and move to England."

"And what's so bad about that? We'd all get a free place to stay when we visit on vacations." Caro threw back at her.

Toni and Starli both laughed, then Toni spoke. "He wouldn't consider living here?"

"He wanted me to hire a good manager and chef to run the restaurant. Said we'd keep our hand in the business—from a distance, of course." Starli couldn't help the trace of sarcasm in her voice, but the sadness in her heart overwhelmed her feelings. She blinked several times to hold back the tears. She would not cry.

"Of course, I understand. You've worked hard to make Apple Blossoms a success."

"I don't understand. I would've been gone in a flash if some romantic man had asked me." Caro still frowned. She propped her elbows on the table and rested her chin on her fists.

"Blossoms represents the only success I've ever made of my sorry life, Caro. It's taken a lot of hard work and determination, but at last I'm ready to open a branch. I can't give up my dreams because of a man. I won't make that mistake again."

But I want to. Oh, how I want to.

"Joel is not just another man." Caro

objected.

"And Joel won't work with your dreams?" Toni's steady dark eyes studied her.

"Not if they don't coincide with his."

"That doesn't sound like Joel." Toni's head moved back and forth in denial. Or was it in puzzlement? "We've all gotten to know him and love him."

Starli looked away. Were her friends right? Was Joel right? Was she using Apple Blossoms as a security blanket for all her incongruities?

Dear God, am I wrong?

She shuddered at the thought of depending on another man. Hadn't living with Ryan taught her anything? Why then did her heart feel like it was breaking?

~*~

Joel chopped the spinach with a savageness that belied his own outward mellow expression. He lifted his gaze to the one-way window overlooking the dining room. He couldn't keep away from it. He couldn't hear her voice, what she said, but he could see her lovely face. He could see her lips move and widen into a hint of a smile.

Lord, was he wrong? Was she not the woman for him?

Manny came up beside him. "How are you doing, nephew?"

Tilting his head toward him, his lips twisting in ockery of a frown, he said, "What do you think, when the woman you want doesn't want you?"

Manny's yardstick straight back didn't bend, but he leaned closer. "I am praying she will come to her senses. Don't give up on her yet. I didn't send for you to have this fail."

"I knew you had something up your sleeve when you claimed such an emergency you had to have my presence here in the states immediately. You sly fellow. Quite a matchmaker you've become." Joel chuckled.

"She was worth the trip, don't you think?"

"She is." Joel dropped his spoon and nodded at the three women in the dining area, sitting at their favorite table. "I'd give a lot to know what they're talking about."

"You, of course." Manny straightened and snickered. "Toni and Caro care too much about Starli to let her give you up."

"You put a bug in their ears?"

The maître de walked away, but he tossed over his shoulder. "Sometimes one has to act on one's faith."

True, and the battle wasn't over yet.

~*~

"I want us to pray together about this." Toni reached for Caro and Starli's hands. "We don't want you to make the wrong decision."

Aren't I already doing that? Starli opened her mouth, then snapped it shut.

Toni's strong faith came through in her words. "Lord we ask you to show Starli the way. Don't let the enemy distract her..."

Was Toni talking about Apple Blossoms?

"...but show her the way to your true happiness..."

Am I not happy with my life now that I've made my peace with God over Ryan? Of course, I'm not.

"...Let her light burn brightly..."

I do want God's will. I really do. Starli's

heart leaped in response.

"...We claim that for her. We trust her to you."

Her two friends chorused together. "Amen." Starli squeezed their hands. "Thank you."

"You're welcome." Toni rose from her seat. "And don't forget that spare bedroom is yours if you want it."

After hugs, the two girls were gone. Starli walked toward her office.

"There you are."

"Stu. How are you? Why are you here at this hour? Enjoying this cold snap?" She waved him to follow her to her office.

"Sure." Stu wore a dark blue casual sports jacket, the buttons shiny and bright, over a lightweight turtleneck, his pants pressed, not a wrinkle in them. "Had a couple of items wanted to mention to you."

"What would those be?"

The banker sat in the chair across from her. "We have a problem with your loan request."

"What kind of problem?" Her credit was good, and the income from the restaurant had never been better.

"Some questions were brought up at our board meeting last night about the feasibility of such an expensive oven when the one you have is new and far from being worn out."

"But I submitted all the information and reasons you asked for."

"You did, and did a very good job too." He sat forward. "I don't want you to worry too much, but felt you need to know about a few doubts hovering over the loan request. Would you let me take care of this? Do you trust me to see what I can do? I like to care for my own. I'll ask if I need you to go into more detail."

"Absolutely. You know the financial business side of Apple Blossoms as well as I do." She gave him a warm smile. "Thank you."

He settled back in the chair. "Good. I also thought you might like to come with some of us to the ski resort."

He was a charismatic person. He hadn't risen to the best job at the bank with his dad's help. Thankfully, he'd done that on his own.

"Oh, Stu, I've been wanting to go forever, but I just can't leave today." She was glad she didn't have to pretend disappointment. Skiing today would have been the perfect—or almost the perfect—solution to her blues. "I'm so sorry. I really would have loved going."

He studied her face. "I suspected that would be your answer. Fortunately, I can see you're sincere."

Starli wanted to draw a breath of relief that he wouldn't make a fuss.

"It's too bad really. You're way too attached to this business although I love Apple Blossoms as you do." He took her hands, tugged on them, his face serious. "Seems I'm going to have to ante up my persuasion a little more."

He leaned over and kissed her cheek. "See you later, Chickie." He sketched a wave and was gone.

What had that been about? Had her friend finally decided to move on? Not with the statement about increasing his persuasion. He was a dear though.

She hurried toward the kitchen to check on

tonight's menu, when the door swung open, and Joel stood there. He looked as startled as she felt.

Her heart leaped. How aristocratic-looking he was, but was he thinner? Had the bones in his face sharpened? Worry like dust motes swam in her mind. Was he suffering from those awful kidney stones again? Was he okay?

Of course, he wasn't okay. She'd refused the sweetest thing he had to offer for what? Surely they could come to some kind of better arrangement. Couldn't she have both? Love and Apple Blossoms? Apple Blossoms and Joel?

She reached out to touch his arm with her fingertips.

He gave her a fleeting smile, and for a moment, that old teasing light flashed in his eyes. Then it was gone.

And so was he.

The swinging kitchen door swished back and forth, and only that square piece of wood door stayed with her.

Cold comfort indeed.

Chapter Nineteen

Joel eyed Camille. She was pouting. About what he had yet to discover. Her attitude lately had bordered on sullen, and he wondered if at any time she might not show up for work. His heart still sympathized with her seemingly hopeless plight, yet others had overcome worse life problems than hers.

Could she still be harboring a grudge against Starli? The owner had not given her the manager position, and he seriously doubted it would happen.

I'd kill for the manager's job.

Words spoken not so long ago. Had she meant them or did they come from a careless attitude, not meaning what they sounded like?

He hoped so.

A knife clattered as Louis tossed it onto the countertop, and Joel winced. He was particular with his own personal set of knives and allowed no one—even Louis—to touch them. A chef's knives were expensive, well loved, and intimate objects for his culinary creations. That was one reason Louis would never make a top-notch chef. He didn't care enough.

Was he correct in thinking Louis's attitude had changed? From sulky and angry, he'd morphed into cooperative and anxious to please.

He sent Camille out of the kitchen, and with Juanita at the other side of the room, Joel figured it was now or never.

"Louis, how are you doing? Seems whatever was bothering you has eased up? Doing better, Mate?"

Louis's face filled with shame. "Yeah. Got my head on straight, finally. Sorry about the attitude. I reckon I was a bit jealous."

"You had no need to be."

"Right. Not your fault, and I realize enough to know I'm not the professional chef Miss Starli needs here. Don't even want the job, so why'd I get my tail in a wad I don't know. You fit the bill, I'm thinking."

That was good to know. Thank God for small blessings.

~*~

Joel would be at Toni and Perrin's tonight. Starli knew it. She'd bitten her nails, figuratively speaking, of course. It was such a nasty habit, she'd never literally do it, but spending all day worrying about seeing him did have her mentally chewing. His cold response to her at the kitchen door had done nothing for her confidence.

How could she talk with him when there was nothing to say? What could they talk about? The weather? Apple Blossoms? England?

That tiny bit of worry stung her. Had she irrevocably made the wrong choice with Joel, with the emphasis on the word irrevocably? Had she destroyed the bridge that couldn't be built again? Why couldn't she make him understand what Blossoms meant to her? Was there any possibility he'd change his mind about staying?

She sighed and sat on the edge of her bed.

Her gaze fixed on the three outfits she had laid on the bed, but her mind saw only Joel's face. His tall muscled body as he skated in unison with her, his tan hands as they competently blended ingredients, his face still, as he concentrated, then breaking into fun-loving light.

In the end, Starli slipped into the first thing her hands picked up. What did it matter whether she wore the ice blue sheath or the spring-like green sweater? Joel would notice neither.

As she reached for her car keys, the phone rang. When she picked up the receiver, Manny spoke. "Starli, I'm going back to Blossoms to make out an order for the supplies we need. Was there anything else you wanted?"

"Manny, you don't have to do that. Wait till tomorrow."

"I'd like to see it done tonight. I won't be there long but wanted you to know it should be ready for morning."

An hour later, Starli stepped into Toni's great room. Her gaze darted to each person's face, but Joel hadn't arrived. Would he, knowing she'd be there?

When they settled at the table, and Joel hadn't appeared, Starli's heart sank. Since there wasn't an extra place setting, Starli had to assume that either Toni hadn't invited him, or he'd turned down the invitation.

At the end of the meal, Perrin brought in a huge bowl of the punch cake Toni had prepared, but when the phone rang Toni rose. "I'll get it."

Forty seconds later, she was back in the

room, and went straight to Starli's chair to rest a hand on her shoulder. Because of Toni's Italian heritage, her olive complexion seldom faded, but now, fear pinched it white.

"I...that was Detective Eddie. There's a terrible fire in town."

The chorus of questioning voices drowned out Toni's next words, and she had to repeat them. Her gaze rested on Starli's upturned face. "I'm so sorry, dear. Apple Blossoms is burning."

Starli's world exploded. Or at least it felt like it. The atmosphere swirled faster and faster, her body a minute piece of material caught up in the rapid swirling motion.

Her mind blank, her chest heavy, and her body a numb void, Starli took in the words but refused to understand them. If she didn't think about them, they would go away. There was no way Apple Blossoms...

Toni's voice floated around her. "The problem is, both fire trucks are out on another call outside of town. It's going to take awhile for more to arrive from Beech Creek."

As if an elephant trampled through her heart, it hit her. She jumped to her feet and ran for the front door. Someone threw her light coat at her, and she caught it but didn't take the time to pull it on. She tore down the sidewalk, slowed and ran for her car.

Someone caught her arm. "This way."

Shock at Joel's sudden appearance edged out her fear, but she shoved it away from her thoughts. She veered and ran with him as he led her to his faster car.

"Where did you come from?" Starli pressed

her hand against the dash, willing the car to go faster.

"I was on my way to get you when you burst through Toni's front door."

She could see the smoke even before they reached the street. How could there be that much smoke without damage beyond repair? A groan escaped her throat.

"Hang in there, Princess. We're almost there."

Joel screeched around the corner, his hand on the horn. The moment he stopped, Starli flung open the door, not bothering to shut it. She ran toward her restaurant, but Joel tackled her, wrapping his arms around her.

"You can't go any closer."

"Manny's in there. He said he was going to stop by late tonight to get an order for supplies ready." She shouted her frantic reply.

"Are you sure he said tonight? If he's in there, he'll be overcome with smoke by now." The strain in his voice overran her own concern.

"I'm positive. He's always so good to keep me posted."

"I'm going in. I can't rest if Uncle Lawrence is in there.

Panic spread through her. "No, Joel, you can't."

"You want me to leave Uncle Laurence in there? Look at the kitchen windows. Most of the smoke and fire is still there. If he's in there, he'll be either in the dining area or his office. I think I can reach both without too much trouble."

She clutched his jacket. "The firemen..."

"No time. If I'm not back in five minutes, let them know."

"Joel..." Starli wanted to tell him she loved him, but the words stuck in her throat.

"What?"

She couldn't say it. "Be careful."

He touched her cheek. "I will. Say a prayer, Starli."

Five minutes turned into an eternity. She wavered between closing her eyes to pray for the arrival of fire equipment with watching the window where Joel had entered and wondering if she'd ever see his beautiful face again.

My child.

Starli's heart thumped. Her gaze shot to the window where Joel had disappeared. Nothing. She bowed her head again.

My child, nothing is more valuable than love. You must not only forgive, but you have to learn to trust.

"And I have to learn to trust through a lesson like this?" Anger spurted through her at the wastefulness of the beloved structure burning in front of her.

For you, my child, yes. Will you trust me, now?

The anger seeped out of her. What did she have to lose? Faced with the awful choice—in reality, a gut-wrenching truth—Starli knew her real feelings had literally been dug out of her soul. God had peeled her very being to the core and the unexposed truth lay there for her to see.

She loved Joel. She loved him more than Apple Blossoms, more than enough to go with him, more than enough to trust him.

Starli swiped at her wet cheeks and checked her watch. Six and a half minutes had passed. She edged closer to the window, choking at the smoke rolling from the window. Standing on tiptoe she squinted, longing to see his figure staggering toward her.

And there he was, silhouetted by the fire behind him, carrying...someone. Manny?

"Starli, are you there? Come over here and help me."

Reaching through the window to help Joel navigate Manny's limp form through the window, she almost dropped him. Getting a firmer hold, she did her best to steady him to the ground as Joel guided him down.

"There's someone else in there," he choked out after they had him settled on the ground.

"Joel, no. Don't go, please..."

He reached for her hands, his voice raspy from the smoke. "Would you have me be a coward, Your Majesty?"

She laid her head against his hands for a moment, then she shoved them away. "Go, then. But if you're not back in five more minutes, I'll—I'll..."

His lips tipped up, and he disappeared.

Starli tugged on Manny's feet and managed to move him another two feet or so away from the burning building. Then she knelt by him, listening for the ambulance, and prayed.

Minutes passed like sludging water, and Starli's gaze wavered between Manny's face and the window where Joel'd disappeared.

When at last she saw him there, lifting a body, she ran to help him.

Coughing, Joel clambered through the

window and dropped to the ground, the body easing from his arms.

Starli's arms went around him to steady him when he swayed, and she whispered, "What was she doing in there?"

Shaking his head, he managed a hoarse whisper. "Have no idea."

For just a minute, he rested his cheek against the top of her head, then he moved away and knelt between the two lying on the ground. Bending over, he plucked something clasped in the hand of the girl.

Starli stared down at her beloved maître de and Camilla Findley.

~*~

In the distance the ambulance siren grew louder.

Manny's breathing was raspy but his eyes fluttered open, and he coughed. He reached up a hand and clutched Joel's jacket. His lips moved, his breath wheezing, but no words came.

"What, Uncle Lawrence?" Joel leaned closer. "What did you say?"

Another cough. More lip moving, and then he lay back, and his eyes closed.

The ambulance medics nudged them aside and minutes later, the EMS loaded Manny and Camille into their vehicles. Joel trotted over to Detective Eddie's cruiser, Starli behind him.

"Uncle Lawrence had blood on his head." Joel nodded toward the restaurant.

Eddie shook his shaggy head. "He could have fallen and hit his head. I'll be talking with him as soon as he's well enough to speak."

"I'm wondering if we ought to keep it quiet

that they were in there. Or maybe pass around the word that one or both died?" Starli shook the detective's arm.

"What are you thinking?" Eddie's bushy eyebrows lifted.

"I'm not sure. I'm troubled that they both were in there and that both have head injuries that look suspiciously alike." The quiet suspiciousness that had lain dormant in her brain for several days stirred. "Why would they both have exactly the same injury?"

"You think there's foul-play here?" Eddie sounded as disturbed at she felt.

She met his eyes, letting him see the indecision inside her.

"What are you thinking, My Princess?" Joel slipped an arm around her shoulders.

"Something's bothering me, but I can't quite figure out what it is. I know without a doubt that Manny wouldn't do anything to harm me or the restaurant, so did he surprise Camille or did she come after Manny did for some reason? And if so, why? And the craziest question bouncing around inside my head is: was there a third person there?"

"Why on earth would you think that?" The doubt in the detective's voice hinted he'd not given such a thing even a thought. "Do you have reason to believe there was or is someone else inside the restaurant?"

"No proof, Eddie. Just this weird feeling." Her smile was meant to disarm his doubts. "And what Camille Findley had clutched in her fingers. Show him, Joel."

Joel unfolded his fingers. In the palm of his hand lay a large gold-toned button.

Detective Eddie reached for it. "Why was she holding this?"

"What's so troubling to me is, I saw this button recently. I can't remember where."

"Not sure it means anything useful though."

"Unless she tore it from a *third* person." Joel offered.

"Yeah, there's that."

"Is there any way we could keep Camille's presence from the general media?" Starli knew the police quite often held back information. She just hoped her friend would do so this time.

"What will it hurt, Detective?" Joel squeezed Starli's shoulder. "Give us a few days to figure out what's bothering her."

"Well, seeing it's you, Starli, I guess it wouldn't hurt. I'll try to give you a week to see if you remember something. After that, then we'll have to go with whatever the state fire inspector says. I'm really sorry this happened. I need to go." He touched his forehead and walked away.

The smudges on Joel's face and clothes tore at Starli's heart. "Are you all right? Shouldn't you see a doctor?

"I've burned myself plenty of times cooking." He lifted a hand and looked at the burn on one palm. "Why does this hurt much worse?"

Starli took his hand in both of hers and studied the blister. "You have to have this looked after. Let's get you to a doctor."

"But what about Apple Blossoms?"

She looked up at the odd sound in his voice. "What about it?"

"Are you going to just walk off while it's

burning down?"

Her beloved restaurant was gone, and the sadness tugged at her.

Trust.

She clung to his hand, careful of the burn. "It's just a building. This is what's important now. You're what's important to me."

The smallest hint of puzzlement rode between his brows as he returned her gaze. "What are you saying?"

"I'm saying I've finally got my priorities straight."

"Are you saying this because Blossoms is...gone?"

Was she? Was she choosing Joel because her security in the self-built business was gone? Was she such a weakling she automatically leaned toward another stalwart pillar?

"No. I think not. Even before this..." she gestured toward the blazing building "...I realized what was important to me. For me, Joel, it was a matter of trust."

The smile began in his eyes and spread to his lips. "And you trust me now?"

Starli reached up to encircle his neck with her arms. Almost as if the last weight she'd carried for so long had taken off like a bird, the sudden feeling of freedom gave her the courage she needed. She whispered in his ear. "Yes, Joel. I trust you."

~*~

He looked up at her. "You know, I could get used to this treatment."

She bent and looked straight into his eyes, frowning as severely as she could. "*Don't* get used to it." And then she winked. His laughter penetrated the car even after she shut the door.

She eyed the gear shift.

"Do you know how to drive a standard?"

"Of course, I do." She tossed him a glare. "It's been awhile..."

"Back when you got your first car that stalled in front of your friends, right?"

She wasn't going to answer that one. He'd never let her forget it. But she couldn't resist corner-eyeing him. Just as she thought, he was gloating.

"Do you want to hear my thoughts about all this mess or not?"

"Tell me."

"All along I've felt like all my problems started with Roland, or to be accurate, back with Ryan. But that was because I allowed them to rule my life, to keep me bound with fear and hatred. And recently, I've allowed the same persuasion to rule me."

"And?"

"Give me time. I'm feeling my way through this." She shifted and the car jerked when she let out the clutch too quickly. "What I do know is, Roland has bullied me physically and verbally, the same as Ryan did."

"That's point one. What's next? Camille?"

"Yes. I know she's younger than her years in many ways, but that doesn't excuse the fact that she made a threat to me. Whether it was casually meant or seriously, it was still a threat."

"I don't know if she's smart enough to plan to burn down a restaurant." Joel stared out the windshield.

"I realize that, and I'm taking your opinion into consideration." Starli drew in a deep breath as she pulled into the doctor's parking lot. "Having shared my two points with you, here's my question: something's wrong. Out of portion. If Roland and/or Camille didn't burn down my restaurant—and I'm not saying they didn't—then who did? What am I missing?"

~*~

"I lovingly insist."

How *could* she resist that dazzling smile every time he wanted something from her? The answer? She couldn't, even though she could feel her skin tingle with a tad bit of unease. Not enough to make her draw back for long, or object too strenuously. Long time habits died hard. At least for her. But she'd meant that pledge to God and to Joel. Trust or die trying. That's why she was going along with his idea of talking to Stu about plans to rebuild. But would the bank agree if they already had a problem with a loan for a more up-to-date oven?

She cocked her head sideways to look at the man driving his sporty convertible. Yep. Just as beautiful as she'd thought not a minute before. She chuckled when the vision of him protesting at her latest verbal compliment about being beautiful flashed into her mind.

"Men aren't beautiful, My Princess," he'd said.

But they were. At least, he was. He couldn't win that argument. She laughed now, thinking about their argument, and he joined her, even though she knew he didn't know why.

"Right on time." He didn't bother to open his door, only scooted up in his seat and stepped over the door. He flung open her door and took her hand to help her out. "Have I told you lately how beautiful *you* are?"

"No, you haven't. It's been all of fifteen minutes since you picked me up and informed me of that very fact. Far too long for me to remember it."

Joel tucked her hand in the crook of his arm. "Don't you be sassing me, My Princess."

"Oh, I won't." What fun he was.

"After you."

The bank was busy, and Starli expected a long line of customers. But as she and Joel turned toward the waiting area, Roland's snarling voice penetrated the cozy world she'd been living in since the fire two weeks ago.

"Well, fancy meeting Starl-e-e-e here at the bank after such a tragedy. Why does that not surprise me? After more money? Not likely to get it since I hear you've been shunning poor Stu and hanging with this cad."

Joel stiffened beside her.

"Joel," she whispered. "Ignore him. He'll go away eventually."

"He won't go away, and I'm tired of him hassling you." He turned, took one step, and was face to face with Starli's brother-in-law.

"Were you...yammering again, Roll-e-e-e? I'm beginning to think you sound like a frustrated old woman who has nothing to do but pester others." One side of Joel's lips cocked up in a mocking grin, taunting the man.

"Get out of my way."

"You're leaving? Already?"

"No, I'm not. I'm going to talk with her." He nodded at Starli.

"I think not. I don't want you to."

"Get out of my—"

"Roland."

The voice wasn't particularly loud, but it was authoritive, and those nearby paused and stared. Roland stopped his belligerent move and swiveled.

Chapter Twenty

It was Stu Stroth, standing at the doorway to his office. He beckoned. "Starli, why don't you and Joel join Roland and myself?" When they hesitated, he motioned again, more impatiently. "Come on."

He waited until they'd sat, staring down at the papers on his desk, and not making eye contact with any of them.

At last he looked up and straight at Starli. "I didn't want to tell you this."

"What is it, Stu?"

He hesitated. "I've tried to be there for you ever since you returned to Appleton after you married. You know that, Starli."

"Yes, I do, Stu. I couldn't have asked for a better friend."

"That's why it pains me to drag you into this." He sighed.

What on earth was the man talking about?

"Roland, I've watched you turn from a decent man to a bitter, angry man at what you thought was an injustice against Ryan."

Roland opened his mouth to protest, but Stu raised a hand. "Be quiet, will you, for a change and let me get through this?"

Miraculously, the Stratton brother did as he was ordered, and Stu went on. "Starli is not to blame for Ryan's death. I was with him the night he died. We were at the bar right outside of town. I didn't drink, but he was guzzling. I tried to warn him to slow down, but typical for him, he didn't listen."

"Why are you telling us this now?" Roland demanded. "If you're wanting to slander—"

"Shut up, Roland. I've had enough of your accusations against everyone but the one person you should blame."

Starli had never heard Stu speak so harshly.

"He came to me begging me to cover his debts."

"That's a lie."

Roland was steaming if his red face told the truth.

"Don't forget I handled your father's finances. I know exactly how much he allotted Ryan when he and Starli married. He ran through it all, had to get a second mortgage on his house, bought or charged for whatever new item he developed a craving, and gambled a big portion of it away. If I hadn't covered those gambling debts, he'd been in serious trouble."

"I didn't know this, Stu—"

"You got any proof of all this?" Roland snarled right over top of Starli's comment.

"Do you think I hand out money to every friend I have without some kind of insurance I'll get it back?" Stu smirked at the man. "I haven't gotten where I am today because of stupidity."

"You're not calling Ryan stupid, are you?"

"If what I've told you isn't enough, you hear me out and make your own decision." At Roland's reluctant nod, he continued. "Ryan was very vocal that night about a lot of things, including his treatment of Starli." Stu's eyes rested on her for a moment. "He got quite maudlin for a bit and sobbed out several mushy comments about how good a person she was and what a louse he was."

"A drunk talking." Roland scuffed.

"Not quite drunk enough to pass out though. Just enough liquor in him to get him talking. Fortunately, I got those statements and several others on record."

"What? That's not legal."

"Why not? I didn't give any of that to the cops. It was for my own protection. But that's not all. I saw his accident."

Their collective gasps halted his words.

"You've never told me this, Stu." Starli couldn't believe what she was hearing. Was he making this up to shut Roland up?

"No, Starli, I didn't. You had enough to deal with living with that..."

She understood. Would she have done the same?

"I tried to tell him not to drive, that the road was curvy and dangerous anytime, but in his shape? He wouldn't listen as usual, and since I was ready to go home, I followed him. I was quite a ways behind him so there was nothing I could do to prevent it. He was going too fast, swerving all over the road, and when he came to that S curve, he went right over, almost like he meant to do it." Stu shook his head, the expression on his face revealing a sadness Starli had seldom seen on him.

Starli shuddered, memories from the past flooding her mind. Did she even want to hear any more details? Her gaze flickered to Joel's, but he was watching the banker as if hanging on to every word.

"Then..." Roland ran a big hand over his

face. "I can't take this in. All this time, he led me to believe...I thought it was..."

No one spoke.

"I want to hear this." Roland lifted his head and stared at Stu, then in slow motion he turned to look at Starli. "I have no idea if what he's saying is malarkey or truth, and I can't offer any sort of apology right now. Wouldn't be sincere, let alone warranted, until I can accept what he's saying." He stood. "I'll be back, Stu. Be prepared for another session."

~*~

When the door slammed shut, no one spoke for seconds, then Stu smiled at Starli. "You're probably wondering why I haven't told you this before."

"Yes, I am. Stu, this could have stopped Roland's harassment." It wouldn't be fair to say she was thankful at the moment of possibly never having to deal with her brother-in-law again. Annoyance at Stu was forefront and center. "What were you thinking?"

"Thinking? I was thinking of you." His face reddened a bit. "Why do you *think* I've done everything I've done through the years? Because I wanted the money? Because I felt obligated as your friend?"

Those were exactly the reasons he'd done them. At least, that's what she'd thought. She eyed the man sitting behind the monstrous, polished desk.

"Ryan nearly went bankrupt. I couldn't allow that to happen to you." His gaze implored her to understand. "After his death, I knew your insurance wouldn't pay off your house *and* start your business. I made sure it happened, that you had both."

"What are you saying?"

His expression was grievance inpersonified. "I paid off your house loan."

"You what?" She could see Joel shifting in his seat. Was he as uncomfortable as she was hearing this? "How could you do that without me knowing about it?"

"I run this bank. I can do whatever I want, and make it happen. How do you think you got all those small loans with your credit score?"

"I paid every one of them back."

"Yes, you did, and your credit score is now excellent. I'm proud of you. But you couldn't have without my help in taking that heavy house burden from your shoulders. It wasn't your fault, and you shouldn't have had to pay for Ryan's mistakes."

Just when she thought her life was improving, that things were looking up...Joel was probably planning an escape from the drama queen of Appleton. She wanted to groan. Instead, she lifted her chin.

"I wish you wouldn't have done that, Stu. I'm disappointed that you thought I would appreciate such an act. I insist on knowing what money you paid so I can return every dime."

"Nonsense. That's in the past. And I did it for you. You should know why." He waved away her objections. "We're off topic here. Would you like to be here when Roland listens to the tape?"

"I can't discuss this anymore today." Starli stood. "I'll be in contact later, Stu."

Before she could say another word, a light

knock on the door interrupted, and Crystal Miles his secretary, stepped in. "Sorry, Stu. Janine's here to pick up the items you wanted to send to the laundry."

"Get them from the closet, will you? My wool gray overcoat and the black car coat."

Crystal nodded and pulled out the two coats. She looked at them, then inside the closet again before turning to Stu. "You're missing your black scarf. Did you—"

Stu waved a hand. "Never mind. I misplaced it somewhere. Don't worry about it."

When the woman exited, Stu stood. "Think about it, Starli, and I think you'll see my reasoning. It made sense to do what I did. I was only too glad to do something good for one of my oldest friends."

Starli took his hand and stared into his eyes, not at all satisfied with his explanation or reasoning. It bordered too closely to an even closer relationship with him because of a hold he held over her. Yet she hesitated to argue with him anymore. Was she being obstinate in refusing such a deed from a friend?

"I really care about you, Starli. You should know that by now."

She nodded. "I know you do."

Unfortunately, he didn't know *her* as well as he thought he did.

"I was sorry to hear of that Findley girl getting injured in the fire. Sorry affair. I'm making a private donation to the family to help with her medical bills."

~*~

Joel tucked Starli into the front seat then stepped into his side of the car. That had been a fiasco of a meeting, if he was any judge of Starli's reaction. It wasn't favorable to say the least. How she would respond to Stu's supposedly generosity was another guess. If he had anything to say about it, the money paid for her house debt would be paid back pronto.

Roland Stratton's last reaction had sure been a surprise.

"You're awfully quiet." Starli's subdued voice broke into his thoughts.

"Trying to sort it all out."

"I'm too upset to think clearly right now."

"So you're not happy with what Stu did for you?"

"You have to ask? You don't think I'm over reacting?

"I'd be more concerned if you weren't." Joel hoped his tone wasn't as grim as he felt. "I am troubled by it, but I'll stand behind whatever your decision is. You have my full support, and I mean full. If you feel the need to repay him, it will be done."

Starli laid her head on his arm but said nothing. Seconds later, his shirt was warm and wet. She was crying. He moved his arm, drew her close, and whispered into her soft blond hair. "You're done being on your own, Your Majesty. From now on, I'm your loyal servant."

Her shoulders shook slightly. He'd gotten the reaction he'd wanted. She was laughing.

Now to pursue the clue that'd just been thrown in their faces.

~*~

Starli paced in her kitchen, her steaming cup of tea gradually cooling, as she ignored it in favor of the whirl of ideas swirling in her mind. Joel's half-serious, half-joking comments in the car had lightened her mood. Yet the box Stu had solidly put her in smothered her. His under-stated intent bothered her. He was forcing himself into her life, and she supposed, he hoped into her heart. Almost, but not quite, worse than Ryan's abuse. Because of their friendship, he figured she'd feel too guilty now to say no to his advances.

Wrong, wrong, wrong.

Unfortunately for him, her heart was taken.

Nothing was as it seemed. Ever since Joel had shown up, Camille's sudden display of pettishness for what she wanted had grown. Louis and his unexplainable moods were a surprise because he'd always been patient and good-natured. But since Joel had begun working at Apple Blossoms, he'd changed. Then there was Stu with his increased pushiness...

But only since Joel's arrival. Before that, he'd been easy-going and laid back about any interest he harbored for her.

So was all this Joel's fault?

She laughed. Of course not. But—and it was a big but—his arrival had triggered something in all three of those people. No one else seemed affected by his presence in any serious manner—except her.

What had the trigger been? Hmm. For Camille, jealousy of the new man's interest in her? That was a crazy thought because she'd never had any claim on Joel. And as far as she knew, everyone in town had encouraged Camille to better herself. Kinda far-fetched to imagine either of those suggestions, but maybe.

Louis? Jealous of Joel's ability? Could be, but her assistant chef had always been just that: an assistant chef, and had never shown any desire to be anyone but a hard-working, diligent helper. But then she'd only had the one chef before Joel.

Stu was another matter. They'd been casually in each other's lives forever. They'd never been an item, but he'd taken her to high school functions many times. During their college years, they'd drifted apart. But through her married years, they'd managed to be there for each other. And since Ryan's death, they'd filled the gap when one or the other had needed an escort for an important event.

Only this past year, she'd had to wiggle out of several requests from Stu. Was that his problem now?

He was an important man in town. Maybe it wasn't herself as much as his own pride that hurt at the attention she paid to the chef.

But all this rumination wasn't solving the problem of who'd burned down her restaurant.

Drawing a tablet and pencil from a drawer, Starli sat at her island and scribbled whatever came to her mind.

Reasons to burn my restaurant:

Ugh. That sounded awful.

1. An accident.

Seems to be the best suggestion because I can't imagine anyone wanting to do it. Still, i have to write something.

2. A hate crime against me?

3. A dissatisfied client? Or employee?

4. Revenge?

What a bunch of nonsense. Starli ripped the page from the tablet and tossed it aside. What now? Laying her head down on her crossed arms on the table top, she allowed her mind to relax and tried not to think about any of it.

Her heart expanded with love at the thought of Toni's baby Danni. A chuckle erupted from her at the thought of how Andy Carrington had paid for Caro's meal days ago, and her friend had protested. Too much so. Her heart warmed as Joel's face smiled at her from her memory files. He'd been so supportive and insistent that they visit the bank to see what her possibilities were to rebuild...

And of a sudden, the video of faces halted their rapid circling.

Today, a comment had been voiced; one that shouldn't have been made.

Starli sat up. Could it be? She wasn't entirely sure. She could be wrong. But even as she argued with herself, she reached for her cell and dialed Joel's number. When he answered, a bit breathless, she said, "I need to run over some things with you. When can we meet? I think I might know who was involved in destroying my restaurant."

~*~

"We'll go straight to Manny's."

"How's Manny doing?"

"His voice is still a little raspy, but much better." Joel sped up to pass a dawdling car. "I asked your Detective Eddie to meet us there."

"*Our* Detective Eddie?"

"*Your* detective Eddie. I've not quite forgiven him for that harassment." He flipped on his turn-signal. "Not sure why he should be there, but if we find out what I think we're going to find out, then we may need him."

Joel maneuvered his red sports car into the closest parking spot. "Ready?"

When she nodded, he stepped out and headed to her side of the car. Swinging open her door, he joked, "Your Majesty, let's get this show on the road."

Manny opened the door after they knocked and led them to his seating area where Detective Eddie stood by the electric fireplace, holding a glass.

"What's this all about? Why the secrecy?"

"We didn't want the arsonist to leg it, Detective." Joel nodded at the man.

Eddie's brows lifted. "Leg it? You mean run for it? Speak English, man."

"I am speaking English." And they all laughed.

Manny offered drinks as they settled into their seats.

"First, I wanted to share my discovery." Joel met each of their gazes. "After we left the bank, Starli, something bothered me."

"Same with me."

"Remember when Crystal came to get Stu's coats and couldn't find his black scarf?"

"I do."

"Well, I wondered if there was a way to find out where he'd bought it. You'd mentioned that a store here in town sells them. I figured why not ask?"

"And?" Detective Eddie's voice held a bit of impatience.

"The manager did have a list. A very short

list, but with some very interesting names on it."

"Are you going to share this list with us?"

"In a minute. The thing you need to know is, there are two scarves."

"Two?" Detective's eyes narrowed. "What do you mean?"

"There's the one Stu lost, and then there's the one Starli found on the front steps of her house."

"The same one?"

"Could be, but Stu's name wasn't on the list."

"Well, give man. Give."

"Hold on." He turned toward Starli and took her hand. "I'm sorry, My Princess, but Detective Eddie needs to hear this, to know where we're coming from and to get another perspective of the scarves issue. I'm not sure if you know it or not, Detective, but Starli's being harassed by Roland Stratton."

"Why didn't you tell me this, Starli? You know I would have had a talk with him."

"Yes, and made it hard on yourself when his buddies side with him?"

"I'm not that fragile, my friend. I could have handled them."

"Roland approached her again at the bank with his usual sarcastic remarks, but we were interrupted by Stu Stroth who pulled us into his office. He shared some very disturbing information."

"About the fire?" Eddie's brows drew together in a frown.

"No, about Ryan Stratton's death."

"You know something I don't, Starli? I hope

you're planning on filling me in on this information."

"That's why we're sharing with you now, Detective. We found out yesterday. Today, you're getting the info from us, and whatever else you need, you can talk with Stu."

"Right. Get on with it."

Joel spoke for ten minutes relaying what Stu had told them, with Starli inserting tidbits here and there.

When they both stopped. Detective Eddie rubbed a hand through his hair, weariness lining his face. "That accident has always given me the willies, but I never came up with a thread to give me cause for an extended investigation."

"You didn't finish about the scarf, Joel," Starli leaned forward.

"Right-o." He dug in his pants for the list. "Here you go, Detective."

Eddie scanned over it then looked back at Joel. "Three names from residents here in town. Am I to assume this one name..." he tapped the paper. "...is the one you're bringing to my attention?"

Joel raised a brow.

"Are you going to tell Manny and me?" Starli's head tilted up.

"The names written here are...Mayor Stroth, Rita Mae Simpson, and you, Starli." Detective Eddie gave Starli the serious eye, but the grin on his face spoiled it.

"That's right. I totally forgot. I gave mine as a Christmas gift to Perrin."

"No offense, Starli, but I'd better verify that. Then I'll have a talk with the other two."

"Sounds good. Now, go ahead with your thought, Starli."

"As we were leaving the bank, do you remember what Stu mentioned?"

Joel started to shake his head, then clicked his fingers. "Something about Camille—"

"And we didn't release the information that she'd been hurt in the fire. Did we, Eddie? Do you know if it got out?"

"Hard to know for sure. You can give orders, but that doesn't mean someone hasn't whispered it to their best friend. I haven't heard any rumors though."

"So, do you agree it's odd that Stu knew it?" Starli insisted. "Who told him?"

"That brings us to the question: Why *was* Camille in the restaurant?"

Chapter Twenty-one

"**U**ncle Laurence, I think it's time to tell what you know."

The maître de nodded his head, his expression serious. "When I entered the restaurant, I heard voices and walked toward them. Surprised them, I dare say. Camille saw me, her eyes widened, but it didn't dim that joking attitude she always has, Miss Starli. Her gaze flicked to someone out of my sight, there was a rustle as if that someone was moving—rather quickly."

"Any idea who it was?" Eddie poured himself another glass of lemonade.

"None. When I asked her who she was talking to, she laughed."

"She didn't say why she was there or how she got inside?" Starli sipped her drink.

"Nothing. I questioned her, she evaded answering, and the next thing I knew I woke up in the hospital. I'm supposing it was the second person who hit me. Very foolish of me to turn my back on him."

"That doesn't give us much more information." Eddie shook his head. "If he was in cahoots with Camille, then why knock *her* out too, assuming this unseen person did so."

"Unless they argued." Joel gave the detective a quizzical glance.

"Unless they argued," Eddie agreed. "Or this mysterious second person no longer needed Camille's help if they were in a conspiracy together."

"Or it could have been a coincidence they both showed up there." Starli suggested.

"Right." The detective nodded. "I also have the object you handed to me at the fire."

"The button." Joel met Starli's gaze, and they both asked, "Did you find out who owns it?"

"We'll get to that in a bit."

"Did the fire marshal give you any idea of what started the fire?" Joel held his glass up for Manny to refill.

"His preliminary ruling is arson."

"I'm thinking, Eddie. Wondering if you could call Rita Mae and Mayor Stroth right away. I'd love to have this all settled soon." Starli put all the pleading she could in her voice.

He gave her a look. "Hmm. No reason I can't call them right now, although I prefer talking in person. Give me a minute." He walked toward the hallway. Two minutes later he was back.

"Rita Mae didn't answer, but Mayor Stroth will be right over. Said he'd just finished a business meeting and could be here in five."

"Perfect." Starli beamed at him.

Manny rose. "I'm hungry. Anyone else need some sustenance?"

By the time Manny returned to the sitting area with a tray piled high of delicious-looking sandwiches, a knock sounded at the door. Seconds later, Eddie returned with Mayor Stroth and his son in tow.

"Have a seat, Mayor." Detective Eddie motioned with his hand. "Sorry you had to make the trip down here, but had a couple questions only you could answer."

The mayor's chest visibly expanded. "Sure thing. Ask away, Eddie, my boy."

The detective must have decided to ignore the condescending address and gave a wave of his own at the people gathered. "We've been trying to get to the bottom of several questions we have concerning some incidents. One of them is the scarf Starli and Joel found on the steps of her front porch one night. You do own one of those fine woolen black scarves from Sharon's Favorites, right?"

"Don't wear them. I'm too short and my neck's too thick."

"That's strange. Sharon has a record of you buying one there."

"Nonsense. She's got me mixed up with someone else...Wait." The mayor's eyes slithered to his son then narrowed. "Were you at Starli's home, Stu?"

"No." Stu's protest was a bit too hardy. "I was gone that night, remember? Couldn't have been at her house."

"What night was that, Stewart?" Eddie's dark gaze drilled into the banker's eyes.

As if the detective hadn't spoken, the Appleton Mayor went on. "But Stewart, I gave you a black scarf for Christmas. That's why my name was on Sharon's list of purchasers. What have you done with it?"

"I—I lost it. You know I have a tendency to lose my scarves. That's why you gave me another one. There must be hundreds who've purchased one like it."

"Actually, Stu, there were only three from Appleton. And those three are the only ones we're interested in." If Eddie's voice held a trifle of sarcasm, he well deserved to use it. The detective strolled over to the man and stood behind him, looking down at him. "Then there's that remark Starli picked up on at the bank."

Was Stu just a bit red-faced? Starli studied the banker, the man who'd seemed to be such a friend through the years. When had his pushiness for a relationship gone sour?

"What would that be?"

"More to the point would be the answer to how you knew Camille Findley was in the fire. You see, Stu, we kept her presence at the fire a secret. How could you have known about it? Can you give us the name of the person who told you?" His pause was poignant.

Stu stared at nothing and shook his head.

"Are you indicating you can't tell me who it was or you won't? Perhaps you can't." Again, Eddie hesitated, obviously giving the man time before he prodded him more. "If that's the case, then you must have been there. *Were* you there at Apple Blossoms before it burned, Stu? Were you? Answer me."

Stu's head-shaking was more violent now, back and forth as a dog shaking water from his body, his gaze looking at no one and everywhere at the same time.

"What have you done, Stewart? Is Detective Eddie right? Were you at Apple Blossoms?" Mayor Stroth's tight-lipped response was full of a don't-even-try-to-lie-out-of-it warning.

"And did you start that fire, Stewart Stroth?"

Starli stared at Eddie who sounded every bit the stern detective.

"Will this help you remember?" Detective Eddie tossed a gold button onto the coffee table. "While I was out calling your father, Stewart, our police department was searching your house. The search warrant that we got earlier today was specifically for a jacket with buttons matching this one, and they found it. The right sleeve button was missing. Care to tell me how it happened?"

No one spoke. Everyone waited. At last, Mayor Stroth spoke in the gentlest tone, the love for his son shining through.

"Son, I want you to tell me everything. Now."

For a minute, Stu hesitated, then he nodded. "Right, Dad."

He drew in a long breath, then began. "I was at Apple Blossoms the night of the fire. He looked at Starli. "I'm so sorry. I never meant for it to happen."

Was that tears in the man's eyes? Starli felt her heart softening.

"You didn't know, Starli, but years ago, I had keys made to your restaurant. That gave me easy access if I ever needed it. I didn't until recently when I saw I was losing your interest. I thought by causing a few problems at the restaurant, you'd see how valuable I was to your plans and life. I didn't want to hurt you— ever. Please believe me. All I wanted was for you to turn back to *me*. I wanted you to ask *me* for advice and help like you'd always done, instead of turning to your new cook." Stu flashed a disgusted glance at Joel.

He'd burned her restaurant for her attention? Lame. "You scratched my reception desk and left my freezer door open just so I'd turn to you? Stu, how could you? You knew how much that desk meant to me."

"I have no idea what happened to me. I kind of went crazy. Jealousy? Yes. Fear of losing you? Probably. I always assumed we'd get together after we slowed down with our work. You were always mine."

Really? She lost her restaurant because he'd had a fantasy? Starli gentled her words. "But, Stu, I never gave you any indication that would happen. We were always friends. Good friends, but just friends."

"That didn't mean it wouldn't happen. Can't you see what could have been, what still could be?"

Hardly. The Valentine cookie image with its message, You're Mine, neon-lit in her mind, and Starli drew in a deep breath. It'd been from him, no doubt.

Another thought struck her. "Stu, I need to know. Did you send Helen that threatening note? Did you?"

His expression reproached her, but she could tell. He had written that note, and knowing it, did something to her. She moved away from him, taking a chair behind the gathered group. If her heart could fall any farther than her feet, it did at that moment.

"Tell us what happened the night of the fire." Eddie moved around to stand where he could see Stu's face.

"That was an accident."

"Tell us."

"I went in intending to do some more minor damage. Remember, Starli, I was prepared to cover damages, even though you wouldn't have known it was me who caused them. I didn't want to hurt you. All I wanted was to be your hero."

"Why didn't you tell me this? Why be so subversive?"

"I tried to but you wouldn't listen. You kept refusing dates, and I could see your interest was veering away from me. Scaring Helen off and the damages—all of it was to get what was mine."

Starli groaned inwardly.

"Get on with the story," Eddie ordered.

"That night, as I said, I planned on a minor damage again—I thought a small fire—but after I got there, Camille showed up. I have no idea how she could have known I was there, if it was an accidental sighting, or what, but I couldn't get rid of her. And once she saw me unlocking the door, I had no choice but to drag her inside with me. I wanted to reason with her, but she kept making a joke of it—breaking in, she called it, asking me what was I going to do. She wouldn't shut up."

"Why didn't you leave then? Make some excuse why you were there?" For the first time, Joel spoke up. Had he held his tongue to keep from agitating the man more than he already was?

"Everything happened too quickly. Camille was cooking on the stove, laughing about getting free benefits—a meal at Starli's expense, since she didn't think you were going to make her a manager anytime soon. By then, it was too late. Manny..." he nodded at the man "...showed up, and I panicked. Camille didn't give me away, but I figured he guessed someone else was there. I couldn't have him calling the police or recognizing me, so I hit him. Sorry, Manny."

The maître de said nothing, his features a grim mask.

Stu lowered his head. "Camille went wild after I hit Manny, so we struggled, and I managed to hit her too when she turned her back to run. After that, I figured why not go ahead with a small oven fire? I planned on calling the fire department as soon as I left. Knew they answered calls quickly and would be there before Manny or Camille were hurt seriously. But I forgot about the fire under the skillet Camille had set there, and the container of oil, once we started arguing." He shrugged.

"I can't believe what I'm hearing." Mayor Stroth rubbed a chubby hand over his perspiring face. "Didn't you realize you could be in serious trouble for their injuries?"

"They were as much to blame as I was. I would have reasoned that I was under pressure...or something like that." His carefree answer indicated he was beyond reasoning with.

His dad shook his head.

"But when I left, I met a couple of guys, and couldn't get away from them. Then you called and insisted there was an emergency you needed to talk about."

Mayor Stroth jumped to his feet and strode to the window as if he couldn't bear to hear another word.

"I still thought I was safe—that Manny and Camille would be all right, but the next thing I heard, the fire was out of control. Your restaurant was burning. There was nothing I could do."

Mayor Stroth groaned from his position. Starli was almost sure she heard him mutter. "Didn't I teach the boy anything?"

Obviously not.

Chapter Twenty-two

Three Months Later

Starli stared down at the banks of flowers decorating the church, the letter penned on expensive, embossed stationery from her parents, warming her heart.

Darling, we so wish we could be there to help you celebrate this day, but we can't be physically. You will, however, as always, be in our hearts and thoughts. We can't wait to meet this awesome man you love...

She hadn't expected them to attend, but it didn't matter. She knew how much they loved her, how much they wanted true happiness for her. Their support and acceptance of Joel— sight unseen—was a crowning touch to today.

Her wedding day.

She'd wanted something simple and quiet. Joel had wanted elaborate. She'd wanted a simple pastel gown and no veil. He'd drawn on Toni and Caro to help her pick out the appropriate gown, not trusting her choice for what he wanted.

She'd been perfectly happy to go without a veil. He and Andy Carrington had been in cahoots over the creation of her wedding veil. Starli still had no idea what he'd come up with.

She'd wanted simple finger foods. He'd personally overseen the reception meal.

He'd been so on top of the world, so full of

plans, that she'd not wanted to tell him no. There was no way she could hinder his plans. She loved him too much.

Low murmurs rose from the overflowing wedding attendees below. As Pierre Markus took his seat at the piano, the music she and Joel had chosen floated through the air straight to her heart.

There was a tap on the door, and first Toni, then Caro peeked at her. "Okay to come in?"

She waved them in. Her few moments alone was over. Almost time to go.

Toni carried a tissue-wrapped article. With care, she laid it on the table and looked at Starli. "You want to unwrap it?"

Starli folded back the tissue. Lying under the sheaves of paper lay her wedding veil. She lifted it, then looked at her friends. "Is this thing real?"

"Joel had it made especially for you, so I'd say some of the jewels are. Claimed his princess would wear a jeweled crown on her wedding day." Toni touched it with one finger.

"It's breathtaking. Please help me."

Settling the crown on top of Starli's head, Toni adjusted the layers of tulle, then stood back and gazed at her friend. "Gorgeous."

Caro handed over the pink apple blossoms and baby's breath. "Joel didn't spare any expense for you, did he?"

"I wish he would have. It's too much, don't you think?"

"Not for you." Caro insisted.

"It's meant a lot to him to do things his way. You've been wonderful to give him such a free hand." Toni gripped her hand and squeezed.

A second knock interrupted their chatter, and Manny stuck his head inside. "Lovely, as always, my dear."

"Is it time?"

At his nod, Starli reached for her friends. "Thank you for being such wonderful friends. Let me hug you quickly."

'Romance from String Quartet' filled the air as her maid of honor—Caro, and Toni, her matron of honor, preceded her down the aisle. When Pierre stroked the piano keys, coaxing the first notes of the 'Traditional Wedding March,' Starli squeezed her escort's arm and whispered, "Are you pleased, Manny?"

"My dear, if that scoundrel hadn't married you, I'd have disowned him."

Starli laughed softly, and as the congregation stood, she and Manny began their walk.

Joel stepped forward, his gaze fastened on her face, and not once did he avert it. The minister asked his questions, and Starli responded, caught in Joel's gaze so that nothing else mattered.

~*~

Manny had outdone himself with the outdoor reception organization. He'd insisted on hiring the waiting staff and the band that now played in the background as Joel and Starli stood near the end of Toni's back lawn.

"Happy, My Princess?" Joel wrapped his arm around her shoulder and pulled her close.

Starli laid her head on his shoulder. "Very."

"Not worried about anything? Toni will see that the reconstruction of Apple Blossoms is done. You and I will search for the right chef and manager."

"I'm at peace with everything, Joel. I've been so hard headed God knew it would take something drastic to help me realize His perfect plan for my life. I'm very, very happy."

"And you trust me completely. No doubts, no shadows, no fears?"

Starli lifted her head and stared at Joel. What was that tone in his voice? He was up to something.

"I see I'm always going to have to be on guard around you. What have you got up your sleeve?"

He grinned, then took her by the shoulders and turned her to face the opposite direction.

"What?"

"See it?"

"See what? The trees? Clouds? That perfect sky?"

"There." He laid one hand on her shoulder and pointed with the other, his mouth close to her ear. "See that balloon?"

"That hot air balloon?" Her throat felt as if she'd tried to swallow cotton.

"Watch it."

They stood silent, Starli leaning against Joel's broad shoulder. As the balloon floated closer, Starli spoke again and started to turn toward him, but he held her still.

"It looks as if it's landing. Is it? Is this some kind of gimmick for our guests? A free ride?"

"There, Your Majesty," His voice filled her ear again, "comes the limousine to our next destination."

"Our what?"

This time, he allowed her to turn, and she

knew it really was mischief shining from his very being.

"Remember when we talked about ballooning? We haven't tried it, because of winter, but it's warm now. I found a balloonist near Morgantown and hired him to fly us to the moon."

"To the moon?"

"Or somewhere around Columbus, Ohio, where we'll take the fastest plane we can to Italy, then on to France, and a final stop in England to show you my roots." Joel cupped her face and planted a kiss on her nose.

The large balloon settled on the lawn, and a large knot of her friends circled to watch it.

"You're going to spoil me."

"Ah, now you're catching on. That's exactly what I've got planned for you." He held out an arm, and Starli placed her hand on it.

They walked to the balloon, and Joel lifted her into the basket. Her heart pounded in anticipation. No fear, just the thrill that she was about to embark on another adventure with the man she loved.

As the balloon rose in the air, her friends waved and shouted at them. Starli returned their farewells, her heart in her throat at their love for her. Her gaze sought Toni and her wonderful family, moved on to Caro and Toby with Andy hovering just behind them. How she loved them and wished them as much happiness as God had given her and Joel.

With a carefree laugh, she lifted her bouquet and tossed it straight into Caro's arms. Laughter bubbled up inside her at the bemused expression that settled on her friend's face.

Joel clutched the side of the balloon, and Starli clutched him. They rose higher and higher until the people at her reception were mere dots. Then she turned to Joel and hugged him.

Again, he asked the question. "Happy?"

"Delirious."

Her heart swelled with love for this wonderful man who'd come into her life just a few months ago. She placed a hand on her heart and knew that the fears, the terror and the bitterness she'd carried for so long were over. There wasn't room any longer for those things.

God and Joel had seen to that.

Epilogue

Starli bowed, bowed again at the enthusiastic audience of clapping people. Waving, she swept off the stage. The concert she'd given tonight for a hundred or more of some of Joel's government associates was over, the response overwhelming and gratifying. Once behind the curtains, she went straight into Joel's arms and let him wrap her in his love.

"You were magnificent. A real queen tonight, my dear. And did I tell you that you look stunning in that black thing you have on?" He crooned in her ear.

"About ten times, you did." Starli grinned, then pouted at him. "But what about my playing? Was that any good at all?"

He held her off. "Now you're coaxing for compliments. Shame on you."

"I suppose I wasn't half bad. At least the crowd seemed to appreciate my talent." Starli murmured as they walked from the building to their car.

"From their response, I'd say you're on your way to being a popular concert pianist."

How could she get any happier? Once they'd settled in England, after their honeymoon and a quick trip home to check on the progress of her restaurant's rebuilding, Joel had surprised her with the purchase of a year's training with the best master pianist he could find in England.

The year had flown by while Joel fulfilled his promise to the throne to raise volunteers and money for third world countries.

This evening had been the culmination of that year for her.

Once inside their apartment, Joel drew her into their bedroom. "I received some emails today."

"From our friends?"

"One from Appleton's best policeman."

"Detective Eddie?" Starli whirled. "What is it?"

"Stu waved a trial. The judge set sentencing for next month."

She whispered the words. "You did tell them I didn't want to press charges?"

At his nod, she sank to a loveseat. "What took so long?"

"Because of your testimony for Stu, Eddie was working with the prosecutor to get the best deal he could for him." Joel scowled. "He mentioned Roland too."

"What's happened?" Starli knew he was remembering Roland's threats and harassment.

"He had a talk with him that perhaps it was time to move on. Roland resigned and moved to Charleston."

She laid a hand on his. "God has helped me forgive, Joel. Let's not remember any of that, but thank God for the life He's giving us now."

"That sounds like an excellent plan from my business-minded wife." His blue eyed-gaze searched hers, then that lovely smile of his spread across his lower face. "One more thing he mentioned, and then we need never bring the name up again."

"Am I supposed to guess?"

"Eddie said Camille had been put on six months' probation for breaking into Apple Blossoms." Joel hesitated. "I didn't tell you sooner, but I did a little investigating, and found out on my own that it was Camille who stole your skating outfit from the cleaners. If you want, I'll call Detective Eddie and give him what information I've got to carry through however he sees fit."

Starli walked to the window, staring out for seconds before returning to stand in front of her husband. "No, Joel. I think we'll keep that misdeed and the culprit behind it to ourselves. I've had to learn to forgive and this is another time I want to practice that."

"Are you sure?"

"Yes, I am. I'm not sure I was right in not encouraging her more. Perhaps some of her problems came from that."

"I doubt it, but it's your call, and I support you totally."

"You do? Totally?" She edged up to him and smiled.

"Completely."

"Then that's settled. And the second email?"

"Mayor Stroth. Stu is giving up his inheritance to pay for the fire damages. I'm sure it was the good mayor's doings. Probably figured it would go well with the judge if he made restitution."

"Whatever the reason, I'm glad he was

willing. I'm sure Mayor Stroth will make sure his son doesn't go to his grave penniless."

Starli walked to her dresser, pulled out the pins that had held her hair on top of her head, ran the silver brush through her hair and flung it back from her shoulders. She watched as Joel walked to the open window. When he didn't move, she went to him.

"What are you thinking, Joel Peterman-Blair?" She stroked his cheek, the beginning stubble biting into her fingertips. "Have I told you how much I love you?"

He turned and tucked her close to his side. "Only about a zillion times in the last year."

Starli cocked her head at him, then again smoothed his cheek with one hand. "And you've made me very happy."

He laid his head on top of hers, and she stared out the window with him for a long moment. She could feel his heart beating, loved the pressure from his head on top of her's, the stubbiness of his chin occasionally brushing her forehead.

She turned and curled her fingers against his chest. "I want to give you something that I hope will make you as happy as you've made me."

"A gift for me? I don't need anything at all as long as I have you."

Starli loved his condescending tone and assurances. "You're going to be a daddy."

"And if you want another trip to West Virginia, I absolutely approve of that plan...What did you say?" He gripped her shoulders, holding her away from him, his eyes, a blue fire of intensity.

"I said you're going—" she repeated, her heart skipping at the sight of his pale face.

"I know what you said. What did you mean?"

"I'm pregnant with your baby. We're going to have a baby, Joel, together." She leaned into him.

He touched her stomach, and she could feel his trembling fingers through her gown. "I thought you said you couldn't..."

A shadow threatened to touch her heart, but she shooed it away with her words. "Ryan always said it was my fault we had no children, but I never had a doctor check to be sure, and Ryan refused to see a doctor. I just weakly believed what he said."

Concern dripped from his voice as he ticked off his thoughts. "You bully well must be careful. Don't lift anything too heavy. Are you eating right? Taking vitamins?"

"I'm fine. Stop fussing. I've got two more concerts this month. You have to finish your final speeches and appointments, then we can take some time to go to West Virginia and let our friends know."

"Have you seen a doctor?" The anxiousness still hovered in his eyes.

"Oh, yes. Yesterday. Everything's fine. I'm healthy, and the baby's healthy."

Only then, did Joel lift and whirl her about the room. She laughed against his chest. When he settled her on her feet again, she felt something drip onto her cheek. Wonder at his tenderness filled her. She touched his cheek yet again. "You're crying."

"Nonsense. Men don't cry."

"Of course, they don't, my darling," Starli agreed, thrilled at his pleasure.

"And I think..." Joel hesitated, the fun creeping into his eyes again.

"What do you think?"

"I think that after we kneel beside our bed to offer thanksgiving to God, that we need to discuss some important issues."

Starli followed him to their bed. "What issues?"

"Baby names. We need to decide on what to call the little fellow when he gets here." Joel took her hand and they knelt together.

"Or her." Starli whispered.

Joel heard and squeezed her hand. "Or her."

The End.

Turn the page for a sneak peek at Book Three in the Appleton Romantic Mysteries. Enjoy the first chapter of *Undiscovered Treasures*.

Carole Brown

An Appleton, WV Romantic Mystery

Her life was spinning out of control. Just like the ballerina on the shelf.

Undiscovered Treasures

ANTIQUES/CURIOS/COLLECTABLES

Undiscovered Treasures

Chapter One

"**I**'m depressed." Caroline Gibson yelled as she staggered under the weight of the books she carried from the storage room.

Her brother didn't bother to look up from the computer where he typed. "You're always depressed."

"Am not. And if I could get some help around here, that storage room would get cleaned out faster."

Toby looked up then. "You're doing fine. I've got to go after those two other pictures Andy promised us."

Caro sniffed. "That's what's making me totally depressed. I cannot abide..." she loved that old-fashion word "...that man's drab paintings. Why doesn't he paint in pastels? Or something..."

The toe of her sandal caught the ragged edge of a floorboard, and she tripped. She tried to catch herself, floundered, held on to the books for a second, then let them go in a desperate effort to keep from hitting the floor. Again.

Ouch.

Lifting a hand to rub her arm where the edge of a counter had scraped it, she winced.

Silence, then Toby's head appeared at the end of the aisle. "Are you okay? Didn't break anything, did you?"

"I didn't break any bones, if that's what you're asking."

"I meant any of our treasures." He grinned when she scowled.

"It's all Andy's fault."

"How on earth do you figure that?" Toby huffed and rubbed his chin.

"If I hadn't been so depressed over those horrible paintings of his, I'd have seen that aggravating board."

Toby did laugh then as he walked away. "Yeah, yeah. You've tripped over that same board how many times?" He stopped at a shelf and twisted the key in the back of a ballerina music box. The tinny music began playing as the dancer twirled. Toby looked back at her. "There. That will give you something to listen to while you're lying there feeling sorry for yourself."

Caro started to sit up when a thin hand appeared in front of her eyes. Had she hit her head? Was she having a vision? She studied the hand. Tan. Stained fingers and well-kept nails. Altogether a rather nice one. She let her gaze lift to the owner of the hand.

"Need some help?"

Andy Carrington, artist of the paintings she'd just labeled horrible, bent over her, a concerned look on his lean face. His outstretched hand still dangled in front of her face.

Oops. She'd done it again. She gave him a sharp glance. He didn't look offended. His gentle features seemed as placid as they always did. Maybe she could squeeze out of any explanations for her vociferous

2

declarations of hatred for certain paintings.

Ignoring his hand, she scrambled to her feet. He dropped to his knees just as she stood and began gathering the scattered books she'd dropped.

An exasperated puff of air escaped from between her lips. Should she get back down on the floor and help or walk off?

He always placed her in a dilemma. Why couldn't he peddle his work somewhere else? Just because Toby liked him didn't mean she had to, did it? Or that they had to display that stuff he called art in their shop.

Without a thought, she tapped a foot in agitation--or was it nervousness? Of course not!--and when Andy glanced at it, she cringed and walked away. Let the books stay on the floor.

She bent over Toby's shoulder as he pecked away at some chart on his computer and whispered. "Your friend's here. Probably with some of his ghastly art."

"Stop it, Sis." Toby's rebuke came with a severe look.

"Why?" Oh, dear, why did that perverse streak have to show up every time she didn't want it to?

Toby sat back in his chair and sent her one of "those looks." "Because you're not being nice. Because Andy's our friend. Because Andy is nice, and I don't want you hurting his feelings."

She tried for another sniff, then gave it up. After all, she really didn't want to hurt the man's feelings either. Hadn't Pastor Hagg just preached Sunday about being kind-hearted?

And she tried her level best, as her grandmother used to say when she was alive, to follow the Bible's teachings.

But that didn't mean she had to like his paintings or want to deal with his puppy love. Why on earth couldn't he forget *her?*

Andy appeared around the aisle, his arms loaded with books. "Where do you want these, Caroline?"

"It's Caro, not Caroline." She waved vaguely at the old church bench that served as a catchall. "Put 'em there. Thanks."

"Hey, Tobe, how are things going?" Andy deposited the musty books.

Toby shut down the computer. "Good on my side. What're you doing in town on a weekday?"

"Needed a break. Brought those two paintings you wanted."

Caro shot Toby a dirty look. Toby flashed a smug look back at her. *See how nice he is*, his eyes said.

Wimp, Caro flashed right back at him.

"You look kind of peaked. Are you sure you're feeling okay?" Toby stood.

"I'm fine. Just busy. Let me get those paintings."

"I'll help. Caro, how about rustling up some grub for us?" Toby baited her with his goofy imitational cowboy slang.

"What am I, your servant?" Caro frowned. Toby was the greatest amateur actor in town, but she hated it when he put on that Wild West act.

Come to think of it, she was hungry. The refrigerator didn't hold much. She'd neglected to restock it last week because of her friend Starli's wedding. She hadn't had time to think about food.

She looked at the contents with greater interest. Hmmm. Sandwiches would do. They had plenty of peanut butter in the cupboard. Pickles, bananas, and honey would serve as toppings. Nutritious and delicious.

She checked for mold, then sliced the last of the homemade bread, set the peanut butter jar on their small table, and poured tall glasses of iced tea. Perfect. Fit for a king. Not that that description fit either Toby or Andy.

After the blessing, Andy reached for two slices of the bread, smeared peanut butter lavishly, laced it with bananas, and took a big bite.

"So, how's the painting going?" Toby bit into his own creation of a peanut butter sandwich.

"I've got a problem. I think."

Great. *He thinks.* Caro choked on the giggle and peanut butter combination that was preventing the snort of laughter threatening to erupt.

"What are friends for? What's wrong?" Toby grew expansive.

Toby was laying it on pretty thick, if you asked her. Caro leaned back in her seat and slid a disgusted look in his direction.

Andy laid his sandwich down on his paper plate. "I'm pretty sure I'm being robbed."

"What do you mean?" The frown between Toby's brows tightened.

"Someone's stealing my paintings."

"What?" Caro laughed, then bit her lip. Who on earth would want those ghastly things? But it was none of her business. Let Toby deal with it. Andy was his friend, after all.

"Yeah. I thought I'd misplaced the first one, but then when the second one disappeared, I knew someone was stealing them." A small frown wrinkled his forehead.

"Do you have any idea who?" Toby reached for the peanut butter.

"Not really. I mean, whom am I going to suspect?" Andy shrugged. "The mailman? The delivery guy? My assistant who's doing a great job of keeping me organized?"

"Well, someone's doing it, unless, of course, you're getting senile." Caro wanted to slap a hand over her mouth. Why couldn't she keep quiet? Andy would think she was really brilliant with that deduction.

Andy's gaze flashed to her, but he shook his head. "Since I'm still on this side of thirty, I doubt that. But you're right, someone is definitely doing it."

"You call the cops yet?" Toby poured a mound of honey on top of the peanut butter.

"I couldn't decide whether to or not for awhile, but, yes, I finally did. It's not as if my work is valuable. Yet."

Yet? Did he really think they would someday be so? Ha. She hated to clue him in, but that might take a few years. Like never.

"There's only one thing I can think of. New York Regency's local office has offered me a contract. A very good contract." His shy smile took in both brother and sister with his good news.

"Seriously? That's great." Toby reached over and slapped his friend on the shoulder.

Regency's was THE art center of the world. Supported by a patron like them meant something big. Who knew where one could go from there?

But those paintings of his? What were they seeing that she missed?

Still, it wouldn't hurt to be nice. "Congratulations."

Andy smiled at her, his eyes a warm oak brown, and Caro felt herself smiling in return. Then she blinked. What was she doing? She felt almost friendly with the worst painter in West Virginia. Best to switch the topic back to the thefts. "So what are you thinking? That someone feels threatened and is trying to eliminate the competition? Or someone thinks they'll grab your work and make a mint when it gets valuable?"

"I haven't the foggiest. I am having a new security system put in. I guess there's not much else to do. When my agent convinced me to call the police and report it, they came by and looked things over, but didn't sound promising."

"You can't leave it to the cops in this town." Caro stopped when Toby and Andy stared at her.

Her defenses rose when Toby's dark hazel eyes twinkled at her in mischief.

"Well, he shouldn't. I mean, how much can we trust the cops after what just happened?"

"They're not all crooked, just because Roland was." Toby shook his head. "Look at Eddie. Good cop through and through."

"They wouldn't believe it though, till faced with the evidence. Even after all those threats

Roland put Starli through." Caro shoved aside her plate, her hunger gone.

"Okay, say you're right. What can we do? I know nothing about investigating anything, and I don't think you do either." Toby layered his peanut butter-and honey slathered bread with pickles.

Caro held up a hand and ticked off her points. "First, we're above average in intelligence, wouldn't you say?"

Her brother burst into a guffaw. "Well, Andy and I are for sure. Not quite convinced a cute sister of mine is."

"Says you." Caro wrinkled her nose at him. "Who scored higher on their SATs at college?"

"Just because she got a college degree, she thinks she's got the right to brag." He gave her an exaggerated glare. "Go on."

With a smirk, Caro continued. "Secondly, I've read a lot of mysteries. And you guys aren't immune to that sort of thing. Why can't we figure it out any better than any other amateur? I say, let's try."

"Oh, brother." Toby smacked his forehead. "The next big Nancy Drew."

Andy laughed. "Maybe, but Caroline does have a point. Why shouldn't she try? I can't afford to keep losing paintings especially if Regency's predictions for my work comes true."

"It's Caro. That is exactly my third point. It has to be stopped, and if the cops aren't motivated to do something, then...?"

Toby looked from Caro to Andy, then back to his sister again. At last, he raised his hands, but a sly glint sparkled in his eyes. "Fine. Go for it. But I can't help. I'm making a quick trip to Charleston for an estate auction."

Caro eyed her brother. Was he up to something? Trying to throw Andy and her together? She wouldn't put it past him.

Yet the chance to solve a mystery intrigued her. She'd wanted to try her hand at it for a long time. Could she do it? She wouldn't know unless she seized this thrown-in-her-lap opportunity.

She threw a "I-know-what-you're-doing" glance at him. "Fine. *I'll* find the paintings."

Toby's suddenly pleased expression sent the hounds of doubt baying at her heels again, and she wanted to groan. Not again. Why couldn't her friends get it in their heads that she and Andy would never be an item?

She weighed her options. Hanging around bad artist Andy—the guy who wanted more than friendship from her—against the chance of solving a mystery.

Yeah, she could handle it.

Other Books by Carole Brown

Denton and Alex Davies Mysteries:
Hog Insane
Bat Crazy

Spies of World War II
With Music In Their Hearts
A Flute in the Willows
Sing Until You Die

The Appleton WV Mysteries
Sabotaged Christmas
Knight in Shining Apron
Undiscovered Treasures
Toby's Troubles

Troubles in the West
Caleb's Destiny

Women's Fiction:
The Redemption of Caralynne Haymen

Misc
West Virginia Scrapbook
Christmas Angels (WW II short story in the Anthology *From the Lake to the River*)

Award winning author Carole Brown loves to weave suspense and tough topics into her books, along with a touch of romance and whimsy.

She is always on the lookout for outstanding titles and catchy ideas.

Carole and Dan, her pastor husband, reside in SE Ohio and have ministered and counseled across the country. Together, they enjoy their grandsons, traveling, gardening, good food, the simple life, and did she mention their grandsons?

Carole loves to connect with her readers. You can find her at her blog:
Sunnebnkwrtr.blogspot.com/
And facebook:
www.facebook.com/CaroleBrown.author

If you enjoyed reading this book, let others know... and bless Carole Brown with an honest review.

www.ingramcontent.com/pod-product-compliance
Lightning Source LLC
Chambersburg PA
CBHW031659170626
46808CB00005B/1517